Oxford University

The Richard Jackson Saga, Volume 8

Ed Nelson

Published by Eastern Shore Publishing, 2024.

Table of Contents

Other books by Ed Nelson

The Richard Jackson Saga

Book 1 The Beginning

Book 2 Schooldays

Book 3 Hollywood

Book 4 In the Movies

Book 5 Star to Deckhand

Book 6 Surfing Dude

Book 7 Third Time is a Charm

Book 8 Oxford University

Book 9 Cold War

Book 10 Taking Care of Business

Book 11 Interesting Times

Book 12 Escape from Siberia

Book 13 Regicide

Book 14 What's Under, Down Under?

Book 15 The Lunar Kingdom

Book 16 First Steps

In the Richard Jackson World

Mary, Mary

Stand-Alone Story

Ever and Always

Cast in Time Series

Book 1: Baron

Book 2: Baron of the Middle Counties

Book 3: Count

Book 4: Earl

Book 5: Earl of the Marches

Dedication

This is dedicated to my wife Carol for her support and help as the first reader and editor.

Also, the BHS class of 1962 just because.

Professionally edited by Janet E. Rupert

Quotation

That is exactly how it happened, give or take a lie or two.

James Garner as Wyatt Earp, describing the gunfight at the OK Corral in the movie *Sunset*.

Copyright © 2019

Chapter 1

I had just barely finished breakfast Monday when I had a phone call from Mr. Monroe. They had some footage from my reveal as Lew Wetzel that he thought it important that I review. Not having anything scheduled, I told him I would be there within the hour.

In the small theater, they played daily rushes for me. I couldn't believe what I was seeing. They had made me up to look scary dark. It was more than that. It was downright diabolical. The brief look I gave the camera made me look like evil personified.

"Rick, for the movie it works great. For your image, I don't know. Can you live with this?"

"I'm not certain, my team and I had talked about me having a goody two-shoe image. This would certainly take care of that."

"Who is your team?"

"My parents, Susan Wallace, Sharon Bronson, and Anna Romanov are the core; my brothers and sister also have input."

"That's a good group. Why don't we have them all over to review this footage? It could have an impact on your career. Assuming you make more movies. It will open up a wide range of options for you."

"I doubt I could get everyone together in the next few days. Could we schedule a showing this Friday?"

"We can wait that long. Why don't I host a lunch, and then we view it after that?"

"Thank you, Mr. Monroe. That sounds good. I will make the arrangements."

"Regarding your travel plans, remember the telethon at the end of the month."

"I will be back from England before that, so no problem."

"Okay, see you Friday for lunch."

I returned home and got on the phone, calling everyone I had mentioned. Sharon Bronson was the only one with a prior commitment, and she would try to change that. I couldn't talk to my family until dinner, but I was certain they would be available. Well, I hoped they would.

After that, I spent time reading one of the five English history books I had bought. I doubted that my American history courses would do much for me on the English exams. I wouldn't be able to go in-depth, but I would at least have some idea of what had happened if not the nuances.

I did get a phone call in the middle of the afternoon. A patent search on my beer can pull tab had come up clean, so I had to have prototypes built and tested. I called the engineering firm that Dad had recommended. They had built the tooling needed to cut the various depths of metal and would be making test lids on Wednesday, and I was welcome to come in and see them.

Knowing the test lids would be available, I called Mexicali Delight Brewery and talked to their general manager. He was intrigued by my idea and agreed to use my lids at the end of the day's run on Wednesday. I then called back the engineer, Warren Smith, to let him know about the filing, and invited him along. He was all for it. He liked the idea, and Mexicali Delight was his beer of choice, so it was a win-win for him.

After that interruption, I was too psyched up to sit and read, so I drove in Dad's Ford Fairlane to the airbase on the other side of the park. When I got there, I found nothing had been done. That was not surprising as Dad was still negotiating with the Forest Service. I did take another run around the perimeter of the base.

I then went into the open hangars, hoping against hope to find some old airplane parts or equipment, even though I had looked before. I found a set of stairs going down in one corner of the furthest hangar. I had to go down even though I didn't have a flashlight with me. At the bottom of the stairs was a closed door. It wasn't locked, and I was able to pull it open. You could tell by the force needed that it had been a long time.

Beyond the door, as expected, it was pitch black, but I could see the edges of wooden crates. I managed to drag one out, but I would never get it open without any tools. Remembering the tire iron in the Ford, I raced back to the front gate.

After returning to the hangar, prying the top off the wooden crate only took a few minutes. Inside were stacked gold lacquered cans labeled C-Rations. They all had a paper label in the process of coming off. I guess the glue had deteriorated over the years.

The date on the cans was October 1941, so I wasn't about to try them. There were meat and beans, meat and potato hash, plus meat with a vegetable stew as the main meal. Some of the cans were labeled bread and dessert. I had no urge to try them.

Not a very good start to a treasure hunt! I returned home for a flashlight, hoping to find something better deeper in the room. After a dirty, dusty two hours, I realized that this must have been the storage for an emergency food supply. Taking a selection of the cans with me to show the family, I returned home and cleaned up for dinner.

When I showed them to my parents, it was obvious they had no fond memories of these meals. On to a more pleasant subject, I told them about the rushes from the movie. They agreed that they would come over on Friday to see them. Even the kids could come, as their school did not resume until the following Monday.

In a surprise move, both Mum and Dad wanted to go to the brewery on Wednesday. Of course, they were welcome.

After dinner, Mum and I joined Dad in the English room. He had an update for Mum and me about the contents of the safe. The biggest news was about the old one-hundred-dollar bills. They had auctioned off for a total of three and a half million dollars.

The loose gems went for a million point-six. He had kept a selection of diamonds he was having made into a tiara for Mary. She wouldn't receive it until she "came out", which meant when she was sixteen. The only other item that Dad had kept was an old opal ring. This didn't have great value but looked like an heirloom. He had it resized for Mum.

After dinner, I returned to my study of English history. It was really interesting as you could see how our modern world had emerged. Reading history will put you to sleep no matter how bloodthirsty those competitors for the throne were.

After my morning routine on Tuesday, I contacted our travel agent and arranged for a trip to England with an open return. This included a suite at the Plaza on the Strand and a car. I also called the British Consulate in Los Angeles and asked for their thoughts on my US Marshal status, especially on being armed. I didn't know it was possible to have kittens over the telephone. Under no circumstances was I to attempt to bring a weapon into the country.

They had no problems with a longbow and war arrows even though they killed at a greater distance than my pistol. A saber was also allowed. The British were very traditional in their weapons. It was not could it kill; it was how it was done. I had no plans to take my bow or sword, so it was all moot. I had a nice long ride on George, joined by my brothers and sister on their mounts. It was a nice outing. Way up the trail in the park, we came out on the main road and found an ice cream store. What a nice day.

The late afternoon and the evening were spent in the history books.

Mum took the kids to register for school starting on Monday. I rode into the office with Dad. I had to look into getting another car. While the Ferrari was still on my mind, I knew it wasn't a practical car. While the T-Bird had been perfect for me, I felt like I was ready for something new. Since I was leaving the country, there was no hurry. Besides, if I spent much more time in England, I would need a car there.

Jim Williamson gave me a business update in about half an hour. Everything was moving well, and the money was rolling in. It was also rolling out at a fantastic rate. Fortunately, it was still more in than out. The monthly cash turnover was over a hundred million as the various governments met their commitments. Of all that money only ten percent was considered profit. My God!

Jackson Enterprises' latest venture was the freight forwarding portion. It was taking off like gangbusters. More and more US industries were exporting products, and they wanted a source that could take care of all areas they were shipping to.

Our initial plan was to partner with freight forwarders in various countries and then purchase them when the business reached a critical level. It appears that once our services were known, they instantly went critical. We were buying brokerages as fast as we could. I can say it is wonderful to have a staff.

Now, the issue was merging all these different companies into a common business model. Besides different forms, currencies, and laws, there were also many languages. It is really wonderful to have staff. Along those lines, Jim informed me we would have to expand. Our landlord was making two more floors of the building available. I thought that a lot but discovered we probably would outgrow it in six months. It is great to have Dad as a landlord.

One of the next orders of business was to set up a full HR department for local hiring and then integrate all of the foreign offices with headquarters. It would be a daunting task. The first thing HR would have to do is hire someone to run the division. The Scottish Lines staff was proving helpful in identifying people worldwide to bring on board. No matter how I hated it we would also have to hire some relatives of important leaders in many of the countries. It was a reality of doing business.

After the briefing, I had to head to the Mexicali Delight Brewery, where Warren Smith and my parents were waiting. Warren had brought the sample lids, which had been cut at different depths. He had fifty of each of the three cuts.

The Mexicali GM, who for some reason looked familiar to me, showed a lot of interest in the project. After a tour of the brewery, and just before they shut down for the day, my lids were fed into the line. They passed the first test of going onto the line without bursting.

After they were filled, each of us opened one can of each thickness. Again, they all opened with no problems. Next would be warming the beer up while having it undergo a test on a shaker bed for twenty-four hours. We would have a product if warm beer could be shaken at the same amplitude as a semi-truck bouncing down the road.

As we were saying our goodbyes, the GM, Mr. Echeveria, asked Mum to say "Hi" to Mrs. Hernandez. It clicked that he was the man at the Christmas dinner.

Chapter 2

My morning started well with a pleasant run. After cleaning up, I joined Dad at breakfast. We had plans for the day or at least one project.

One loose end had to be tied up before I went to England. We had tried to drop a box with Jason Talmadge's bones off Catalina Island but were foiled by a fly-in breakfast. I rented a plane in Ontario and met Dad at the same airport as before. This time, the restaurant only had two cars. I landed, and Dad brought the box over and got on board.

The flight was only an hour round trip, and Jason was now to be found where the authorities thought he would be. Of course, if that box were ever brought up and his remains identified, it would open many questions. I doubted that would ever happen, and it was so long ago that no one would care.

The box had been stored in the safe located in the sub-basement. Dad mentioned that the only thing left in the safe other than some cash and gold coins was that box with that old clay cup. Did I want to do anything with it?

After a few moments of thought, I told him I had no idea what to do with it and that it would wait. By the time we dropped the box, returned Dad to the little airport, and I returned the rental plane to Ontario and got back home, it was lunchtime.

After lunch, I hit the books for three hours. From Alfred the Great to the Domesday Book to Macmillan, I felt like I was getting a handle on the subject. I think after Churchill, Disraeli was the most interesting of the prime ministers. Without question, Lord Nelson was the quintessential British sailor.

That session mentally exhausted me for the day. I drove down to the beach and checked out the beach house construction. Progress had been made, but it still seemed to drag on. After that, it was back home to the English history books.

I wanted to do well in the examinations. English history was simple when compared to the rise and decline of the British Empire. What a glorious mess they made of things. And mess it was, looking at maps of the Middle East and what they had created, I could see no good end in sight.

The first thing Friday morning was to call Mr. Norman in England. I was put directly through to him. After an exchange of pleasantries, I explained why I had called.

He told me he would have to make phone calls and would have information ready for me by the time I got to England. He seemed intrigued by the idea of me being in England for an extended stay. I asked him and was told that having a young-looking messenger opened up several possibilities. Most of the messengers were very competent forty-year-old military retirees. They were considered to be as hard to identify as policemen.

After talking for a few minutes, we made an appointment for Tuesday afternoon.

I would have to do very well on O-Levels and passing at least four A-Level exams would be best. If I did that, the possibilities were open.

I then had a long run, which helped me wake up. I mean, no one should dream of the Crusades. A hearty breakfast followed, and I then went for a ride on George. When I was in England, Ben would exercise the horse.

He didn't seem to mind ensuring that our entire stable had their workouts. It may have something to do with the fact that a female farrier would join him many days. I finally found out her name was Jane Linville.

After a long ride, I cleaned up and joined the family in a limo for our luncheon date at the studio. It wasn't Mary's as no pictures were taped to the back of the seats. How many five-year-olds have a limo dedicated for their use? Spoiled? Nah.

Susan Wallace, Sharon Bronson, and Anna Romanov met us at the front office. All the ladies did the kissy-face thing even though they had seen each other in the last few days. We guys managed to avoid it. Mary announced that she wouldn't push herself forward as children should be seen and not heard. I think there is part of the concept she doesn't get.

Mr. Monroe was a perfect host for the luncheon set up in the executive dining room. There was pleasant conversation until after we had dessert and coffee. At that time, he brought up the fact that we would be seeing daily rushes from *Over the Ohio*, which had the potential to change my image as an actor.

I asked those present to view it and give their thoughts on this possible game-changer. From there, we proceeded to a projection room. This one was nicer than those out on the sets. This was more like a miniature movie theater. Eddie even asked if they had popcorn.

Susan Wallace asked how he could even consider eating after that large lunch. He replied that it was not for eating but to throw at me on the screen. We had to explain this was common practice in the Jackson House basement. I thought this *lese majeste* would horrify those present. Instead, Mr. Monroe stated he would see about installing a machine as he frequently had the same urge. Maybe a basket or two of rotten tomatoes should be kept on hand.

The projectionist started the film after we were settled. It began with the unknown killer shooting the Indian father and then knifing the mother. The camera then followed him chasing the young Indian girl with a tomahawk raised. At one point in the run, the camera position is changed, and we see the killer's face for the first time in the movie.

Since I had been in the picture and seen the rushes earlier, I wasn't surprised like the others present. The gasps told the story.

They all had an idea of what was coming, but the reality was shocking.

The film stopped, and the lights turned back on. At first, my family and friends just sat there. Then they started talking all at once. I heard words like evil, devil, malevolent, demonic, and terrifying.

No question that the shot raised an emotional response.

One person had said nothing. She just sat there sobbing. I stood up and moved over to Mary. I knelt and asked her what was wrong.

"You changed; you are different, and I don't like this scary Rick."

"You know I am not scary. That is just the makeup and me acting."

"When we talk while waiting for our turn to audition, the other kids say that you can only let out what is inside you. Do you have that evil person inside you?"

Anna Romanov stepped in and probably saved my life.

"Mary, those kids have it only partly right. A great actor can be a different person from what they are. They are acting a part. They are not the part. Before today, Rick was a character actor. He has played Rick and what is inside him. In this film clip, we see Rick be something he isn't. That is true acting."

Mr. Monroe said, "Now Rick needs to make a decision, and he wanted your thoughts on this. Does he want the world to see him as an actor and if so, does he want them to see this? Some people will be confused and think this is the real Rick. Others will think he has stepped up his acting to a new level."

"I can't answer for Rick. I can answer for the studio. This scene will make the movie. What started as a B-movie is now a brilliant piece of work worthy of an Oscar. Not only that, but it will also make money, a lot of money. If this scene is cut and redone with a lower intensity, it will go back to being a ho-hum show."

At least my sister had stopped crying. A discussion started amongst the group. All agreed with Miss Romanov and Mr.

Monroe's thoughts. I had taken the first step towards being considered an actor. Also, as it stood, the movie would play strong in the marketplace.

I was of mixed thoughts. I wanted the movie to make a lot of money. It would vindicate me as an actor and also as the one who had come up with the movie idea.

The next question was, do I want to follow up on it? I had been ready to drop out of Hollywood and concentrate on school. If this movie played as we all thought, I would have to follow up on the success. I might be able to wait six months but not much longer.

We talked about all these issues until we started going in circles. Susan Wallace finally summed it all up.

"By using the scene, we have a strong movie that will showcase Rick as an actor, plus making it profitable. Going this route does not lock him out of dropping movies and going to school. It just keeps his options open."

Mary said, "I can always tell Patty that my scary big brother will get her if she is mean to me."

It sounds like we have a plan. I told Mr. Monroe to leave it as is.

Now the professionals Mr. Monroe, Sharon Bronson, Anna Romanov, and Susan Wallace discussed how to leak insider information on this scene to build some industry buzz without giving the climax away.

At that point, our family returned home. Well, after stopping at a Dairy Queen on the way. It was weird going to a Dairy Queen in a limo. For some reason, people stared. I did hear my name in the background, but no one approached for a nice autograph.

I changed clothes at home and saddled up George. I rode over to the new old airfield to see how things were going. Dad had mentioned the cleanup had started.

For some reason, I pictured a hundred guys with trash bags picking up beer cans. A hundred guys were working, but only three were on beer can duty. One was driving a D5 Caterpillar tractor, shoving them into a pile. Then a front loader gathered them up and put them into a dump truck, hauling them to a pit dug in a corner of the field. It looked like all the trash would go there and then be covered up—very efficient.

The entrance road had been cleared of weeds, and even the tree in the middle was gone. You could tell where the stump had been ground down. A simple resurfacing of the road would put it in good condition.

I hadn't been there for more than a few minutes when a Jeep came driving up. A man in a real smoky bear hat asked me what I was doing on government property. I explained who I was, and he relaxed. He was aware of the whole story. I was told I was welcome anytime.

I was paying for the whole operation through my company, so that seemed reasonable to me. He seemed to think he was giving me a gift. I hope that wasn't going to be a problem down the road.

I was wearing a vest to cover up my shoulder holster. When I leaned forward to shake his hand, he saw it. From the expression on his face, I quickly pulled out the wallet with my marshal's badge. Whatever he had been going to say got lost as he turned, got in his Jeep, and drove away.

I guess I would find out someday what was going on.

Rather than wear out my welcome, I left. I had seen what I had come for, the progress being made. At home, I told Mum and Dad about the whole incident. They were as puzzled as I was.

Dad made a phone call to his higher-up contact at the Forest Service and got an answer. The Forest Service was not armed except under exceptional circumstances like a grizzly bear needing to be put down. To have an armed person from another service on what they considered their private property was disconcerting.

The guy in the field had called his headquarters for clarification. There was no problem. He just wanted to know if their partnership was with another federal agency or Jackson Enterprises, as he had been told.

It turns out that I was reading way too much into the incident. You would think the Soviets had made me paranoid or something.

Speaking of being paranoid, I had decided that being out on horseback with only a pistol was not enough. I was going to buy a scabbard and a new Winchester lever-action rifle for heavier firepower. I didn't feel any need to ask Mum and Dad if this was okay. I'm emancipated now.

Besides, you could rely on them to always be on the side of heavier firepower.

After dinner, it was back to the textbooks. This time, it was calculus. I had heard this was the bane of college students. For some reason, it almost sang to me, yeah flat and out of tune with no sense of rhythm.

Eddie had a scout patrol meeting on Saturday, so at 10 a.m., I took him over to his patrol leader's house. I once again drove the Ford Fairlane. There was nothing wrong with it other than it wasn't my T-Bird. I had planned to wait in the car while Eddie went in for his forty-five-minute meeting. They had to plan a menu for their next camping trip and decide who would bring what and what skills they would work on while there. The troop planned to work on the Hiking Merit Badge so they should pick something along those lines.

Eddie had barely gotten into the house when the patrol leader's mother came out and invited me to join them out at their pool. I hemmed and hawed but gave in. I got an eyeful when we got to the pool. There were three girls about my age in bikinis. One was the sister of the boy Eddie was visiting, and the others were next-door neighbors.

Mom asked if I wanted anything to drink. As she went in to get the requested Coke, I was joined by the girls. It quickly became apparent this was a bit of a setup. They knew Eddie was coming over, and that me the actor was his older brother. It turns out that the patrols normally meet at the Scout House, but they had convinced Donna Masters' little brother Billy to have the meeting here instead.

They confessed all this cheerfully. I could be churlish to resent this, but hey, three pretty girls went out of their way to meet me. Who was I to complain?

The other girls were Linda Harrison and Nancy Houston. Mrs. Masters brought me my Coke and joined us. I think this may have foiled part of the girls' plans. What those plans might have been, I could only imagine. I have quite an imagination.

Anyway, it turned out to be a get-to-know little about you and your life session. It was a pleasant conversation. In passing, I can share that two of the girls were very well-endowed blondes. The third, Nancy, was slender and dark-haired.

As our conversation went on, I found that I appreciated Nancy's dry wit over the other girls' appearance. There was not enough time to get to know the girls well or for us to let the others know how we were reacting.

When Eddie and the other guys came out, we stood to leave, and Donna handed me a note. It had three names and three phone numbers. Now I'm a guy, and by definition, not very smart when females are involved, but I was smart enough to know this was the social equivalent of a stick of dynamite. Call one, and the others would want to claw that girl's and my eyes out. Fortunately, they were only five-digit numbers, and the first was the same on all of them. After a glance, I handed the note back to Donna.

When we got into the Ford, I pulled a pen out of the glove box and wrote the four digits I had memorized on the back of my hand.

While Eddie filled me in on their camping plans, I tried to figure out how to call Nancy without causing war to break out. It would have to be after my trip to England, so maybe the other girls wouldn't be upset when I called her and not them. One can dream, can't one?

Boring as it may seem, other than exercising, I spent the rest of Saturday and Sunday studying and packing for my Monday morning flight.

Chapter 3

I was able to get my exercises in before leaving for the airport. Mum went over things with me before I left. Yes, Mum, I have my ticket; yes, Mum, I have my hotel information; yes, Mum, I packed clean clothes including underwear; yes, Mum, I have my passports; yes, Mum, I have dollars and pounds. Boy, forget to pack shirts on a trip just once, and they never forget.

I also remembered the textbooks I was studying, so I read them on the way to LAX. That drive seemed to get longer all the time. I would be glad when the airstrip out back of the forest was finished, and I could fly to LAX. That reminded me I had to price out hangars or rental facilities at LAX. A rich man's work is never done.

As usual, I was flying TWA. From the moment the curbside skycap took my luggage to exchange my ticket for boarding passes, the staff recognized me. This made the whole event smooth and cheerful.

The lady at the check-in desk was taken aback after she asked if I had my passport.

"Yes, Mum," was not what she was expecting. She quickly recovered by asking if I remembered clean underwear. At that point, I gave up and nodded yes.

I had coffee in the Ambassador Club. They paged me to their front desk. They had a cart ready to take me to my gate. What service. It also had me signing autographs at the gate rather than in the hallway while trying to get to my flight. As they say, not their first rodeo.

It was easy to disengage when my flight was called for boarding. They called me up separately and before other passengers. That way, I was able to get an aisle seat in row two. The rest of the first-class passengers had to scramble to get their desired seats. Maybe someday they will be able to assign seats before boarding.

It would make it easier for everyone. I hated to know what it would be like in coach class. Looking to the back of the aircraft, you could see the aisle and window seats filling up as people boarded. This continued until all of those were taken. Then, the center seats started to fill in. Fortunately, not many people carried their luggage on with them.

A big, beefy guy sat next to me on the leg to St. Louis. He pulled out a spreadsheet and was making notes before we got off the ground. While he did that, I had more coffee and then breakfast when we were airborne. He kept working the whole trip. I pulled out a textbook and read until I felt the urge to nap.

As we were taxiing to the gate at St. Louis, the guy spoke up for the first and only time on the flight.

"Enjoy it while you can kid. It won't be as easy when you have to earn a living."

"Good advice."

What else could I say? We didn't have time for a conversation, and I didn't want to be rude.

I didn't bother to get off the plane as it was a short layover. I did give the flight crew autographs while we were waiting. The floodgates didn't open up since I was the only one in first class who didn't get off the plane.

Well almost. Murphy caught up with me as they announced a half-hour delay due to a minor maintenance issue. One of the flight attendants asked if I would go to the back of the plane and give autographs to the coach passengers. It would make the time go faster for everyone and keep them from getting restless.

Luckily, I had a stack of studio photos in my briefcase. An announcement was made to those who had stayed on the plane that they had arranged for a Hollywood star to have an autograph session.

I proceeded to work my way to the back of the plane. Besides giving out over fifty autographs, I collected seven phone numbers:

three from young ladies, three from not-so-young ladies, and one guy. I also got pinched on the butt. I swear the lady that did it was seventy-five if she was a day.

When I glared at her, she said, "At my age, you get what you can when and where you can."

I couldn't refute that logic, so grinned and moved away.

The leg from St. Louis to New York was uneventful. I had a three-hour layover and boarded for London. The nice thing about being in New York was no one recognized me, or if they did, they ignored me.

The flight to London was boring; well, nothing was happening on the overnight flight. I finally gave up, covered myself with a blanket, and slept like most of the other passengers.

Breakfast was served about two hours out. I had packed a small carry-on with clean underwear, a shirt, and my shaving kit. I then went into one of the small restrooms on the plane and cleaned up. I wish I had a film of the contortions I had to go through to change clothes. It was worth it. I looked and felt fresh with new clothes, washing up, and shaving.

I had learned the value of a good appearance in Hollywood. While most of the other passengers looked like refugees, I came across as put together. A final cup of coffee and it was England, here I come.

At passport control, I used my updated British passport, which listed me as Sir Richard Jackson. They processed me politely, but I didn't feel my title gained me anything.

I had nothing to declare, so my entry was easy. Outside the International Terminal, a limo from the Plaza on the Strand was waiting for me. The driver whisked me to the hotel, where my luggage disappeared while I checked in. The bellhop who escorted me to my room was all Sir this and Sir that. I figured it would cost me about a dollar a Sir.

Once settled in, I took a nap, being certain to phone for a wake-up call in two hours. After a nice sleep, I showered and dressed in jeans, a shirt, and a heavy pullover sweater. I then went for a walk around the area.

I ended up at Westminster Abbey, so I went on a tour. After that, it was a roundabout trip through Kensington and Piccadilly Circus. It was then back past Waterloo Station and St. Paul's Cathedral. It was a long, windy trip, but I enjoyed it immensely. The weather was typical English for January, cold with a misty fog that was slow to clear. At the front, January.

After being out all afternoon, I was ready to return to my room. I took another shower, donned a suit, and had dinner in the main dining room. I was the youngest one there by almost fifty years. Not a place to go for excitement. After dinner, I spent the evening studying and called it an early night.

On Tuesday, I felt great. Dressed for a run, I talked the front desk into having me driven over to Hyde Park for my morning run. As I was running along Rotten Row, a person on horseback almost bowled me over. They and the horse were paying no attention as they approached me.

I had to jump out of their way.

I let out a sharp, "Watch it!"

The person, a female by the clothes, didn't acknowledge me other than with a rude hand gesture. I did notice the markings on the horse. It had a white blaze between its eyes, continuing down its nose.

That certainly had my heart rate up. From there, I turned and jogged back to the hotel. I had found trying to run at my full, well still not that fast, speed on city streets was not a good idea. I could run into things, and it got police attention as though I were a thief running for it.

The return trip did cool me down. A hot shower, a full English breakfast of bacon, sausages, eggs, baked beans, fried tomato and mushroom, fried bread, coffee, and juice, and I was good to go for the day. Since my appointment with Mr. Norman was after lunch, I went to the British Museum.

I could spend days in this group of buildings. This morning, I browsed through the recently rebuilt Coins and Medals Department. It had been destroyed in the war. The more ancient coins reminded me of that cup in the safe at home. I wonder what its story is? I wouldn't even know where to begin.

I had lunch at a greasy fish and chips shop and then had to find a place to wash my hands. A look into their loo drove me away. It was still near the museum in Bloomsbury, so I used one of their public water closets. I was trying to think in British English to fit in.

From there, I caught a black cab to Buckingham Palace. I thought the cab driver would be impressed with my destination, but apparently, he took people there all the time. Thinking about it, he probably did. They called them tourists!

I remembered to wear my Greyhound pin on my lapel so that with my passport and a phone call to prepare them, my arrival was expected. A footman led me to Mr. Norman.

After the usual pleasantries and inquiries about my trip, I brought up the subject of my journey. What were the requirements for me to sit for my O-Levels and possibly the A-Levels?

He explained that anyone could pay for and sit for the levels. The question was, was I ready for them? We both agreed that the O-Levels should be no problem, but the A-Levels might be because of differences in the US and British instructions. Approved private companies gave the tests. The same company could also provide a readiness test for each exam you wanted to sit for. It was common for students outside of England to want to sit for the exams, so provisions had been made.

He had set me up with a group called International Testing. They specialized in seeing where foreign students fit within the English curriculum. Another advantage of their service was that they didn't have testing seasons. Normal testing groups had registration deadlines, exam dates, etc. They needed this as they were handling the bulk of English students.

International Testing did everything by special appointment. Of course, they charged about five times as much per test. This seemed to be the best route for me, so Mr. Norman called and confirmed an appointment for me to meet with one of their counselors tomorrow morning.

After that, he and I had a conversation about where my life was going. He wanted to know if I was doing more songs with Frank Sinatra. I told him that Mr. Sinatra was on me to do another duet. He asked if he could get a recording when released and have our autographs.

It seemed so weird that this stern-looking older man was a fan of such music. You would think he would attend Beethoven concerts or listen to highbrow chamber music. As we conversed, I found out that he did.

He was most interested when I told him that I had a six-passenger plane being delivered in March or April. He wanted to know if I planned to bring it to England if I attended school here. I hadn't thought about it, but it would open a world of possibilities.

Mr. Norman told me that it opened possibilities for the Messenger Service. They were mostly comprised of retired military personnel who traveled on commercial airlines. A young man like me might help with transportation when needed quickly.

We went on to talk about what university I might attend. I told him that I wanted to look at the engineering program at the Imperial University in London. He asked me if I was in a hurry to obtain an engineering degree.

I thought that an odd question.

He explained, "Richard, from what I know, you will never actually hold a job; well, I guess your singing and acting are jobs, but you know what I mean."

So, the question becomes, why are you going to school? There are two valid reasons for a man: obtain a technical degree to earn a living or make contacts that will stand you well in later years. Which is the most important to you?

I had never looked at it that way. It was similar in reasoning as Mum had put it in the past to wanting socialization and relating to my peer group. I started to open my mouth and remembered something else I had learned. If you have time, don't plan until you have given it mature thought.

"That is a lot to think about, Mr. Norman. What you are presenting is similar to what my parents have talked about in the past. I have to think this through. In the meantime, I will take the evaluation exams to see where I stand. If I do poorly, this may be all for naught."

At least he laughed at that.

"I don't think that will be a concern, Sir Richard."

He glanced at his watch.

"We have an appointment with Her Majesty in five minutes, so we had better move on."

This was news to me.

Her Majesty was very welcoming. She asked the usual questions about my trip. She then came out with the real reason I was here with her.

"I understand from your Mum that you are undecided in which direction to go with your education, a technical degree, or an opportunity to socialize with your peers."

Well, I didn't have to give this any more mature thought. Mum and Dad were pushing in a direction and were joined by the Queen of England; the writing was on the wall. Next, I would get a phone call from the president of the United States.

The Queen continued, "In my last conversation with President Eisenhower, your name came up. He agrees that it is important for you to make acquaintances with those you will be dealing with later in your life."

"What would your Majesty suggest?"

"If your exams go right, and I'm sure they will, it would be most pleasing if you applied to University College at Oxford."

I heard the royal "We" in that sentence.

"If they accept me, I will consider that."

"We are certain they will."

Well, that fix was in.

After that, I was dismissed. I made sure to back out of the room. Fortunately, the door was nearby, and I didn't tip over any vases.

I was driven back to my hotel, where I collapsed and thought about what had transpired this afternoon. The way I read it, my parents had connived with the Crown to get what they thought best for me. Maybe they were right. I noticed recently that my parents seemed to be getting smarter than they were several years ago.

After dinner, I worked on formulas from my book on statistics. I could see where this could be very handy when interpreting a mound of data. Another good thing about statistics is it can put you to sleep easily.

Chapter 4

Wednesday morning, after my morning routine, I headed to my appointment with International Testing. Unlike California where my sports coat and polo shirt were standard, in England, it was a suit and tie. Informal was not wearing the waistcoat.

I was informal for my interview. My appointment was with a man named Mr. Clark. He had me describe my education to date. He frowned and smiled so much while I was describing it that I had no idea how it was being received.

He was able to put my worries to rest, or at least calm them.

"Sir Richard, you appear to be very driven with self-education. There is no doubt this is the best way. The only need by doing it that way is that you learn the correct material."

After discussion, I decided to take the evaluation examinations for English Language, English Literature, Modern History, Latin, Economy, Spanish, Mathematics, Additional Mathematics, Chemistry, Biology, and Science (including Physics). He was a little taken aback about my refusal to take a Music exam.

Each practice exam would be one and a half hours; the actual exam would be three hours. I was asked when I could sit for them. I responded that I was ready today. Since these were only evaluation exams, they were able to sit me in a room with the testing materials and a proctor.

After writing a cheque for an insanely large amount, at least in my experience, I was allowed to start the tests immediately. I wrote the English Language portion before lunch. With an hour's break for lunch. I had a pot pie at a pub next door. After lunch, it was English Literature, a half-hour break, then Modern History. They were given in the order I had discussed with Mr. Clark.

I felt that I had at least passed each of the exams. Did I pass them enough to be recommended for the full examination? Time will tell.

Since it was my money, I was free to pay for and take any of the exams. They were giving their estimation of my ability to pass the full exam. It was all at my risk.

I had no problem falling asleep at an early hour.

The following day, I went through my normal routine, then appeared at International Testing, or IT, as they called it. Two exams in the morning, two in the afternoon, and I didn't have two thoughts to rub together. After changing into comfortable clothes, I went for a long walk by the Thames. It was raining and those umbrellas that I had been sneering at suddenly looked good. I might carry an umbrella but never the homburg.

Friday was damp. I took a taxi to Harrods and bought an umbrella. From there, it was to IT for the last of my exams. By the time I finished the last one, brain dead was too kind. Not only did I not have two thoughts to rub together, I'm not certain I had even one. I was to return Monday morning to review the results and decide on a further course of action. I would either take revision courses to pass at least seven O-Levels or if I passed seven, the evaluation tests for A-Levels. I felt confident about passing enough O-Levels to take the actual exams.

It was nice to have the weekend off. I went for a long run around Hyde Park. There were several groups of riders, but none of them had a horse with a large white blaze on its face. I ate lunch at a small outdoor café on Piccadilly Circus, on or in. I'm not confident how to say that.

There were street vendors galore with interesting and not-so-interesting items. I picked up small gifts for the family. Nothing exciting, just things from England. I bought Mum a set of Coronation Flags from every king and queen back to Victoria. Dad got a whistle from World War I, which had been used to signal going over the top of the trenches for an assault.

I looked at the adverts in the Daily Telegraph for flats to rent. Staying in a hotel was already getting old. After reading the ads, I was more confused than ever. I didn't know the neighborhoods in London, and I realized I had no idea how long I would be in London.

It was late enough in the day I called home and talked to my parents for over an hour. That would be some phone bill. I didn't care because they helped me in several ways.

After thoroughly discussing the benefits of going to Oxford vs. trying to start at London Imperial immediately, I realized that maybe I was pushing too fast. Why not settle into college life without the academic pressure?

Of course, it all depended on how I did on my O- and A-Level exams.

Another thing I hadn't thought of was renting a full suite here at the Plaza. Apparently, you could redecorate your rooms and even replace the furniture on a long-term arrangement. As Dad pointed out, I could afford the rooms forever if I wanted. It would be very pricey, but I would always have a place available in London.

I decided to talk to the hotel manager and see what could be done.

Not one to put things off, after hanging up and telling everyone in the family I loved them, I went to the lobby.

Since it was the weekend, an assistant manager was running the office. He had all the answers when I explained what I was looking for. Expensive answers but good answers. There was a penthouse three-bedroom suite available with separate living and dining rooms. There was also a full kitchen. He took me up to show me the rooms.

What he hadn't mentioned were the large rooms. The furniture was too heavy for my taste, but I was assured they could put it all into storage while I used whatever I wanted.

There was a large patio off the living room. I mentioned it was a shame there was no swimming pool. The assistant manager laughed and told me the old girl (the hotel) couldn't stand the strain. Two reserved parking spaces in the garage went with the room and valet parking privileges. The normal hotel room services would continue if I wanted to host a party by special arrangement.

That all sounded good. The suite was available for a mere ten thousand US dollars a month. The assistant must have thought this price would freak me out. However, I knew what was paid in Hollywood and at the Waldorf in New York, so I was prepared for the price. Knowing all that, I had time to think about my finances and realized there would be no strain. Based on that, I told him that I had to see some exam results on Monday, and if they were as anticipated, I would take them.

Changing into jeans and a sweater, I went to the movies. I had so much to think about, I don't remember the movie. After dinner, I pulled out a new novel. It was about a monastery in the American Southwest that was preserving scientific knowledge after an atomic war.

Sunday, the sun peeked out, so my morning run was pleasant. There was still no sighting of the horse with a large blaze on its head. I had pretty well gotten over my peeve of the reckless rider. It had been a foggy day with poor visibility. I still wondered what the girl looked like.

I wandered the streets of London for the rest of the day, but nothing caught my attention. Well, there are a lot of pretty girls in London, and it was a sunny day, so it wasn't a waste.

When I returned to the hotel, the assistant manager was waiting for me.

"Sir Richard, you will understand that we took the liberty of making certain you could afford the penthouse and that your parents would support you. We didn't realize you are emancipated and have the funds in your own right."

He must have spoken to Mum.

"I'm very sorry if you are offended by this, but we needed to do due diligence."

Yep, he had talked to Mum.

"I understand. You have a business to run, and it is a large sum of money."

"Thank you for your understanding, Sir Richard."

He gave a deep bow when he said this. It was so deep I thought he would tip over.

Now I know he had talked to Mum.

I asked him if they knew of any decorators who could help me redo the suite and purchase new furniture. Of course, they did. The decorator would be available as soon as we signed a contract. I told him that I hoped it would be tomorrow afternoon. I would know where I stood with my exams by then.

This led to a brief talk about what exams I would be taking. He seemed impressed that I was considering eleven of them if my evaluations came out well.

After that, it was to my room to finish the book about the monastery and an early night. I was anxious to see what the morrow would bring.

Chapter 5

I was waiting at International Testing's door when they opened on Monday. My appointment was the first thing, and I wanted to know how I had done. Mr. Clark followed me in the door. He didn't seem surprised that I was already there. I asked him and he replied that many students were there before the doors opened.

As we walked to his office, he told me, "For you, it's good news, bad news situation."

With a sinking stomach, I asked for the bad news first.

"You can take all the exams. The good news is you passed all the evaluations."

I may have shot people for less or at least thought about it.

In his office, he went over each of the evaluations with me. The only ones that appeared to be on the edge were Additional Mathematics and Biology. Neither was a surprise. I had done well enough they encouraged me to take all the exams, but if I were to have trouble, it would be on those.

Eleven three-hour examinations, whew! Mr. Clark encouraged me to take one today and then no more than two a day and leave a day between exams. If I started today, it would take the next two weeks.

As much as I wanted to get them over with, that schedule made the most sense. When we discussed the order, I only asked that the Biology and Additional Math be left until last. That made sense to Mr. Clark, and he even offered me study packets for the two courses that were directed at the exam.

We agreed on English as the first exam. Since I had hours until lunch and the exam, he set me up in an office with a study packet. This set the pattern for the next two weeks. I would go over the study packets for a specific exam. In my other free time, I worked on Biology and Additional Mathematics. I was worried about Biology the most as I didn't have the opportunity to cut things up as was done in a formal class.

After my first exam, I signed a contract with the hotel on Monday. They would start the process of emptying the Penthouse Suite for me and painting it where needed. Since the walls were all a neutral white, I had no issues. I put off talking to a decorator until after my exams were done.

I spent every waking moment either exercising, studying, or taking exams. It was as an intense period of my life that I could remember. Thinking back to final exams in Bellefontaine, they were nothing.

It seemed to take forever and seemed to fly by. I finished up on a Friday afternoon and had to wait until Monday for the results. Again, I was at the front door when they opened. This time, Mr. Clark beat me in and waited in his office. He didn't try to make it suspenseful this time.

"Rick, you did well on all your examinations. Your worst grade was a C in Biology."

"You received an A in English Language, English Literature, Modern History, Latin, Economy, Spanish, Mathematics, Chemistry, and Science. Then there is a B in Additional Mathematics and a C in Biology. Overall, passing eleven O-Levels are very impressive results. This would be the top for a person in year twelve."

"So, what should I do for A-Levels?"

"If I were you, I would take all of those for which you received an A."

"Did I miss an A in Additional Mathematics by very much?"

Mr. Clark reviewed the exam and results and told me no, only by three points.

"Then I think I would like to take it also. I suspect Biology is hopeless."

"Your C is a low C. I think we can count that out."

"So, should I do the same sort of schedule as the O-Levels?"

"That would work, but I want you to take the next two days off. The last two weeks have been stressful for you. I know you had the weekend off, but you had to be thinking about the exam results. We have found students do better if they have some time to decompress."

"I can't argue with that, so I will take two exams every other day starting on Wednesday?"

"Yes, that will finish you off, Friday week."

"Sounds like a plan."

"What are your intentions for the next two days?"

"I'm going to practice archery, quarterstaff, and swordplay. I thought about studying, but that would be self-defeating at this point."

"Good, I'm glad you understand. If I may ask, where can you practice in the city?"

"I usually go to the Tower or a Queen's Park outside town."

"You must know someone of influence."

"Queen Elizabeth is my godmother."

"That would do it. See you Wednesday morning here at nine."

On the way back into the hotel, the assistant manager caught me. They had the rooms cleaned out and repainted. Would I like to see them? Of course, I did.

The rooms were enormous without anything in them. I had been window shopping on my walks through London, so I had an idea of what I wanted. The rooms would look like the 1960s rather than the 1860s.

In particular, there was an Eames lounge chair in brown leather that I had to have. The furniture by Jacobson and Saarinen is particularly nice, while a Knoll couch would be perfect.

I asked if the decorator would be available tomorrow. She would. From there I changed clothes and called Mr. Norman. I owed him an update on my test results, and it also gave me a chance to ask about going to the Tower to practice quarterstaff work.

We chatted briefly and hung up while he made another call. He called me right back and said nobody was available for the next several days. That took care of that thought.

So, it was back to the good old run until you were ready to drop. It certainly took my mind off the examinations. After that, I called Jackson House and updated them on my exams. I received words of congratulations and encouragement from the family.

Mary wanted to know when I was coming home. I told her it would probably be a few more weeks. Her sigh made me think my little actress had gained a new talent. I asked Mum about that, and she confirmed my thoughts. Mary had been practicing sighing for several days. Would I like her shipped over to me?

Tuesday was a nothing day. I tried running but was bored quickly. Returning to the hotel, I tried reading fiction and studying, but neither worked to distract me. After lunch, I met with the lady decorator. My first reaction to her was that she was a snob. Once we got talking furniture and went through the catalogs she had brought with her, she became a different person.

You could tell she enjoyed what she was doing. She was enthusiastic when I told her my thoughts about 1960 rather than 1860. She asked if we could be followed by a photographer. The redoing of the Plaza Penthouse would make an excellent magazine layout.

There were many pictures of the before penthouse, so that would not be an issue. I initially wondered if people knowing where I lived would be a problem but then realized it was not a state secret.

I told her she could proceed with the entire project. To say Dorothy May Kinnicutt was happy was an understatement. She had been designing for a while but needed a breakthrough to gain an international reputation. She told me to call her Sister as all her friends did.

When I told Mum about it, she asked for Sister's phone number as she had some questions. Not being completely dense, I asked Mum if she would coordinate everything with Sister and present me with a finished product. I told her I was impressed with how my office was done up in LA and would like that carried through.

From her response, I knew I had dodged a bullet. It worked out well. Mum was happy. Sister had a project. I would have a suite of rooms in London without having to do the scut work. Good job, Rick!

Wednesday was a test day. I ensured I had a good night's sleep and a moderate workout followed by a light breakfast. This was followed by taking a cab over to IT for the first test.

After that, I ate a slightly larger lunch and spent the balance of my time walking.

Then, I took the second A-Level of the day.

Thursday, I spent two hours revising materials provided by IT. This was mainly passing papers submitted for previous tests. It gave an idea of what was being looked for. Today, it was to be in essay form. It seemed to follow what I had seen previously on a Latin test. Bend the answer into the material you had already put together. So, I did exactly that.

The next day, the exams flowed, or at least they seemed to. The only hitch was if I had read the requirements wrong. If I had, it would be a disaster. Time will tell.

For the weekend, Mr. Norman had arranged for me to go to the Queen's Park I had been to previously. There, I met several men who were from different branches of the service. It was a fun day of martial arts, sword fighting, quarterstaff work, archery, and even some boxing.

I held my own in all but boxing.

Sunday was a day of revision and preparation for Monday's exams.

The following week was a repeat of the previous as I took care to have plenty of rest, eat well but not overeat, and get exercise. I was so glad to see the end of the week. Now, all I had to do was to get through the weekend and see how my test results came out. That would decide what I would do for the next several years.

I was wrung out enough that the thought of going to Oxford for three years and working on a low-pressure BA sounded good. It could be fun as I would be with guys more my age. While sixteen would be young, a lot of the first years would be seventeen. That was not a wide gap since I would be seventeen in October. Plus, I would be bigger than most of them so they wouldn't even guess my age.

Saturday, I went to a park and watched a cricket match. I had no idea what was going on. It was like attending a baseball game in that the crowd was laid back most of the time, and then some excitement when something happened. Somehow, I don't think it is a game for me. Watching the pretty girls on the sidelines was a nice way to spend the day. I didn't try to introduce myself to any of them as they were probably there to watch their boyfriends play.

Walking back to the hotel, I made an American mistake. I didn't look in the correct direction as I stepped off the curb. A sharp honk of a horn saved me. The driver of the car, a young lady, made an obscene hand gesture as she went past. She looked familiar. Nah, it couldn't be.

There was a message for me at the hotel. I returned Mr. Norman's call. He asked if I had any plans for the rest of today and Sunday. I told him none whatsoever. He asked me to take an overnight boat across the channel and deliver a small package to the British Embassy in Paris. I replied I would be glad to as I was just wasting time until Monday when I would receive my A-Level results. I took a black cab to the Palace where the package and my tickets awaited. It would be a quick trip. Train to Dover, ferry boat to Calais, train from Calais to Paris, drop off a package, return to Calais, then overnight to Dover where I would catch a train to London.

That sounded tiring, even reading the itinerary. I called Mr. Norman from the front desk and asked him if I must take the trip as laid out. He wanted to know what I had in mind. I told him I would like to fly to Paris in the morning, drop off the package, and return later in the day.

"Sir Richard, you can do that, but it would be at your own expense. We have a budget to maintain, and the ferry and train tickets are much less expensive than airfare."

"If that is the case, I will fly. I will leave the tickets here at the desk."

I returned to the hotel and talked to the concierge, who in turn called a travel agent. Just like that, my trip was arranged. It would be an hour's flight to Paris and an hour back, all on the same day. This was a much better use of my time.

Clever boy, what would I do for the rest of the afternoon? I may have outsmarted myself.

That solved itself. I was paying off my cabby at the hotel when a group of boys my age ran by, not at a dead run, more like a jog. I asked what that was about. It turns out they were Hashing. A person called the Hare would lead them on a chase. The Hare would mark their trail with bits of paper or flour left at the turns. The object was to chase the Hare until you found the pub they were finishing at and have a party.

Since I had been to a cricket match, I was dressed in jeans, a polo shirt, and running shoes. Having nothing better to do, I finished paying the cabby and took off. Tally Ho.

I caught up with their tail-end Charlies in short order. I was content to run with them until I understood what was going on. The pace was such that we could talk. They quickly realized that I was a Yank with no idea what was happening. They couldn't have been nicer.

It turns out there were no winners or losers in this run unless you made a wrong turn and lost the course. Some clubs tried to be tricky, but this one wasn't. They called themselves the Hash House Harriers after an earlier famous club.

It took us another hour to finish the course. It didn't seem too difficult. In the center of the intersection where we had to turn, there was a dash of flour. Then you had to decide which way to go—right, left, or straight. About fifty feet down the correct route was more flour. This gave course confirmation.

Of course, when twenty people got to an intersection, they would split up and go in all three directions. Once the correct one was identified the others would turn back and join them. Depending on your choices, you could have a long or short day. I noticed many people held back, especially those who looked older. They let the kids do the running.

Even though I was a kid, I decided to let the youngsters run. This gave me a chance to talk to the other runners. They were of all ages and occupations. I just identified myself as Rick Jackson, an American at loose ends for the day.

It was fun, and at the end, more people introduced themselves at the pub. I got roped into a game of darts and quickly found out that these people were serious about their darts. One game was enough for me, and I suspect, them. Overall, it was a pleasant evening with nothing accomplished but relaxation. Maybe I should have more of these.

Sunday was an early flight to Paris. Going through immigration and customs was ho-hum. They took one look at my passport, asked when I was returning to England, and waved me through. Using a cab with one of the craziest cab drivers I ever had, I dropped the package off at the British Embassy. I had no idea how long I would be inside, so I paid the driver off, hoping the next one would be better.

I wasn't in the embassy for more than ten minutes. They had a car and driver to return me to the airport. I discovered that they would have picked me up if I had called them. Good to know.

I sat in the first-class lounge for several hours reading the afternoon paper and then had an uneventful trip back to my hotel home. The newspaper did carry a story about an explosion in a stateroom on one of the cross-channel ferries. Fortunately, the room wasn't occupied.

Chapter 6

The next day, I was about to go down to breakfast when there was a knock at the door. This time of day was very unusual, so I used the keyhole window in the door. There were two men in suits standing there. I left the chain on the door and edged it open. The frontman held out a badge wallet case with an ID card.

"Sir Richard, we are from MI5 and would like to have a word."

Every spy story I had ever read went through my mind.

"I must check out your identity before I allow you in."

To say they were not pleased was an understatement, but it wasn't my job to please them. They passed two business cards through the door. I looked up the public number for MI5 and inquired. It only took several minutes to establish they were for real. I let them in after that.

"Why are you so cautious, Sir Richard?"

"Some Russian lads have it in for me."

"That may tie into why we are here. You were booked on a cross-channel ferry last night, but then you canceled the reservation. Last night, there was an explosion in that room that would have killed you if you were there."

That left me cold.

"Why did you cancel your reservation?"

"I decided to fly instead. It would be a much easier trip."

"Why were you taking the trip?"

It then dawned on me the right hand did not know what the left hand was doing. I told them to wait a minute and retrieved my diplomatic passport, which identified me as a Queen's Messenger.

This took them aback.

"You said some Russian lads were upset with you. Who are they?"

"The KGB."

"Sir Richard, I think this is deeper than our remit. We were told to interview the passenger who didn't make the crossing and find out if they had any idea what was happening. It seems this is a lot deeper than we thought."

"I suspect it is. I suggest that someone in your organization contacts the Palace and MI6. They can give you a clearer picture, also the CIA and FBI if you have time."

You could see them getting more nervous all the time about what were they getting into.

"Do you have any official standing other than as a Queen's Messenger?"

I collected my US Marshal badge and wallet with my ID and showed them to them.

"How old are you?"

"Sixteen."

The more senior-looking of the two asked if he could use my telephone. He called his office and was having a spirited conversation. When he hung up, he asked me a question.

"Is your mum Viscountess Jackson?"

"Yes, sir."

They left shortly after that with a caution to be careful. Now, that was helpful.

I had to miss breakfast to make my appointment at IT to see my exam results.

I passed everything with at least a C.

"You received an A in English Language, English Literature, Economy, Spanish, Mathematics, Chemistry, and Science. B's in Modern History, Latin. Then, there is a C in Additional Mathematics. Overall, passing ten A-Levels are very impressive results. You would be accepted by any university in the world. Sir Richard, you have our congratulations and best wishes."

"Thank you."

About that time, a secretary knocked on the door.

"Sir, a ride is waiting for Sir Richard."

Now, I hadn't asked for any rides. When I looked out the front door, there was a familiar face. James Barclay was standing next to a Bentley. As soon as he saw me, he opened the car door, so I made a beeline for it.

"Until this is sorted out, we thought we had better keep track of you."

"I appreciate it."

We didn't drive to the Palace; instead, we went to a nondescript building with an indoor garage. There was a guard at the entrance to the garage. He raised a gate for us to enter. Once inside, we exited the car and went up an elevator. Upon exiting the elevator, James had to show some identification to a guard sitting at a table across from the elevator door. The guard had a short-barreled shotgun on the desk. I would bet there was a round chambered.

We went to an office that can only be described as civil service nondescript. It was probably issued around 1930. It matched the drab green of the walls. The only thing hanging on the wall was the obligatory picture of the monarch. The portrait reinforced my estimation of the year as it was George V.

The man behind the desk did not fit the room. This is how he would look and dress if there was a real James Bond.

He introduced himself as Bond, James Bond. The look on my face must have been priceless as he and James Barclay roared with laughter.

"I always wanted to do that to someone."

"Well, you got me good."

"My real name is Nigel Montgomery, a very distant relation. This is an MI6 office we try not to use very often to keep it safe."

"Do you have any idea who and why someone is trying to kill me?"

"We do. It was a very amateur attempt by a low-level IRA gunman. He worked on the ferry. When he saw your name on the passenger list, he saw an opportunity to use the quarter stick of dynamite he had lying around. It doesn't seem to go any deeper than that. We had you picked up as soon as we knew what was happening. Don't want you going Cowboy on us."

I don't think I will ever live my Secret Service call sign down.

"Well, that's a relief. I wondered if I would have to return to Jackson House and stay inside for the rest of my life."

"We think you are safe for now. However, you are a high-profile person in certain circles and could become a target of opportunity, so use some common sense where you go. Now, James, I think Mr. Norman would like to talk to Sir Richard. Please take him to the Palace."

I was whisked through Palace security like it wasn't there. Mr. Norman was standing in his office waiting for me.

"My poor boy, we didn't think for a moment anything like this would happen. It was to be a boring messenger run, to show you what it is really like."

"Well, the actual trip was boring; it was afterward that it got interesting, and I was never in any actual danger once I varied my route."

"Yes, and that is a lesson well learned. We are going to be reviewing how all our messenger trips are organized. I'm afraid we have gotten too complacent."

"That can happen."

"Yes, well, I wanted to reassure you that this was far from ordinary. In the meantime, Her Majesty would like to have a word."

"Yes, sir."

James led me to the Queen's apartment and waited outside. The Queen was there, so I entered the room, giving the small head bow and formal Your Majesty.

"Sir Richard, are you alright?"

"Yes, Ma'am."

"I'm so glad. I just got off the phone with Peg. She told me you would handle it well, but I wanted to know myself, now on to more important matters. Congratulations on your A-levels. Have you decided what you are going to do about schooling?"

"Ma'am, I'm going to see if one of the colleges at Oxford will have me."

"They will. Which one do you want?"

"I don't know enough at this point to choose."

"Understood. I will have you briefed on what is possible, considering that you should keep a low profile. Now, young man, I must see you off. I have a luncheon, and I suspect you would eat somewhere other than with a bunch of old fuddy-duddies."

You come up with a good answer to that!

"Yes, Ma'am."

At that, the Queen laughed, and I backed out of the room.

It was early afternoon, and I was getting hungry. Another of the Palace's fleet of Bentleys dropped me off at my hotel. Bentley would never go out of business as long as there was a monarchy. Instead of going into the hotel, I went around the corner and down an alley to a fish and chips shop I had found.

I think Victoria was Queen the last time a health inspector had been in. The wooden floor was worn down to a grey patina. The walls got darker the higher you looked from many generations of cigarette smoke. The ceiling was an embossed metal repeating design.

The fish was a white, flaky North Atlantic cod; the large cut chips were golden brown with just the right amount of salt. The vinegar was malt vinegar but must have been a secret recipe. Mr. Treacher was the perfect host, making one feel like they were in a high-class restaurant instead of a hole-in-the-wall dump.

Dump or not, the food was wonderful. I wish they had this in America.

From there, I took a cab to the British Museum with the intention of browsing until dinner. I was looking at the exhibit of drawings from the Hans Sloan collection. The drawings were okay, but I was more impressed by the fact that he was credited with the invention of chocolate milk.

I was leaving the area when I saw a young lady stumble into a life-size statue. It started to tip, so I lunged towards it and caught it before it went completely over. The only problem was I was off balance, and the statue was very heavy. I couldn't hold it up, so I yielded to its weight as slowly as possible. In this manner, I was able to lower myself and the statue without harming it.

Of course, I was then trapped on the floor with about five hundred pounds of statue pinning me there. I wheezed out to the girl who had stopped and turned. She gave me a crooked grin and then made a crude hand gesture. I recognized that hand!

A museum guard had seen the whole incident and had the statue lifted in a few minutes. I must say they seemed to care more about the statue's condition than me. By this time, the young lady had disappeared. I wondered what she had against me.

After they helped me up and dusted me off, the guards were more attentive.

"Young man, that was a fine thing you did, risking your life over a marble statue."

"Well, it was not thought through. I saw it topple and grabbed it."

About that time, a group of museum authorities showed up and wanted to know what had happened. The guard who had witnessed the whole event described it in detail. The young lady, who I swore had fair blonde hair, became a brunette. She went from tall and fair to short and dark-skinned.

I looked at the guard when he was done with his description. He winked at me and mouthed, "It was an accident."

It was, so I let it go. Still, she should stop with the gestures.

Of course, I had to give my name, and they made a fuss about me being the man who had saved the Queen. Just what I needed: more publicity. A member of the press, the *Times*, had a few questions. From the tone of the questions, it was what sort of gormless person would jump under a five hundred pound falling piece of marble.

When I thought about it, he was correct. Anyway, I called it a day. It was back to the hotel. My new digs weren't ready yet, so I was stuck in my small suite. Oh, woe is me. Well, I had survived the O- and A-Level exams, so now had to get into a college at Oxford. I now had to wonder if any would accept a gormless American. After that, I should head back to America and see what was happening at home.

Chapter 7

I had a lot of things to do after my exercise and break on Tuesday. The first thing was to arrange a flight back to the US. Then I had to pack. That wasn't hard to do. A trip to the concierge desk took care of the flight, and as I left most of my clothes in place, there would be no checked baggage. I did take a shaving kit and reading material.

Leaving clothes there made me think about what clothes I had in the US. It wouldn't take much to have similar wardrobes in each country. That way, I would never have to check bags again.

Next was to call Mr. Norman at the Palace. I had to see him about my attending Oxford. My timing was fortuitous as he was about to call me. If possible, I was to come to the Palace at 2 p.m. for a meeting about Oxford. It was possible.

So, after my hard work for the day, all forty-five minutes' worth, I read until lunch and then caught a black cab to the Palace. It still seemed weird getting into a taxi and saying Buckingham Palace, please. It never startled the cabbies until I told them the visitor's entrance. They took many tourists there, but few who would visit.

The guards at security were beginning to recognize me. They still required identification and checked me for weapons (after asking if I had anything to leave for safekeeping.) Still, they were pleasant, and the checks were perfunctory. I wonder what would happen if I brought my US Marshal ID and weapon. Some thoughts should remain thoughts.

Mr. Norman was waiting with Mr. Merton. He knew everything there was to know about Oxford.

There were several items of importance. First, I was totally outside of the normal registration scheme. That would not present a problem as I had a sponsor, and an exception would be made. That would be Her Majesty, of course.

Next, they would prefer if I sat for the SAT examination as soon as possible. My strong Levels would get me in, but a high SAT score would be the icing on the cake. I could take the test in the UK or the US. I told them I was returning to California tomorrow, so it would be best to take it at home.

I was to enroll with an alias! How cool was that? It would only give me a low level of security and provide some protection from outside sources such as paparazzi. Any serious groups would be able to find me. Inside the university, I could use my real name.

As far as the college itself, Mr. Merton recommended Trinity. It was large enough with 400 undergraduates and another 400 graduate students. I could remain in the background if I desired.

It was too late in the year to obtain a room at the college, so I had to find a flat outside of the school. This shouldn't be a problem other than the expense. I assured him that I could afford it.

As far as degrees went, after a lengthy discussion on courses available, I chose Engineering Sciences. This would give me a good foundation across the entire field. Mr. Merton was concerned to know if I had shown any inclination toward Engineering. I assured him that I did and, as a matter of fact, held several patents.

This led to a discussion on what I held.

He then educated me about what would happen if I performed any work on my ideas at Oxford. They would own a majority of my work.

They may think that, but I knew some good lawyers. I would have to sign agreements with Oxford but would be certain to exclude any patentable ideas developed by Jackson Enterprises. Of course, any ideas I had would be developed through Jackson Enterprises.

I was assured this shouldn't be a problem as very few undergraduates ever had an idea worth any money. It was aimed at graduate and doctoral candidates who were doing serious work. I didn't quite know how to take that.

Mr. Merton would obtain the paperwork for me to apply to Trinity. He would also talk to the Master of the College to pave the way for the various irregularities in my admission. It appeared that without the support of the Crown, this would never happen.

I brought up that I had committed to play in the US Open Golf tournament in June and that I would need several travel days. Mr. Merton didn't think that would be a problem but was glad that I had brought it up now. It was best to have these details sorted upfront.

This meeting took several hours, so I was glad to leave and stretch my legs. When I got back to the hotel, I checked on how my new suite redecoration was going. It would be available by the time I got back in two weeks.

I made an early night of it as I had to be up at 4 a.m. to catch my flight.

At least I was able to get coffee in the morning. That is the nice thing about a hotel. The hotel also had a limo to take me to the airport. It was easy to check in with no bags to worry about. A simple holdall did the job.

The flight boarded on time, and the takeoff was smooth. I would be home in time for dinner. Most of the flight continued to be smooth, but the part that wasn't smooth was called CAT, clear air turbulence. We hit it somewhere over the Atlantic. One moment, we were cruising along nicely; the next, we dropped several hundred feet.

The drop wasn't bad enough to hurt anyone, but it did make a mess of the plane's interior. It happened in the middle of a meal, and everyone's food and drink stayed where it was while the plane dropped. This put the juice from a glass of grape juice I was drinking up in the air. It must have studied Newton when it was in a bunch on the vine because it knew what goes up comes down. Came down it did, all over my tie and white shirt. Luckily, the suit jacket and pants were spared.

The flight went fast after that as everyone was involved in cleaning up the mess or their messy selves.

I took off my shirt and tie. My only replacement was a white tee shirt that went with my suit coat, or at least it didn't clash too much. Once the mess was cleaned up and everyone settled back in, I was approached by another first-class passenger.

She was a fashion photographer. She thought my impromptu outfit looked fairly good. It was a juxtaposition of formal and informal that would show the wearer to have self-confidence in their position in life and not be held back by artificial boundaries. Her words, not mine.

I went along with it, figuring the photos would never see the light of day. She was a true professional and had a set of releases for me to sign. She was very much aware of who I was and felt that this could influence the fashion of the affluent young. Would this make me a member of the Sloane set?

I was proved wrong later when I was sent a copy of *Teen Fashion*, which predicted that this would be the "In Look" next year. Fortunately, that prediction didn't come true.

I was so glad when I stepped off the plane at LAX. People had been staring at my clothes through every airport and plane change. They must have thought I was the dork of all dorks. If any of the airports had shops where I could have bought a new shirt, I would have.

Having complained about all that, I must say wearing a T-shirt was more comfortable than a shirt with a boiled egg collar and tie.

A guard from Jackson House was waiting for me with one of our limos. I was glad to see someone I recognized. I was getting more conscious about my security all the time. Maybe I'm paranoid, but there are people out to get me. They won't leave me alone, so I take care of them. They started it. Gee, I sound like I'm five again.

Anyway, it was good to be home. The guard asked me about my new fashion look. I told him it would be all the rage in six months or the twelfth of never, whichever took the longest. Hmm, twelfth of never, would that work in a song?

The whole family was waiting for me. They were all ready for dinner and waiting for me before eating. I got hugs from all. Mum told me I could sit down for dinner despite not dressing properly. I tried to tell her it was the latest fashion in London, but she didn't buy it.

I broke down and told them about the plane dropping down and spilling everyone's meal and my grape juice. The kids all thought that was funny. Mary told me I would have to wear a bib when I flew from now on. She also gave me some grief about allowing someone else to beat her to a story. Brat, now I know I'm home. It feels great.

We kept the conversation light during the meal, mostly about my new suite at the Plaza on the Strand and all the tests I had to take. The kids thought that was horrible.

After dinner, my parents and I withdrew to the library for coffee and a serious discussion about my trip. I had called about the IRA gunman, and Mum had talked to the MI6 people, so they were up to speed on that.

I told them about Oxford and Trinity College. Again, Mum and Elizabeth had discussed that, so she knew what was going on. Her only thought was, since I had to get a room in Oxford, why not buy a place? That way, it would be nicer than those ratty old rentals she remembered. I asked how she remembered those, but she deflected the conversation. Dad didn't seem happy about the subject so I guess I would leave it alone if I knew what was good for me. Some cans of worms, like your parents' dating life, you don't open.

I told her I didn't know the area or would feel comfortable buying a house. Dad thought that was funny after I spent a small fortune on a hotel penthouse suite that I probably would only use a dozen days a year.

I thought it would be double that, but again, some arguments must be avoided. Mum told me not to worry. She wanted to visit England and her family again, so she would pick me a place. I told her to remember I only made a million and a half a year, so please price shop. She gave me a funny look and told me she would buy something appropriate.

I updated them on my need to take the SATs while I was here. Plus, the real reason I was home right now was for the telethon this Sunday evening.

From their side, I had to return a call from Mr. James, the Director of *Over the Ohio*. I was surprised that the original name stuck. They usually were changed half a dozen times. They probably had a retake needed.

Also, I had to have a business meeting and update while I was in-country.

I had a question for them that had been bothering me for a while about Mrs. Hernandez.

"I thought Mrs. Hernandez's husband was in prison in Cuba, but she now seems to be dating."

"Oh, you weren't here the day she got the news, and we forgot to tell you. Her husband died several months ago, and the news never got out. Castro probably executed him. That happened about eight months ago. She was upset about his death, of course, but it didn't come as a surprise, and she had not seen him for over five years. She asked her priest how long she should mourn. He told her under the circumstances, six months would be appropriate."

"I wondered."

The next morning, I returned the phone call to Mr. James. He asked if I had time to come to the studio as they had a question for me that was best asked in person. That sounded like trouble, but I told him I would come right over.

Mr. Monroe was with him when I entered his office, so I knew it was trouble. They got down to business after the normal greetings.

"Rick, we have tested the scene where you appear as Death Wind. It tests out incredibly strongly with audiences. We think it would be stronger if we had one scene with dialog."

"What do you have in mind?"

"We think something simple, Wetzel talking to Simon Kenton. Kenton is telling him that there is a chance for true peace in the Ohio Valley and you reply not while you are alive. It is already set up that the family he kills in the last scene is the son, daughter-in-law, and granddaughter of the chief that would have signed the treaty."

"The trick to it will have you in your 'good guy' Lew Wetzel outfit, but your face that of the evil one."

"It will have to be tomorrow or Friday as I head back to England right after the telethon."

Mr. Monroe stated, "I forgot to ask, how were your exams?"

"Very well, I passed enough A-levels that I can get accepted at any university in the world without a high school diploma."

"You can always take the GED after you get your Ph.D."

"Very funny, but I might just do that to send a message to the State of California. I just remembered I have to take the SAT exam yet so I may be here into next week, but I would still like to get this scene out of the way."

"Be here at 9 a.m. tomorrow and go right to make up."

"Yes, sir, see you later."

Chapter 8

Out of curiosity, I drove the Fairlane to the Forest Service airport. That is what the new sign said at the beginning of a paved road. The old Air Force sign had disappeared. Now, the entrance had a landscaped look. New trees had been planted to flank the gate. There was an attended guardhouse at the entrance.

When I showed my ID, they directed me to the main office, which now looked like an office. I was issued a parking permit for the Ford. If I got another car, I would have to get a new one. They were nice about it. Maybe they knew who was paying for all this.

A young ranger, still older than me, gave me a tour of the operation. Everything was completed except the septic system; he thought it would be operational next week. The Jackson hangar was up and looked good. It was in the Jackson green with both Mum's and my coat of arms on the door. Now, it only needed an airplane.

I asked about what happened to all the C-rations that had been in storage. He told me they were taken away one night. They were supposed to be taken to a dump, but rumor had it they had been sent to US Department of the Interior locations as emergency supplies. I had heard of inter-service rivalries, but that was plain mean.

I returned home and reviewed my wardrobe, not that I was going to take any of it to England. I started a list of what I should buy to have over there. Most of it was Western gear. Before dinner, I brought up my plan with Mrs. Hernandez and Mum. They volunteered to take care of everything. All I had to do was give them money. Now, what could go wrong with that?

Naturally, I jumped on it, and let the women have fun shopping. It would be worth the money not to have to do it.

I spent the evening playing Monopoly with the family. Once more, Mary sweet-talked her way into Park Place and Boardwalk.

Soon she had won it all. There appeared to be a trend going on here. Who cared? It was fun to be home with my family.

I was at the studio on time Thursday and went directly to makeup. I didn't get out of there until lunchtime. I was told I couldn't eat until after my scene. Fortunately, everyone was on set and ready to go. We did a few walkthroughs while the grips did light and sound checks.

I said my lines and was asked to say them again with more passion. I did this six times in a row and was beginning to get a little upset. The seventh time I practically screamed into Simon Kenton's face. I was getting frustrated and hungry. I must have shown that in my presentation because the director yelled and cut. "Rick, you have it. Now once more for a safety shot."

I'll safely shoot him, I thought as I went through it again. The intensity must have gone up because he demanded another shot. I did it and must have sounded like a maniac. He loved it and said that was the shot he would use. That would have to do because I don't think I had it in me to do again.

The actor who played Simon Kenton's eyes had gotten big, and he started to back away from me on the last shot, so I guess it reached the intensity level the director wanted. I noticed everyone on the set had become quiet and were eying me as though I might start to scalp them.

The director came over to me.

"Rick, you came through as a completely different person on that last shot. The audience will understand that you are playing a complete psychopath. I don't doubt that some people will think that is how you are. Considering this was supposed to be a B-movie, I think it will win some awards and earn us a lot of money."

"A lot of money is good; I don't know about the psycho bit."

"Don't worry about it. You are just acting. When interviewed, tell how hard it was to get you frustrated enough to deliver the lines."

"That sounds good. Thanks for the advice."

"Rick, I think you have it in you to be a real actor, as in the sense that you could convince people that you are many different characters, not just a character actor."

"I doubt if I will ever get in that deeply or care to."

"The stage's loss. Now, I have to go have a late lunch."

"My missing lunch is why I sounded like a psycho."

"Rick, be sure to share that."

I had lunch at the studio canteen as it was the closest food. I wasn't kidding about missing meals.

After that, I went to the schoolhouse to see Miss Sperry. I wanted to share my O- and A-Level exam results and had brought copies. I was proud of what we had accomplished together. She didn't teach me, but she sure guided me in the right direction.

She wanted to know all about England and my taking O-Levels there. She was thrilled to death when I shared those results and the A-Levels. Well, she lived, but she was excited. Using one of the new copying machines, she copied all the results. They would go to her home office and be used in their continuing war with public education.

Seeing all the fighting between institutions, which should be concentrating on educating children, was an eye-opener. It was also very discouraging.

She did know what I had to do to take the SAT exam. They were an authorized examination administration center. She would arrange for a proctor to be there on Monday. All I had to do was show up and take the exam. I felt no stress about taking it so soon. Boy, talk about having taken too many exams recently.

Most kids worried about the SAT and took prep courses and practice exams. I only saw it as something minor to be addressed. Of course, my recent successes hadn't given me a swollen head, at least not much.

I spent the rest of the afternoon with my sister. She was home from her half-day at school. The boys were in class all day. Would you believe we had a tea party? There was Mr. Bunny, Mrs. Bear, and Bond, Jane Bond, the Barbie doll.

Everyone enjoyed their tea and crumpets, though I had to taste test Jane's for poison before she would try them. I don't know what was the strangest, Mary having a spy Barbie doll or me thinking it made sense to taste test.

I was getting very good about keeping my pinkie finger out while drinking tea. Well, since my finger wouldn't fit in the cup, it was the only way I could use it. At least I didn't spill any of my nonexistent tea on myself.

I had to get dressed for dinner. Since there were no guests, I got away without a tie. After dinner, we had a good game of Clue. This time, it was Mr. Green in the Conservatory with a Candlestick. I was the murderous Mr. Green.

Friday was a nice January day in California, mild enough to wear a light sports coat to my office for my business briefing. The way Mum acted at dinner when I got home, I suspected something was up with my finances. I hope what I spent in England wasn't going to cause any problems.

There was something up with my finances. They were almost out of control. So much money was coming in that the accountants were having trouble avoiding the highest tax rate of 91%. I agreed with Dad that at this point, Ike wanted too much!

I was advised to spend money on as much property as I could, as it could be deducted. My million and half a year salary had to go up to five million at once to keep corporate salaries in line. Anyone who worked for me made more than the industry's top rate for their position. My company was in danger of causing national wage inflation. Also, besides an increased salary, I had to take corporate dividends of fifteen million dollars.

This was all because the container industry had taken off like gangbusters. Plus, the freight brokerage business we were putting together had filled an unforeseen need. As such, we went from a zero-dollar business to forty million a year in a matter of months. There was talk of it going over a hundred million a year.

Then there was my beer can opener idea. The patent had gone through. Our first licensee was Mexicali Delight. After that, Coors bought in. Again, a fortune was to be made. My only money problems were that I had to spend it faster or give it to the taxman.

I didn't want to be stupid, so I asked what charities we could support. There were several in the US. I also asked that Trinity College at Oxford be contacted to see if I could contribute to their endowment fund. Just like that, I had spent fifteen million dollars, ten to US charities, and five to my new school. I hope I had something left over.

A Ferrari was sounding closer and closer.

It took all day Friday to go through the details of my businesses, not running them, just for me to understand what was going on. Detroit Faucet was the easiest to understand. There was a nice fifteen percent growth over last year, and projections for next year were at eighteen percent.

Mark Downing and Sharon Bronson were a couple in love. At one point, I even laughingly told them to get a room. Sharon's blush was Technicolor in its brightness. They were planning a spring wedding, and Mark asked me to be the best man. I had no idea how I would make it happen but told him I would be most pleased. Would he let me know the dates as soon as the ladies told him?

The biggest problem the container business faced was growing in an even manner. This meant we had to have the workforce and facilities to build cargo containers to fill the ships that had to be built to use the ports that were being converted. All had to be in balance.

One choke point was the availability of steel. My team was looking at making a significant investment in South Korea to have steel available for our Asia expansion. We would become the majority owner of a large mill. As such, the government wanted to meet me, the owner. That meant that I would be going back to England the long way.

I asked about possibly doing my Asian parts of the documentary while I was there. That meant stops in Japan, Korea, Hong Kong, Australia, Taiwan, and New Zealand. That meant two days at each stop plus travel time. It would take me two weeks to return to England. It would be an exhausting trip.

It could be done but would take a while to set up. Following a long discussion, we decided everything could be in place in two weeks so that I would spend three weeks in February on this project. The leaders of the various countries would be contacted to revise their schedules to be available for our filming.

That was mind-boggling, prime ministers and presidents conforming to my schedule. This was more than a long way from Bellefontaine.

It also played heck with my wardrobe requirements. Susan Wallace, who would accompany me, suggested I hire an assistant for the trip to see to these details. That sounded like a good idea, so since she had thought of it, I gave her the assignment of recruiting someone.

Since there would be a bunch of us, we decided to charter a jet. Besides Mum and Dad and Popeye and Sybil, there would be Sam Wingate, our corporate attorney, and Todd Goodson, president of Jackson Transportation. Todd had started in charge of container production but had proved he could handle the larger job. There would also be several assistants and secretaries. Then there was the whole production crew for the film and their equipment. There would be at least fifty people on the flight.

At the end of the day, everything appeared to be under control. If control could be defined as being strapped to the front end of a freight train entering a dark tunnel with no light at the end.

It was all exciting.

At home that evening, we watched some television. Mum and I discussed England. She was flying over next week to visit. Her mum was okay but couldn't get out and about very much. Mum wanted to spend some time with her. I made a note to see Grandmum when I got to England and also to catch up with the cousins.

Mum would also take a look in the Oxford area and see if she could find lodgings for me. I suspected it would be a small room with a landlady who kept a sharp eye on my comings and goings. She would also have a direct line to Mum, at least Mum's telephone number and the ability to call collect.

Sunday was the day of the telethon. My role would be to answer telephones. They had set it up in a studio at Warner Brothers, which was convenient for me. A lot of movie actors were involved, but most of the telephone people would be students who had been at the so-called sock hop.

TV cameras were there to show us at work, and we would be interviewed. As usual, while the charity pitches were being made, the acts being put on were all in another studio across town.

It didn't start until early evening, so I had the morning and most of the afternoon to myself. I went surfing as it would be my only opportunity for a long time. It was fun in a lazy way. It was work in the water, but there was no hurry about it. There were good waves but not many people out on the water.

After a lunch of hotdogs from a beach cart, I headed back to the water. It was fun, tiring, but fun. A few more surfers showed up but not enough to crowd the area. I did this until about four o'clock and headed home for dinner and to prepare for the telethon.

The telethon itself went as all those events do. For those at home, it was made to look busy as all get out. The reality was that they had overstaffed the phones, so we were doing well to get a call every ten minutes. I played each call straight as far as getting the donation information, such as name, address, and amount. I was told that a certain percentage of those would never come through.

Of course, you could not tell which ones weren't in good faith. You treated all with equal politeness. I wondered if those who kept me on the line with personal questions were the ones who would default.

We did well against our announced goal. Of course, I have learned enough about the business to know the major studios would never allow the goal to be missed.

When I was interviewed, I was asked about my eleventh-grade plans. To me, that was an old, old issue. I explained that I had gone to England, taken all the exams there, and passed them well enough to apply to any university in the world. I used the line about taking the GED after I had my Ph.D. Take that, California.

I found that being on the telephone all evening was very tiring, so I headed home as soon as we were off the air. I was told later that the after-party got pretty wild, and some reputations were destroyed. Sometimes, being tired is good. Besides, I had the SAT in the morning.

Chapter 9

After a light workout and breakfast, I headed to the studio to take the SAT examination starting at 9 a.m. At the little one-room schoolhouse, Mr. Dawson was waiting outside with someone I didn't know. He proved to be a Mr. Knight who would be proctoring my examination.

We shook hands politely, but the nature of our interaction was professional.

Miss Sperry was teaching a class of younger kids, so I would take my test in one of the conference rooms at the main office. We made our way there and attended to our preparations. For me, that was one last bathroom trip.

I hung up my sports coat. It was more to show that nothing was written on my arms than anything else. Besides, a polo shirt was more comfortable in the office.

Mr. Knight reviewed my file and told me my six-dollar fee had been paid. I had brought half a dozen Number 2 soft lead pencils as directed. They were sharpened. As a precaution, I laid my pocketknife out. I looked at Mr. Knight to see if it was okay, and he nodded yes.

The basic SAT would take three hours. I would be allowed one hour for lunch, but I had to stay in the conference room. Arrangements had been made for lunch to be delivered from the commissary for Mr. Knight and me.

The afternoon would have three one-hour sessions, the first on English Composition, the second on Science, and the third on Math.

The morning flew by. I went through the test, answering those questions that I knew absolutely, and then I went back and slowly went over those that I had to think about. After that, I went over the entire test once more. I still finished up one-half hour early.

I turned my test sheets over to Mr. Knight, making sure that my name was correct and that I had filled out the test sheet completely. Plus, I double-checked that I didn't pencil outside the lines or leave any smudges that would mess up the grading machine. Picky, picky, picky.

After he had my paperwork put away, he asked me what it was like working at the studio. I told him that it was a lot of hurry up and wait, followed by doing the same thing over and over until you were sick of it. Then you find out that they had decided not to use the scene, and it hit the cutting room floor. Other than that, it was a ball.

After that, I went on to tell him how great it was to see all the different people, actors, and trades doing their jobs. Then, there was what went on behind the scenes. Most people on the set were normal, but then there were the actors, a high-strung bunch if there ever was. They did nothing by half measures. It kept the gossip columnists busy.

Mr. Knight commented he had seen my name in print several times and that I seemed normal. I reminded him not to judge a book by its cover. That got a laugh.

About that time, lunch showed up. As usual, it was good food. We continued our conversation in this manner, never once referring to the examination.

The afternoon was like the morning, the only difference being that I took the whole hour on the Math exam. Still, I felt good about the experience. When we were done, Mr. Knight asked me how I felt this compared to the English A-Levels.

"Very close, different ways of asking the same question, but the overall knowledge seemed the same to me."

"That debate goes back and forth in our office in New Jersey. I wondered what a person who had taken them would say."

We shook hands at that, and he departed after telling me I would hear the results within two weeks. I didn't feel washed out like I had some test days. I think stress had as much to do with that as anything. Since these tests were a formality, there wasn't as much stress.

When asked how my day went at home, I replied, "Fine."

Mum didn't have to throw a pillow at me!

During dinner, I told everyone how the exam flow went. It may have to do with the extra dinner rolls Mum had sitting next to her.

Dad informed me that he had received a telephone call from the State Department.

"You mean the United States Department of State?"

"I don't know any other."

"What do they want?"

"They have heard about your trip and want to send a team with you."

I inquired, "What for?"

"They feel that putting a teenage boy across from world leaders without their supervision is not a good idea."

"I don't care if they come along, but they have to pay their way."

"I already told them that. We have had to charter a 707 as it is, and they don't come cheap."

"How can they help?"

"What is the title of the head of government of New Zealand, and what is his name? Also, party affiliation and beliefs, what the government hopes to achieve, what support will they provide, oh, and how will they pay for their share?"

"Maybe we shouldn't charge them for their seats."

"Nah, they're the government; they can afford it."

That night, I read about Fort Repose. That was a scary story because it could happen.

I now had the next two weeks to get ready for my February world tour as I thought of it. At breakfast, Mum let me know that she had a change of plans and would fly directly to England to visit her Mum and start looking for a place for me to live. She then asked me if I had thought about what gifts I would present to the world leaders. What gifts?

She explained it was a tradition to present a gift when visiting foreign heads of state. I wanted to give them some passes to my movies, but she thought that would be a little tacky. When I suggested copies of my records, she almost had tea come out of her nose. That would be worth at least ten points in the "I got Mum contest" I held with myself.

Alas, it didn't, and I admitted my songs weren't gift-worthy. Then I had a thought she approved of. I would ask the studio to make up a plaque with a note of our meeting, dates, and each leader's name. On the plaque would be an arrow from *Bandits of Sherwood*. The plaque would be titled Forward Progress Together.

So, my next stop was to the studio to bum some of the arrows from the movie. The arrows were kept in the studio armory for use in any movie. I was able to pick out twenty in good condition. The extras were for visits to other countries in the future.

I stopped by Mr. Monroe's office, and he was available. I updated him on my trip to England, exam results, and the planned trip in two weeks. He asked if a studio photographer could join the entourage for publicity pictures of me. At that point, in for a penny in for a pound, so I said yes.

Of course, it made my requests for the woodshop to make my plaques easier. He told us that they would do it as soon as they found out the names of the leaders of each country to be visited. I would call the State Department and have them contact him with the information in return.

I borrowed a phone in a conference room and called Dad at his office to get the number of the State Department gentleman who had called. Dad had it handy, so I called the third assistant to the second undersecretary. I kid you not.

I explained what information was needed and why. He thought it was a good idea and would pass it to Mr. Monroe to start the process. However, he would have to brief the second undersecretary, who, if he thought the idea had merit, would create a study group to decide if it were a good idea and, if so, what the actual gift should be.

It sounded like a bunch of nonsense to me, but it didn't matter. When the information was given to Mr. Monroe, he would have the gifts made, and I would present them. I bet we would be done with the trip by the time this committee had a recommendation.

After leaving Mr. Monroe's office, I headed to the stunt area. Since I had a lot of free time in the next two weeks, I wanted to see if I could obtain the black belt level of instruction in unarmed combat. As normal, Mr. Palmer was training boxers. I didn't know the studio had such a need for boxers, but apparently, they did.

When he had a break, I even asked about that. He explained that every movie with boxing had multiple boxers in the background as extras. It was cheaper for the studio to keep training the list of working extras so they would be available when needed. I could see where that would also benefit the regular extras, keeping them employed.

He explained that worked to a point. After a while, the extra would become a known face. The extra was either dropped or considered as a bit actor. They might get a supporting role if they did well as a bit actor. The people who got beyond that were few and far between. Out of the millions of people in the world, less than a thousand were recognized movie actors. Out of that thousand less than one hundred were considered names. It made me realize how lucky I had been.

After that diversion, I explained why I had stopped by. He told me if I could give him four hours daily, Monday through Friday for the next two weeks, he could get me there. I committed to being available from 8 to 12 every weekday for the next two weeks.

After that, I hunted up Mr. Bell, who was practicing his archery and joined him for forty-five minutes. It felt good, but I could see from the soreness on my fingers where callouses would build up if I kept it up. It also meant there was something wrong with my form. Mr. Bell agreed to watch me during a session later in the week.

Next for me to see was Sammy Dawson to practice the sword. He was busy with a student, so I paired off with another stuntman. I was either fairly good, or he had a long way to go. After fifteen minutes, he gave up. By this time, a short line had formed to try their hand at me. I had worked up a good sweat by the time I was done and had not been touched by any of the dull practice blades. I had numerous scores on my opponents.

By that time, Mr. Dawson was free, so we had a sword bout. It was sharp and quick. Somehow, I disarmed him. He yielded at once. I asked him if I was that good or if he was having a bad day.

"Rick, you don't appreciate what your physical fitness brings to the party. Your fitness, along with your reach and hand-eye coordination, makes you a fearsome opponent. Plus, you have put in some serious practice time. You are almost on a par with Basil Rathbone, considered the best swordsman in the world. Don't let it go to your head, but you are good. Still, don't bring a knife to a gunfight.

Well, that was a good way to end my visit to the studio.

On the way home, I passed a Ford dealership. I couldn't help it; I stopped in to check out the new 1960 T-Birds. There was one of those square-looking T-Birds in Monte Carlo red with Kelsey-Hayes wire wheels. The retractable hardtop sold me. After a test drive, I tried some half-hearted negotiations, but the salesman knew he had me.

Without fighting, I bought it with only a minor discount. I had my revenge when I wrote out a check for the full amount. At first, he didn't want to take a check because I was too young and needed my parents to sign. I carried my letter of emancipation for these very circumstances.

Since there was no trade-in, I arranged for the car to be prepped and delivered to Jackson House. They told me it would be there first thing in the morning. That turned out to be 9 a.m., which would be too late to make it to the studio, so I arranged to pick it up here at the dealership. It had to be ready on time as I had an appointment at Warner Brothers.

I think that is when the salesman figured out who I was. I then had to go through being introduced to the entire staff. I think it was from the owner down to the guy who washed cars. Of course, I was used to this by this time, so I put on my professional face and glad-handed everyone. They were all nice people, so I had no reason to be resentful.

I made it home just in time to rush around and change clothes for dinner. Everyone had a decent day, from the sounds of it. At least the boys must have because they both responded "fine" when asked.

Mary and her friend Patty were on the outs again. I'm not sure, but I think Davey had woken up to the fact there were girls in the world, and he picked Patty. That would do it.

I played some pool with the boys. They knew both could beat me. I rationalized my losing as being good for their self-confidence.

From there, it was to read more about the nuclear war and its outcome in Florida before I fell asleep.

Chapter 10

A limo took me to the Ford Dealership to pick up my new T-Bird. When I got there, I told the driver to wait. I may need him to take me to the studio. The dealership had my car ready; there was no doubt about that. It was sitting out front with a large bow on it. There were also about fifty people there, and cameras were set up.

I had intended to stop and drive my new car away. They intended a lot of ceremony and publicity for their dealership.

I saw the salesman standing with the owner I had met yesterday. I went over to him. He had his hand out to shake and a large smile. That got wiped out quickly.

"I told you I have an appointment this morning. I will pick up the car this afternoon. And I will not be giving you free publicity. If you want to pay, that is fine."

I said that, looking at the dealer. He was not a happy camper, but I couldn't care less as I turned and walked away. If they had listened to me, I would have cooperated later, but they hadn't listened.

I spent my morning in unarmed combat, as agreed with Mr. Palmer. A light lunch at the canteen and it was boxing, archery, and swords.

A studio runner found me as I was finishing up.

"There is a man at the front gate with a new Thunderbird, which he says is yours."

It was the dealer who had smartened up and had the car delivered. The salesman who had sold me the car was the driver. He asked me to drop him back off at the dealer. I told him I would, but I hoped there would be no more games.

He said there wouldn't be, but I didn't trust him for some reason. I stopped half a block from their drive and told him that was as far as I was taking him. He wasn't happy but got out of the car. As I drove by the entrance to the dealership, I saw a small crowd and cameras. Some people never learn.

Other than a sour taste from the dealership, I loved my new car.

When I related the day's events at dinner, Dad asked me, "Are you going to call Ford?"

"What do you mean, Ford?"

"Ford Headquarters; that conduct is unacceptable."

"I think I will."

In the morning, I did just that. Detroit was three hours ahead of us, so I had time. I made a long-distance connection with the Ford Headquarters switchboard. Once there, I asked for the complaint department. Then the run-around started. I finally ended up with someone in their Quality Control Department.

When I explained my problem, he told me I had the wrong department. I needed to call the Dealer Relations group. He even offered to transfer me. I declined and dialed the switchboard back.

"This is Sir Richard Jackson calling for Henry Ford the Second."

I didn't expect to get through to him, but at least I could talk to someone in authority.

I was put through to an executive secretary who inquired as to the nature of my call. When I relayed it, I was told I needed to talk to their Dealership Relations group. I told her my next phone call would be to the press and left a number if someone desired to call me.

Within five minutes, Mrs. Hernandez announced I had a call from the Ford Motor Company. It was Mr. Thompson, the Vice President of their Dealer Relations group. He was not impressed with my complaint. He thought their dealer was acting responsibly in getting them good publicity.

I thanked him for returning my call. I also remembered this was the same team that introduced Edsel.

I wondered what to do next and had a bright idea. Do nothing. Why let those jerks upset me? I had the car I wanted, and they had nothing. I think Mr. Ford should consider changing his management team soon before he loses his company.

It was another day at the studio stunt area, practicing all my skills. At dinner that night, Dad told me that the arrangements for our trip were coming along nicely. Mum had left for England this morning, so it was a quiet group at dinner. I never realized how much she contributed to our conversations.

After dinner, I called Nancy Houston, the girl I had met at Eddie's patrol leader's house. She was surprised to hear from me. I asked if she would like to go roller skating on Saturday night. She hesitated.

"I'm not allowed to car date by myself. The only other friends I could invite are those you met swimming. That might not be the best thing to do."

"Well, can I come over on Saturday afternoon, and we can sit outside and talk?"

"That would be great. Of course, you would have to meet my parents."

"I think I can handle that. I have met a lot of people."

"But my dad has always threatened to be cleaning a gun if I brought a boy to the house."

"It won't be the first time."

"Okay then, why don't you come over about two in the afternoon?"

"See you then."

The next day was more of the same. At lunchtime, a studio runner found me in the canteen.

"Mr. Monroe would like to see you in his office when you can."

That was better than the time I was dragged there in full costume. When I got there, he asked me why I had to keep shaking things up.

"What have I done this time?"

"I just got off the phone with Henry Ford the Second, Chairman of the Board, Ford Motor Company. It appears they feel they may have offended you."

"Not really; they just look at the world differently."

I proceeded to explain what went on. He agreed with me. In our world, publicity is a commodity bought and paid for. They seemed to think it was their right and that all would bow down to them.

Mr. Monroe had been asked to intercede for them and requested that I do the publicity shots. Wow, Ford and I weren't on different pages. It was different planets.

He dialed Ford back and put us on Mr. Monroe's speakerphone. After the opening greetings, I started the ball rolling.

"I get paid for public appearances. What is your proposal?"

"We thought you would allow your picture to be taken as a goodwill gesture."

"Will you give me a Lincoln Continental as a goodwill gesture?"

"Well, no, we make our living selling cars."

"And I make mine by acting and selling my image to the public."

I think a light started to go on.

"Sir Richard, we have committed a huge error in handling this. How would you like to go forward?"

"Simple, I bought a vehicle. Now leave me alone."

"That hardly seems cooperative."

"There has been no incentive to be cooperative."

"Could we meet face to face next week?"

"Next week, I have appointments with the president of South Korea, the prime minister of Japan, the Royal Governor of Hong Kong, and the president of Taiwan."

There was silence on the other end for a moment.

"What about the following week?"

"Then it is the prime ministers of New Zealand and Australia."

"I'm afraid to ask, the following week?"

"The Queen of England is on my schedule."

That was a fib. I would probably be with her, but it sounded better this way.

"I believed you until the Queen of England."

Mr. Monroe broke in, "Believe him. This is Jackson Enterprises, not the actor.

"You mean the container people?"

"Yes, Sir Richard is the founder and owner of the company."

"We have misunderstood Sir Richard's position. After meeting with the Queen, when will you return to America?"

"The following week I will have meetings with the State Department and probably the White House on my return, but I could probably drop by Detroit on my way home."

"Please try to do so and keep us posted."

When I hung up the phone, Mr. Monroe just looked at me for a while."

"Where is that mild-mannered kid from Bellefontaine, Ohio?"

"I think he grew up. They started this mess, so it is on them. I don't want to take it anywhere, but they insist on keeping it going."

"You are going to see all those people, aren't you?"

"All of them for certain; the Queen is up in the air. She and Mum may have other plans for me."

"Rick, excuse me, I'm going to my office and have a belt."

I returned to the lot wondering how I had gotten into a verbal fight with Ford Motor Company. I hoped they didn't try to take my T-Bird back.

My heart wasn't up for more practice, so I took the afternoon off and drove around Hollywood.

At dinner, I updated the family on my conversations with Ford. I called Mum later and brought her up to date. As one would expect, Mum was ready to declare war. Fortunately, Dad had a better idea. He called the White House.

I don't know what was said, but the upshot was that I would not be disturbed by the Ford people again. Dad did say that Ike had his uses after all.

The next several days went as planned. On Saturday afternoon, I went over to Nancy's house. Her dad wasn't cleaning a gun. He was washing his car. After introducing me, Nancy whisked me to the backyard. They didn't have a pool but a nice patio. Her mother was sitting there with a neighbor lady.

After introductions, the neighbor excused herself. It didn't take rocket science to figure out she was the mother of one of the blonde girls. Oh well, it's not my fight.

Nothing was said about it, so I left it alone. Maybe I was wrong. Nancy's mom left us alone but was working in the kitchen so she could keep an eye on us. That left us nothing to do but talk.

I had a good time talking to her. I made sure that she had to speak as much as I did. She had a hundred questions about the life of a star. I had a hundred questions about real life.

I found out that Nancy had a good sense of humor. At one point, she convinced me that two Spanish gentlemen had invented Pepsi Cola and that the name meant *Pep Sí*!

We talked and laughed our way through several hours. When it was close to four-thirty, I said my goodbyes and asked if I could see her again. We made a date to go out for ice cream next week. She would bring her little sister. I would bring Eddie, who was her age. That would take care of the not-alone-in-a-car rule.

I would probably have to pay Eddie.

I took my brothers surfing on Sunday. We had a good time. On our way, we checked out the construction on the Beach House. It seemed to take forever, but we could see real progress had been made. At the rate it was going, I would spend all my time in England and never get to use it.

It was a blustery day at the beach, even in the water, so we didn't stay long. Katin's was crowded as the beach crowd looked for shelter, so we left after a few quick hellos. We made an In-N-Out stop to stave off starvation on the way home. That was my weekend.

The following week was more of the same. I made progress in unarmed combat. Brushing up on my other skills was a good idea. It is amazing how fast one can lose one's edge. This is not a sword joke.

The week's highlight was ice cream with Nancy and her little sister. It was really cute watching Eddie and Cindy together. When I did something for Nancy, like opening the car door, Eddie would do it for Cindy. It put Nancy and me on our best behavior as we were in the position of setting examples.

After a while, we forgot about it and had a good time. We drove around the girls' neighborhood with the top down so all their friends could get a good look. Cindy was the big winner there as she saw and waved at half a dozen girls. She would be the talk of her school tomorrow. Eddie was a good sport about it all. For the record, I didn't have to pay him.

I asked Eddie what he thought of Cindy on the way home. He told me she was okay for a girl.

Sunday night was spent making certain I was ready for tomorrow's flight to the Orient. Our first stop would be Japan. I had done some research and knew I would be meeting with Prime Minister Nobusuke Kichi.

Chapter 11

Our chartered flight was leaving on Monday morning from Ontario. It was so much easier to use than LAX. Dad and I took a limo to Ontario, and all seemed to be in order. At least it appeared that everyone was there. The cameraman from Warner Brothers was taking pictures everywhere.

A problem arose early on. A gentleman who identified himself as being from the State Department told me there was a seating problem. They had decided to bring another aide and now they didn't have a first-class seat for him.

I asked why they had to be in first class. He looked at me like I had two heads.

"Well, it is only proper that this important trade mission shows us the respect we deserve. Besides, we must be up front to advise you on how to behave on the trip."

Sometimes, the devil makes you do things. I walked the gentleman to our check-in counter and had another first-class seat assigned to his party. He thanked me in a way that made it clear it was their due.

What he didn't know was that I had given them my seat. I now would be sitting in coach. This was not the hardship it would appear. Since the flight would not strain the 707 capabilities, they had removed every other row of seats so there would be an enormous amount of legroom.

The center seat on each side was built so that the back was split. The front half of the back would lower onto the seat, making a nice armrest on the side, with the center being a flat surface for trays and other stuff. If worse came to worst, there was enough room between the seat rows for one to lie on the floor.

So, I had a nice seat and didn't have to listen to the State Department the whole trip. Another plus was that I was sitting with the production crew, who I certainly had more in common with than the political types.

It was a long flight. My definition of a long flight is when your body starts to eliminate the first meal of the flight. It was a long flight. We refueled in Hawaii and at Midway Islands.

We were allowed off the plane at both stops to stretch our legs, but it was only a few hours at each location. I wondered if I could tell people I had been to Hawaii, which was true, even though I had never left the airport.

The State Department people deigned to come to the back of the plane to talk to me. They had good advice on what not to do and how to do certain things.

Who was to know that when exchanging business cards in most Oriental countries, you did it with both hands? You extended the card, holding it between the forefinger and thumb of each hand. You never took the card and put it directly in your shirt pocket. If at a table, you set the card in front of you. This was handy as you positioned the cards to face each person at the table. This helped when you forgot their name.

Standing, you held it the entire time. The card was considered an extension of the person and was to be treated as such.

Popeye explained to me why you didn't eat with your left hand. We won't go into that. Poor Mary was left-handed. She would have a terrible time here or change their cultural traditions. I wouldn't bet on either outcome.

We had lost a day crossing the International Date Line and the flight had taken another, so it was Wednesday when we arrived in Japan. Welcomed at Narita Airport by the State Department counterparts, we were mercifully taken directly to a hotel where we all slept for twelve hours. Of course, this had us all awake in the middle of the night.

The hotel was geared for this and had their restaurant staffed to feed people in the middle of the night. I noticed airline crews from all over the world, so this seemed to be a specialty of the house.

We had no plans on Thursday as our bodies adjusted to the dramatically different time zone. Dad and I took a taxi tour of the city. On the concierge's advice, we took several matchbooks from the hotel.

The matchbooks had the hotel address on them in English and Japanese, so worse came to worst, we could show someone the matchbook and where we needed to go. Downtown Tokyo was amazing. I had never seen so many people on any street.

We avoided street food vendors as we didn't want to have upset stomachs. That was another piece of advice from our concierge. We did play the pachinko machines, which were endemic to the area. I lost interest quickly as I wasn't into this type of game. Dad went a little longer but lost his balls. Well, that's how I put it.

Friday, we went to the Kantei building, which is the office of the prime minister. It is close to the Diet, where the Japanese Congress meets. Of course, we had a tour of both buildings and pictures taken. Some things are the same the world over. Politicians and photos are one of them.

Prime Minister Nobusuke Kishi met us, and we did the bowing thing, then shook hands Western style. We chatted for a while about such important things as how was our trip and what we thought of Japan so far. The trip was tiring, and we loved Japan. What else could I say? This was all through an interpreter. I suspect his English was better than mine.

We did this to allow time for the cameramen and film crews to get set up. Once they were ready, we did the official exchanges. I presented my gift of a plaque with an arrow from my movie mounted on it with the occasion, participants, and dates listed with the slogan, Moving Forward Together.

The lead gentleman from the State Department gave a speech on how this project would benefit trade between both nations. He was correct, but why did he have to use so many words to say it?

The Japanese surprised me with a gift of my own. The prime minister told me they had discussed at length what to get a young man my age. He told me that a Geisha Girl came in second to what they decided upon. I wish....

What they decided was appropriate was the highest Boy Scout award in Japan. It was the same as the American Eagle Scout Badge. So, I was now a Kiku or Chrysanthemum Scout. It was a cool-looking badge. The chief Scout executive of Japan pinned it to my suit lapel.

After that, we were loaded into a series of limousines and given a tour of the dock area where our equipment was being installed. Again, we chit-chatted while waiting for the various camera crews to set up. I was asked about my plans. He didn't seem so happy when I told the prime minister I planned to attend Oxford. He thought I would do better at a Russian University.

On the trip over, I had been told about his pro-Nazi, pro-Russian stances and the fact he was a convicted war criminal who had seen the light as far as the United States was Japan's best bet for recovery. The fact that *Big Mo* had sat in Tokyo Bay may have had something to do with that. Anyway, I knew not to touch politics with this guy.

We walked around the harbor area, pointing a lot at the new construction. Here, Popeye was in his element, pointing out all the different features of the new container systems. Once the footage was together, I would do a voice-over, and some quotes from the prime minister would be put in.

We returned to the hotel, which was set up for a press conference. I thought the questions would be put to Richard Jackson of Jackson Enterprises. Instead, they were all about Ricky Jackson, the actor. A bunch of teenage girls had been let into one side of the room, so there was a lot of commotion.

I had experience with this, so I got out with a whole skin and without saying anything bad about the Japanese. I did let it drop that my next movie, *Over the Ohio*, would have a surprise. This was at the request of Warner Brother's publicity. They wanted to build some excitement even though the release wouldn't be until the fall.

At least the flight to Seoul, South Korea didn't take forever; it only seemed like it. There, we met with President Syngman Rhee. The State Department representatives gave me an extensive briefing on this Harvard-educated man. He had seen the history of this century, starting with US President Theodore Roosevelt and everyone since.

Rhee also led a corrupt government with dim prospects in the elections to be held next month. I was warned that the Rhee government would try to pry, steal, or extort everything they could.

We weren't given a day to acclimate. They took us directly from the plane to the Presidential Palace, known for obvious reasons as the Blue House. Short speeches were given on how they looked forward to doing business with us.

I was set aside as a child with no power. They wanted to talk to Dad. I listened as they explained what would be needed to do business in South Korea. Dad stalled as the cameramen set up. Once that was done, I was allowed to present my plaque. In turn, they must have paid attention to the Japanese as I was presented with the Tiger Scout award, the Eagle equivalent.

Dad took the opportunity to ask me what I thought.

"Get us out of this den of thieves. Maybe we can work with the new government."

Dad told them we were all very tired and needed to go to the hotel that had been reserved. They reluctantly let us go without either side making any commitments or writing any checks.

The hotel was decent, but I was glad I had listened to the State Department people who had told me to pack my toilet paper. They had some, but it was more pulp than paper.

At dinner, we were approached carefully by two gentlemen. They presented their cards. They were from the steel mill we wanted to buy. They appeared nervous. A note was dropped on the table, and they left.

Dad collected the note, and we read it after we returned to our rooms. The note said that the Rhee government was in no position to carry out any promises made and to please wait until after their elections before making a purchase offer.

That was enough for us. Everyone was warned by a knock on the door that we would be flying out at six in the morning. There would be a bus at the front of the hotel.

At six the next morning, we slunk out of South Korea—no other way to put it. We cut and ran. We would wait until after their elections to make contact again. There was consternation at the airport when we went to board our jet. We were told that we hadn't been released. Dad and I argued with the customs agent while everyone boarded with their luggage and equipment. When we saw it was on board, we walked away from him.

He was still talking as we climbed the stairs to the aircraft. Dad had the foresight to bribe one of the gate crew to wheel the stairs away.

Thus, we left scenic South Korea. My list of almost visited countries was growing.

Our next stop, Hong Kong, went as I had thought all our stops would. There was the official welcome after a decent rest. This time, it was the Chief Scouts Award. The Hong Kong shipyards had made more progress than the Japanese. They were loading containers while we were there, so there were some fantastic camera shots.

The Royal Governor Robert Brown Black was a pleasure to talk to. It helps when you have folks in common, like the Queen. We stayed at the Peninsula Hotel and were driven around in their fleet of Rolls Royces. That is one cool car. It was too staid for me but cool. Maybe I should get one for Mum and Dad to keep in England. This being rich makes you think differently.

Again, we were approached at the hotel. This time, I even recognized the person. It was my dry-cleaning lady! She said nothing as she passed by our table, dropping a note as she went. Back in the room, the note told of mainland Chinese interest in updating Shanghai to a container port, and would we be interested in a meeting? If so, take a suit to the dry cleaner when I get back to the US.

Dad and I immediately met with the State Department people. They were thrilled, to say the least. They had to pass it upstairs, but they were confident I would be taking a suit to the dry cleaners.

Not that Dad and I were cynical, but we also decided to call President Eisenhower when we were in Australia, where there was a low chance of the phone being tapped.

After Hong Kong, we met with Generalissimo Chiang Kai Shek in Taiwan. He was very formal with us. I had been told that the US was providing foreign aid to modernize Taiwan as a bulwark against Communist China. This time, I was given the National Flower or Plum Blossom Award, the same as our Eagle. I wouldn't have room on my uniform for all of these. Even wearing the square knot ribbons would have rows down to my knees, well, okay, my belt line.

They also had made progress on the use of containers. Like Hong Kong, they didn't have the huge overhead cranes installed yet so were using mobile ones. The ships couldn't take all the containers in their holds, so they stacked them so high on the deck that I thought they would tip over.

Again, you could tell Popeye was on top of all this. I made a mental note to find out what we were paying him. I know he was getting a percentage of the profits, but he was going above and beyond.

I would be so glad to get to Australia, where we had three days off before eeting with the government.

Chapter 12

The fight to Australia met my definition of a long flight. I slept on the floor a good part of the way. I was gradually adapting to the time change. When I first got to Japan, it felt like I had the flu for the first two days. I was almost back to normal now.

We stayed at a hotel right on Bondi Beach, a suburb of Sydney. Canberra is the capital, but the container facility is in Sydney, so that is where our meetings were to be.

It is something waking up in February and going out on your hotel balcony to a wonderful summer day. I immediately did my exercises, which had been done poorly, at best, on most of the trip. I then went on a run following the one-kilometer beach from end to end.

The south end was a bit smelly as a sewer outfall was close to shore, and the wind was blowing the wrong way. I decided not to swim in that area. The sweet spot of the beach for swimming and families was the center, with no smells or rip tides.

The north end had wicked rip tides that one had to be careful with. To make up for it was some wonderful surfing. While I watched, I saw a series of barrel waves I would love to have been riding.

Instead, I went to breakfast. The rest of our crew was struggling down to the hotel restaurant. I sat with Dad and the gentleman from the State Department. I had been introduced to him but had promptly forgotten his name. Now, I was too embarrassed to ask, so it was "sir." I think he preferred this.

Anyway, the man from State gave us a rundown of Robert Menzies. From a United States view, it was all good. It sounded as though he had a long and illustrious career in government and would continue for some time. He was a huge fan of Queen Elizabeth, so we had that in common.

After breakfast, I excused myself and, after changing, went down to the beach and rented a surfboard. It was a great day for surfing. I caught many a wave. I also had lunch with a couple of girls who were real lookers. It was a casual meeting on the beach and was destined to go nowhere, but still, it was nice to talk to girls my age, especially pretty ones in bikinis.

While we were eating, a sour-faced man came up to us with a tape measure in hand. He had the girls stand up, and without touching, measured the size of their swimsuits. I could hardly believe it, but the town of Bondi Beach had swimwear regulations and enforced them. The girls didn't seem bothered by this. It was a game to them to see how far they could push the rules. One of the girls, Sheri, told me that she wanted to go topless on the beach one day. I told her to let me know, and I would fly back to Australia to view the occasion.

We went to a steak place for dinner. This time, it was Dad, Popeye, and Susan Wallace. We reviewed what we wanted to accomplish here. Mainly it was the filming for the documentary but also more government support for our project.

Australia has strong unions, and they were resisting. Popeye's strong arm could only reach so many people. We came up with a plan to present to Prime Minister Menzies. It was a combination of support for scholarships for the children of union employees and underwriting some of the cost of containerizing ports in Malaysia and Indonesia.

Higher education interested the prime minister, and the unions would like the scholarships. Australia had strong trade agreements with Malaysia and Indonesia that would be helped by being able to handle containers. We hoped this would be enough to move the project along.

The unions weren't stonewalling it, so it looked like they just were holding out for a little extra for their members. That was their job, so we didn't consider it adversarial.

Susan was more interested in publicity for my upcoming movie. None of us could come up with anything that didn't look contrived. The media would spurn anything that looked staged from the US. Susan said she would call around the movie production companies and see what was being made currently.

I spent the next day surfing some more. I paid a price for two days out in the sun and had the worst sunburn in years. I wish they would come up with waterproof sunscreen. I had applied some before going into the water, but it didn't last.

I quit after half a day in the water. At lunch, I looked for the two girls from yesterday, but they weren't to be found. It dawned on me later they probably had skipped school to go to the beach. What a life! In Bellefontaine, about the only reason to skip school was the first day of hunting season.

I had the bright idea of renting a plane and touring the area. For some reason, no one wanted to rent to a sixteen-year-old from another country. At least I had asked the concierge to call for me rather than driving all about.

I was sitting by the pool under a shade when Susan found me. It turned out that a movie, *The Sundowners*, was currently under production. It had Robert Mitchum and Peter Ustinov in it. They were doing some studio work, and I was welcome to do a no-name walk-on. The no-name part meant I would be in the movie but wouldn't be acknowledged in the credits.

This was fine. It would give a reason to bring up movies during a press conference. From there, I could segue to *Over the Ohio*. I was learning more and more about how the movie business worked. Now, if there was only a way to get this message out worldwide.

I was to be at the studio for makeup first thing in the morning. I was there early. It turned out they were giving me a line. I had to work hard to remember it, "Yes, sir." I think I could handle it. However, that line had me receiving credit if the scene didn't hit the cutting room floor. Even if it did, we would have won because it gave us a current talking point. Later, that was exactly how it turned out. I never appeared in the movie, which was a shame. It was a hit.

As usual, the movie day was hurry up and wait. It turned out that Mr. Ustinov knew Mum from the war. He had been involved with intelligence. He ran with David Niven and that crowd. I found out that Niven had made a pass at Mum, and she shot him down. That is, if she shot him, he wouldn't be here. She didn't miss.

That explained why Dad didn't like Mr. Niven. I didn't know what to make of it. It was hard to think of my parents and youthful romance.

During the downtime, I saw a couple of the extras playing with a boomerang. I had read about them but had never seen one in action. They were kind enough to show me how to use it. I had to have some to take back to the US. They told me about a shop that sold the real thing.

There were several types. Returning was mainly used for fun and non-returning was used for hunting. The returning kind had more of a curve to the airfoil so that it would come back. The hunting boomerang was a stick that could be hurled with enough force to bring down small game. Some hunters used a returning boomerang to flush birds out of hiding and then took them down with the hunting ones.

I had my driver stop at the shop on the way home. I ended up spending a small fortune as they had them in many different sizes, shapes, and colors. They even had a small pink one, which would be perfect for Mary. I paid them to wrap and ship them to Jackson

House. The shop was run by an old aboriginal. I think I made his week, if not his month, by the amount I spent.

As I was leaving, he handed the shop keys to his assistant and said, "Walkabout."

Maybe I made his year.

The next day was a workday. Well, I had to do the official appearances.

Mr. Menzies was the consummate politician. He was charming and knowledgeable, and there was no doubt that he was as hard as iron. During our get-to-know-you period, he asked a lot of questions about my education. He had been briefed on the highlights but not the details.

He knew that I had been on an aggressive course of self-study. He wondered if that could be instilled in students in Australia. He had to slow down when I told him about my run-ins with the Los Angeles school board. He didn't want to have problems with the various Australian teachers' unions.

Even so, he appeared impressed with what I had accomplished. I also told him how the container system had been developed, that I was working as a deckhand on a freighter when the idea occurred to me.

He thought that was wonderful but asked how I took it from the idea stage to reality. Many people had good ideas but never made them happen. This led back to me having a team in place, which started way back with the hairdryer. That was two years ago!

I think he and I could have talked all day. We finally segued to business. Dad, Popeye, Mr. Goodson, and the State Department gentleman were there. Since I seemed to be on a roll, I explained our problems with the Australian dockworkers and construction crews slowing us down.

We discussed how Australia could have more international trade now that the Malayan emergency was about over. There was little communist activity there now.

I was careful not to make it a blame game so the prime minister didn't have to get defensive about his countrymen. We recognized that the unions hadn't seen enough benefits yet. Yes, what we were offering was more than fair, but their job was to get more. Ours was to figure out how to give more without impacting the long-term financial plan.

If we offered higher wages, that would cause long-term problems. A one-time bonus might address the issue, but we didn't see it in our best interest to set that precedent. What we proposed was the setting up of a scholarship fund for the children of the union workers.

You could tell from his body language the prime minister liked this creative approach. It was a fresh idea and hit his higher education hot button. This was our incentive to the unions.

Of course, he didn't get to be prime minister by not getting something his party could take credit for. This had been part of our dinner conversation last night.

For the Australian government, we offered to help their trading partners in Malaysia and Indonesia by offering our expertise in setting up container handling systems. Of course, we hoped our free consulting would result in contracts to perform the work.

The prime minister liked that idea so much that he offered to include some Australian foreign aid money in the package. The gentleman from the US State Department spoke up and said that the United States would match whatever the Australians came up with.

There would be some happy people in Malaysia and Indonesia when they heard about this. Their rice bowls would be full. Thinking of Jackson Enterprises' rice bowl, I asked if construction bonds could be tied back so that we would be the sole provider. As such, we were prepared to take local hiring recommendations in non-sensitive positions.

Both the Australians and Americans thought this would be a good outcome for all concerned. My last thought was to have some high union officials present at our photo opportunities. It is hard to back out when there are pictures.

We were then taken down to the harbor and given the obligatory tour of the new construction. While we were standing near a new crane going into place, a worker spat on the ground next to me and said, "Bloody toffs."

I couldn't let this go. While not imagining this event, I had thought ahead enough to bring my union cards with me in my wallet.

I stepped up to the worker and asked who he was calling a toff. I worked for a living. At that point, I pulled out my Seamen's Union and Oil worker's cards. I didn't think my SAG card would impress him as much.

It did set him back a bit. He quickly grew apologetic. His mates gathered around and asked what was going on. They had a good laugh at him about it, and he would be taking the piss for some time to come.

While my tour group, the prime minister, and all stood watching, I asked the workers what they thought of Jackson Enterprises paying for a scholarship program for their kids. I continued that the prime minister had twisted our arms until we saw the light. Their reaction was positive.

Not one to miss a beat, Mr. Menzies stepped up and took credit, but then shared it back as we had been an easy sell.

This was better than any news conference. It would be the talk of every pub and union hall in the area before the day was over.

The prime minister hosted a dinner for us that night. He asked if I had ever considered moving to Australia. I told him that I had never given it any thought.

"Good, don't. I would hate to run for office against you. Your instincts are spot on."

"Well, I have a good team behind me. You know what we had to offer was all thought of before our meetings."

"I thought so, but you know when the timing is right. That bit with the dockworkers earlier was inspired. We couldn't get that level of worker support no matter how we tried. Normally, it is top-down. This is going to be bottom-up. I bet you will see construction times improve immediately.

The next day, we had all the photo ops for the still cameras. We even had one of the prime minister and me signing a "contract." It was a blank piece of paper. The legal people needed time for the wording.

Two high union officials were there. They both grumbled a little about interfering with their communications with their workers. How could they take credit with the workers since the prime minister already had? Mr. Menzies told them that their previous private consultations had brought it about. They were bright people, so they went along with it. I wonder how often that sort of thing happened.

Last on the photo list was me receiving the Australian Scout Medallion. I wasn't going to sew these all on. I would hire a tailor.

After the photo ops, there was a press conference. It started with the official reasons for the visit. The scholarships to be administered by the dockworker's union were a big hit. The two union officials were front and center with how they made this happen after consultations with Mr. Menzies and his party. The conservatives would never have let this happen.

The news about funding and support for Malaysia and Indonesia garnered some attention. The big announcement was that I had a walk-on part in *Sundowners*. The Australian movie sector had not been doing too well, so it was hoped that it would set off a renaissance in the industry.

This talk of movies gave me the chance to bring up *Over the Ohio*. One reporter said he heard there would be a surprise in the movie. What was it?

"Now, if I told you that, it wouldn't be a surprise, would it?"

This got the laughter I was hoping for and ended the official portion of our Australian visit. We would be flying out to New Zealand in the morning.

Chapter 13

I guess we as a group were getting to be hardened travelers as we all agreed the flight to New Zealand wasn't that bad. Of course, after some of our flights, a mere five and a half hours seemed like nothing.

We still were taking the next day off. That way we would be rested for the meetings and also could do a little sightseeing. We flew into Tauranga, a city I had never heard of. The Kiwis, as they called themselves, had picked it as the harbor for container ships because it was located between Auckland and Wellington.

This avoided a political battle between the two cities. I expressed the thought that they both wanted it. I was put straight. Yes, there were groups in each city fighting for the financial benefits, but there were also groups that did not want it to ruin their beautiful waterfronts. In other words, New Zealanders were people.

Mr. Frank Kitts, mayor of Wellington, was at our initial greeting party. He thought that there was still some political capital to be made. We had just cleared customs and were waiting for our luggage to unload. I sat on one of the many hard wooden chairs in the area.

I had been forewarned about Mr. Kitts. The average man was five foot eight inches tall. He was six foot two. He was notorious for using his height to gain dominance in conversations. He liked to loom over people.

This is what he tried with me. He came close within my personal space. He had not been made aware of my height. I still had enough room to stand. When I stood, I was now bumping bellies with him. My six foot five also loomed over his mere six foot two.

Talking about backing up quickly. He almost stumbled. When he regained his composure, you could tell he was not used to dealing with people taller than him. He introduced himself by name and gave a short welcome to New Zealand and assurance of any assistance we may need. We shook hands, and he backed away. That was the last I had to deal with Mr. Kitts.

Local taxis took us to the Hotel St. Amand. You could tell it had been around for a long time and was looking a little worse for wear. However, it was clean and dry, and they provided good toilet paper.

After settling in, we took a walk around the area. We ended up on Fisherman's Wharf, which served the local fishing fleet. It smelled like a lot of fish. One interesting feature was a water fountain with railroad tracks running through the center. The water fountain had been built in two halves and placed on each side of the track, kind of weird but neat.

We turned in early, as while we had laughed at the short flight, the physical cost of the entire trip was adding up. Everyone had bags under their eyes, including me.

The next morning, we had breakfast at a delightful little outdoor café. No one said anything, but the age and condition of the St Amand was off-putting.

I inquired and found out that there was a park close by. So, I put on my running outfit and went to Memorial Park. It is a very pretty place; the trails were soft ground, so it was easy running. I don't know why the authorities always wanted to pave things over. I guess it was follow the money.

I left the grounds of the park and ran along the roads. Then, I came across a road which ran up a hill. It promised to have a good view of the Bay of Plenty. At the top of Minden Road, the view was spectacular. You could see the whole area. It would be the perfect site for a lookout tower.

After returning to the hotel and cleaning up, I realized I had spent the whole day running around the area, not with a great many miles, but with a lot of stops to view places like The Elms. This historic house, previously a mission, had seen the history of New

Zealand from before the English settlement up to the English takeover.

It was a story of human perseverance in the face of tragedy. It was stirring and sad at the same time. I was told the story by an elderly lady sitting on the house's porch. I never learned her name.

I watched the arrival of the Kestrel ferryboat from Auckland. Those disembarking were some of the people we would be seeing tomorrow. I had dinner with Dad, Popeye, and Susan Wallace. We recounted our days. We had all seen the same sights but at different times.

Popeye had wandered down to the construction area for the new container port. He wasn't impressed with their progress. After talking to a few workers and hearing terms like filthy capitalist and back of the working man, he thought he knew what was going on. The communist-influenced unions wanted no part of this project. If that was the case, we were in for a long-drawn-out battle.

If the New Zealand officials reflected their attitude there wasn't much we could do. There didn't appear to be any deals we could make like in Australia.

The following day, we met at the local town hall. It was the only place in town big enough to hold everyone. The film crews had started setting up yesterday, so they were ready to go in short order.

There was a parade of dignitaries to meet. First was the Governor-General of New Zealand, the Viscount Cobham. He had met Mum during the war but didn't claim to know her well.

Then there was Mr. Walter Nash, the prime minister. He was very personable, like most politicians, but was standoffish. The only personal comment he made to me was to let me know he was also interested in Scouting and had been awarded the Golden Pheasant from Japan. This was Japan's highest adult scouting award.

We did the exchange of gifts, my plaque with the arrow for the Chief Scout Award. This was getting to be silly. I had been told my resume would look good with Eagle Scout on it. I wonder what people would think of it now.

When the talks got serious, it became apparent that while New Zealand wanted a container port, it was not to encourage trade but to raise taxes. They weren't willing to try to influence their unions to quit the work slowdowns that had been going on.

I think Popeye had nailed it on the head. We could deal with a union that was out for financial advantage for their members. Those that had a political agenda were harder. Those that were purely political were impossible. It was a case of apples and oranges.

We would let New Zealand sort it out by themselves. They would fix things when they realized they were no longer competitive on the world stage. All were polite, but no one there was under the illusion that any progress was to be made.

Even so, we took the obligatory tour together and mouthed the words of cooperation and how this would bring New Zealand products to the world.

This trip had certainly been an eye-opener to me. I had seen everything from corruption to cooperation to indifference. It's a wonder some people aren't still living in caves. Oh, wait, many Chinese still did.

We wrapped up the day and had an impromptu party at a tavern next to the hotel. We were headed home tomorrow morning. I sipped beer and decided that it was horrible.

We went around and congratulated each other on a trip well done. This included film crews, state department employees, and my immediate team. The studio cameraman from Warner Brothers was clicking his camera like crazy.

I thanked the gentleman from the United States State Department. I had wondered at first why they had accompanied us. I was almost insulted by them thinking I couldn't handle things. It would have been a disaster without their advice and education on what to expect.

While thanking them, I also asked Susan Wallace, who was stuck by my side, to remind me to write a nice thank-you note to Secretary of State Christian Herter.

The following day, I made certain to get a run in. It wasn't many miles, but I wanted to stretch my legs before the long flight to England. Before arriving in London, we would have refueling stops in Singapore, Bombay, and Rome. I would get off there while everyone else would return to the States, dropping off the State Department people in Washington, refueling in St. Louis, and ending up in Los Angeles.

What a flight. In total, it would take almost three days.

The flight itself was long and boring. We had all talked ourselves out, so we had to find other entertainment. I lost five dollars at gin rummy and gave up card sharping as a possible career. I even got involved in shooting craps on the floor of the last row. A gambler I am not. It only cost me ten more dollars to find that out.

I had been told if you don't know who the mark is in a gambling game, it is probably you. That must have been why I was asked several times to rejoin the games. No, thank you.

The flight did give me time to reflect on what had been achieved. I had a flair for business. I was looking forward to going to Oxford and living an almost normal life. Well, as normal as attending one of the most prestigious schools in the world could be.

I was lost when it involved girls. Every time I thought I had a girlfriend, it fell through. Many young and not-so-young women had let Richard Jackson the actor and wealthy businessman know they were available. I wasn't interested in those. I could recognize a losing proposition when I saw one. I was interested in a girl about my age who I could relate to and have fun with. Yeah, I meant fun in all contexts. Sue me.

Singapore was a quick stop, so we all stayed on the plane. Bombay was a forced eight-hour delay. We were loaded on a bus and taken to a local hotel. The delay was forced by the Indian government to ensure all our papers were in order. This was strange as no one had planned to get off the aircraft.

As someone pointed out, follow the money. Whose brother-in-law owned the bus, and who owned the hotel? All I can say is that Bombay stank. I mean it smelled bad. Too many people, too close, plenty of sewage, little refrigeration. It smelled horrid.

As far as the hotel went, I was afraid to lie on the bed not knowing what critters lived there. After checking out a pillow, I took a nap on the floor. That turned out to be a big mistake, for when I woke up, I was staring eyeball to eyeball with a snake.

I froze. I want to think it was common sense not to move quickly, causing the animal to react. It probably was in total fear. Every type of poisonous snake in India went through my mind. My brain finally got in gear when I realized its head was not the triangle of a poisonous snake. It looked like a rat snake to me.

Knowing that it wasn't poisonous, I grabbed it several inches behind its neck. I had handled rat snakes and corn snakes in Ohio, so I had no fear of them. The snake immediately wrapped its body around my arm. The trick was to grab near the head so they couldn't turn and bite, too close and they went totally crazy and were almost impossible to hold, but I had judged this one correctly. I took him down to the front desk.

The young man had some English, so I was able to communicate. He thanked me for bringing their snake back. They allowed them to roam the building as they kept the mice and rats down. The only problem was that King Cobras liked to feed on them, so they occasionally had to hunt one of those down.

I asked him if I should take him back to my room.

"Oh no, sir, just put him down. Each snake knows what floor it lives on."

Some things you don't question. This was India, after all.

Of course, the Warner Brothers man was there, so he took pictures. I put the snake down, and he promptly slithered under a couch. He no sooner disappeared than Susan Wallace walked in and sat on the couch.

Some days, the devil makes you do it. Today, he didn't. Nothing was said to Susan as we gathered for our ride back to the airport. Once in the air, I had to tell all my story about the snake. I don't know why she hit my arm so hard.

That was the most exciting thing that happened on the way to London. It was really strange when we got there. Steps were brought out for me to leave the plane. I was the only one getting off. Even Dad was returning to Los Angeles. It felt like I was leaving my best friends and a party all rolled into one.

Chapter 14

From the plane, I went directly to my hotel. I was so tired I could hardly see straight. Of course, the manager needed to talk to me. He wanted to let me know there would be several extra charges on my room. It appears my cousins who I had permitted to stay on visits during the weekend had taken advantage of that.

The rooms had been trashed. They had invited a bunch of their friends. The mini bar, which I had never even opened, had been emptied two weekends in a row.

Altogether, it was costing me over a thousand pounds. I wasn't happy. I told the manager they no longer had freedom of my rooms, and they weren't to be given keys unless I gave direct permission by name. I had three male cousins and two females. I didn't know who was involved, so I banned all of them until I knew what happened.

Finally, I was allowed to go to my room and get some sleep. In the morning I noticed that a painting had been damaged. I knew all the paintings were originals, so it must be worth some money. The painter was a guy named Klee, and the painting was titled, "The Red Balloon." I would have to see what it was insured for.

Sister had been insistent that this was handled before I left on my trip. I was really glad that it had. Later, when I saw what it was valued at, I about choked. Luckily, it could be repaired. Even that would cost a small fortune.

I was beginning to question whether or not I should have paintings and other decorations of great value in a place I wouldn't visit that often. Maybe it could be donated to a museum for a tax break. I asked Sister to look into that. She told me that she had a connection with the Guggenheim and would give them a call. She would also look into reproductions for all of my paintings. She agreed that maybe a teenager's residence wasn't the place for works of art. Live and learn.

The next morning, I took a train to Grays. It was interesting to see the British countryside. This wasn't the picture book countryside. It was the gritty side of being a shipping nation. I saw small ports along the way with decayed piers and sunken barges. There were abandoned factories that had been bombed in the war and never rebuilt.

Still, the River Thames flowed with traffic as we traveled alongside. There was every kind of waterborne vessel that you could imagine. Everything from ocean-going ships to kids on homemade rafts. How those kids didn't get drowned or pushed under, I don't know.

On the land side, there was the usual combination of old houses, junk, and a few vegetable garden allotments that one sees beside the railway tracks. At one point, we passed a series of quarries. They were hundreds of feet deep. Mum had told stories about climbing up and down the quarry walls. Surely it couldn't be these quarries.

At the Grays station, I took a cab to 56 Belmont Road, where my grandparents had lived most of their lives. Mum was expecting me today, but we weren't sure of the time. There was hugging all around. My grandmum, whom I only had met the year before, was frail-looking.

She may have looked frail, but her mind was sharp as a tack. I thought of my Mum as a force of nature. Grandmum was the one who raised her and kept her in line as a teenager.

The house was showing its age and could use remodeling. I made a note to talk to Mum about this. We could certainly afford better for her. We made our way to the back of the house to the little kitchen. There, we had a cuppa, a cup of tea, that is. This was strong stuff compared to the teas I had in America.

The tea was considered a black tea or breakfast tea, Lapsang Souchong. It replaced coffee in the morning. It had hair on it; I had to use a lot of sugar and cream, and I was a big coffee drinker.

They had many questions about my trip. I talked non-stop for over an hour. They agreed that the trip had been worth it even though it was disappointing in some places. Grandmum thought it was a shame that the colonies were given their independence as the Crown would have set them straight. Just look at how Hong Kong went so well.

Grandmum had grown up under Queen Victoria and thought the Empire was fine.

I finally got around to telling them about the state of my hotel room and the banning of my cousins. It turned out they knew what had gone on. Paul and David had invited friends to London with them. The friends were the ones who had trashed the place and drunk all the booze.

I could accept that for the first weekend. Why did the boys invite the same people back for the next weekend? Grandmum had no good answer for that. However, she staunchly supported her grandchildren. I would have expected no less.

I finally agreed that the other cousins shouldn't be held accountable for Paul and David, and they would even be allowed back if they asked permission first and told me who would be there.

The talk turned to what Mum had been doing while she was here. On her list was looking at apartments for let in the Oxford area.

My mum blushed as she started to tell me about what she had found in Oxford. Since it was in the middle of winter, or Hillary term, at the University, all the good apartments were taken. What she had seen was small and dingy, to say the least. They were the rejects of college students. That is a pretty low bar.

This led her to look at houses for sale. She had found a nice place only a fifteen-minute drive from the center of Oxford, so it would be close to whatever school I attended. It was only twelve minutes from Trinity.

She described it as in fair condition, with work being needed both on the house and grounds. As she was describing it, she talked faster and faster. My mum was trying to sell me something!

She then changed the subject to Grandmum's health.

"She really shouldn't be alone, you know. She might fall, and at her age, it would be bad. The new house has room for her."

I had this vision of a two-bedroom house shared between Grandmum and me. What could I say with her sitting right there? I would talk to Mum about this when we drove down there tomorrow.

We spent the evening together around the radio listening to the BBC, the Beeb. Grandmum had never had a TV. Some of the stories I heard were new, some old. I was most interested in how Grandmum learned to read and write.

Her father was a supervisor on the East India docks in London. Grandmum Mary's mother died, and he remarried. From there it became the story about the wicked stepmother. Grandmum would be sent outside in the winter without a coat, while her stepsisters would have on nice warm woolen hats, coats, gloves, and fine boots.

When she was twelve, she was put into service. She became the nanny for a six-year-old boy and a seven-year-old girl. She lived at their house in London. She was paid a shilling a week and had off a half-day on Sunday. The parents were nicer than her real parents and allowed her to sit in on the children's lessons.

As she grew older, she caught the eye of a greengrocer boy who sold from a cart in the alleys behind their row of houses. They started walking out on her half-day and while sitting in the neighborhood's private park, she taught him how to read and write. Of course, this was my grandfather. What a different world.

I asked what happened to the stepmother and her daughters. They were all killed in a bombing raid during the war.

After I had a night of poor sleep in a tiny bed in the attic of the house, Mum and I drove up to Oxford. It was a three-hour drive, and I tried to get her to tell me more about the house she had bought.

She told me she had to concentrate on her driving as she wasn't used to the wrong side of the road anymore. I wondered what she was putting off.

Once in Oxford, it didn't take long to find out. Out of town on a small lane, we turned right past a set of gate pillars onto a gravel road. The road ran straight as far as I could see with great old oak trees lining both sides of the road.

The road had a gradual rise to it, and we came to a curve. As we rounded the curve, there was a mansion. No other way to describe it. It was larger than Jackson House.

On the trip, I had been wondering how it would be with Grandmum and me in a shared living space. I could wander for a week in this place and not find her.

"This is what you bought?"

"Yes, the price was right and fits our needs nicely."

"What is the right price for a place like this?"

Mum danced around that question. She told me seven hundred acres surrounded the house. I would love my apartment in the house. Grandmum would have her apartment with extra room for her nurse and companion.

"Rick, you will have to buy a car to get back and forth to school."

This diverted me nicely as I started to think about what I would drive in England.

As we pulled up to the front door, a man in a conservative grey suit came out. Mr. Hamilton had been the butler to the previous owners. He had agreed to stay on. I found out there was a complete staff of a cook, two maids, and a gardener. There was also part-time work for various people in the nearby village as needed for seasonal work. The home farm was worked by a local farmer on a lease agreement.

The house came completely furnished down to suits of armor in the hall entrance. It was one of the most elegant places I had ever been in, including Buckingham Palace.

"Mum, what did Dad have to say about this place?"

"Oh, I haven't had a chance to talk to him yet."

I would love to hear that conversation. Yet again, I had to get used to the idea that we were rich and that while this place must have cost millions of pounds, it was no big deal.

She gave me a tour of the house. It had many rooms. The ones I remember the most are the conservatory, the billiards room with a full-sized billiard table, and several pool tables. Denny would love this place.

There was a great ballroom and a dining room that would seat more than Jackson House. I asked Mum what this place was called. Since it was known as The Meadows when it was built by a coal baron in 1831, we couldn't change it if we wanted to.

The house had been modernized in the last twenty years, so it had electricity and plumbing throughout. I had noticed the sewage drainpipes fastened to the side of the house as we came in. It was the only way it could be done, as the walls and spacing weren't made for plumbing.

"Rick, I have rented an old carriage house near Trinity that will hold two cars. You can drive there daily and keep a bicycle to get around town."

I hadn't thought of that, but the narrow, old, cramped roads would have limited parking, so a bike made sense. If the carriage house were as big as Mum described, maybe I could set up a small workspace and cot to use during the day.

I next had a vision of living in the carriage house while this great monstrosity sat here with dear old Grandmum, her nurse, and staff.

It wouldn't happen that way. The rooms here were too nice; they had a cook, and a maid would clean up after me.

The library was excellent, with many books. When I examined them, I formed the opinion they had been bought by the yard as decoration only. That would change as I brought my books here. I would have my books shipped from Jackson House. I would also have to look into a new typewriter and one of the copy machines now available everywhere.

I would have to order a set of Encyclopedias and an Oxford Dictionary for here. That was cool, an Oxford Dictionary in Oxford. I would have to get the biggest one and have it mounted on a stand.

We even went out to the carriage house. Inside were several coaches or buggies. Mum told me one was known as a four in hand as it would take a team of four horses to pull. It was open with a driver's seat and backseats facing each other. I had seen the like in New York City used for tours. They would be great in a parade.

There was even a Cinderella coach with room for footmen on the back. I wonder how long it would be before Mary was waving to us peasants.

The house was so much more than I ever thought of, but I could see it as the esidence of Viscountess Jackson.

Chapter 15

Mum took me to Oxford to show me the garage she had rented. It wasn't what I had pictured. It was a double-wide, but it also had an upstairs loft that had been used as living quarters. There even was a toilet and a small kitchenette. While I wouldn't want to live in it all term, it would be nice if I had to stay in town overnight.

I still needed to buy a car, but that could wait until I was back for school. A bicycle shop was next door to my garage, facing the back alley. It was run by a retired don who liked to tinker with bikes. We talked with him about bikes for a while. Students would buy a bike from him, and when they were ready to graduate, they would sell it back.

He would fix it up and resell it. Some of the bikes had been bought and sold by him five times. Each bike had a serial number he had engraved on the frame, each fender, and the sprocket set. It was very prominent. There were very few thefts of his bicycles because everyone knew them.

If a bike were stolen, he would circulate the serial number to all the bike shops and post it on bulletin boards with a small reward. Any thief would have to break the bike down for parts or take it to another city. It just wasn't worth their time. The don only charged a few quid extra for this service. I liked his style.

I ended up buying a sturdy old bike that would handle my size. I could have bought a new flashy one made by Huffy with chrome fenders. I went with the thinner European racing style with hand brakes. Its shabby look wouldn't stand out. I suspect I would have enough problems as it was.

After locking the bike in the garage, Mum and I walked to the registrar's office. Now I would see what had been arranged for me. I would hate to think all this money had been spent, and they said, "Go away."

I didn't seriously think this would be the case, considering the support I had and the grant I had made to the college fund.

I was right. Money talks, especially if the Queen of England says you should listen. I was taken to the Office of the Registrar, the headman himself.

"Sir Richard, we can't tell you how pleased we are that you have decided to continue your education at Oxford and especially Trinity. I understand you will take the engineering course for four years and will be a Master of Engineering when you graduate. It is a shame that we can't fit you into student housing. I trust you have found something."

I looked at Mum for an answer.

She said, "Yes, we have bought a house outside of town, The Meadows, if you are familiar with it."

I thought the guy was fawning over us. He positively drooled.

"I am, Viscountess Jackson. I'm so glad you have chosen to join our community."

"Richard and my mother will be living there. I will, of course, visit from America regularly."

"I see. Richard, if you are living out in the country, I should let you know parking is atrocious around here."

I told him about the garage setup Mum had arranged. He thought that a splendid idea. I think if Mum had told him she had me staying in a rabbit hutch, it would have been a splendid idea.

I was given a list of Trinity's required and optional lectures. There was a list of required reading books. Most importantly, I was given my ticket for entrance to the dining hall. This was for meals on campus. There was also a student bar for social occasions.

Someone had paid for everything, including tuition. I had to find out who had done this and repay them or at least include them on my Christmas card list. That reminded me when I was back at my office, I would have a lot of cards to sign. Even after going to printed signatures on employee anniversary cards, I had hundreds to sign.

After best wishes all around, Mum and I headed to a bookstore. There, I loaded a large trolley with the books on the list. I also picked up a student's black gown and other paraphernalia. This included several Oxford T-shirts, sweaters, and pullovers. Hey, I had learned to dress for my parts in the movies. There was even a dark blue blazer with the Trinity coat of arms. I had to have it.

I would have to go through each required reading book to find the suggested reading and purchase copies of them.

When we got back to the house, our butler Mr. Hamilton had a footman unload all my books for the library. I had a brainstorm.

"Would it be possible to have someone go through all those books and order copies of the suggested reading?"

"It will be our pleasure, Sir Richard."

While I was on a roll, I added a xerography machine and the Unabridged Oxford Dictionary to the list.

"You may not be aware, but a set was already purchased last year. Do you wish to have it set up on its stands?"

"I do wish." Well, I didn't say that. What I said was, "Sure."

It would be really easy to get used to this level of service. I made certain to thank both Mr. Hamilton and the footman who had carried my books in.

I tried to make a joke with Mr. Hamilton.

"We will have to order a formal livery for the staff to wear."

"We have that in the former owner's colors. Do you wish to review them to see if they are acceptable? We normally only wear them for formal occasions."

I'm not in Kansas anymore. I hadn't been there in a long time, but this was getting well...it was getting something. I didn't even have words for it. Strange? Weird? Goofy?

Mum, who was standing there, told Mr. Hamilton she would look at the outfits and plan.

The next morning, Mum drove me down to London and dropped me off at Heathrow Airport for my flight back to the States. She was heading back to Grays to start moving Grandmum to Oxford.

I originally had planned to buy a car while I was here in England, but it would now have to wait until I got back.

I had thought that with Dad and the State Department people going to meetings in Washington after dropping me off in London, I would get out of going to DC.

Dad had Mum inform me that I was wanted both at the State Department and the White House. So, my flight from London was to National Airport in Alexandria, Virginia.

The flight was only eight hours, which seemed like nothing after the Asian trip. I was met at luggage by a man with a sign with my name on it. He was with a limo company and took me to The Willard. I had stayed there before when visiting the White House last year.

In the morning, I rose early and got a run in down along the Mall and back. After cleaning up and having a decent breakfast, I walked over to the White House. I knew which gate to go to sign in. There was no hold up there as I had my US Passport and US Marshal's ID with me.

A uniformed Secret Service guard escorted me to the entryway, where the plainclothes people took over. They took me to the anteroom of the Oval Office, where I had to wait for about half an hour. When the door opened, the president was right there to escort me in.

Vice President Nixon and Secretary of State Christian Herter were already in the room. First of all, Ike and Mr. Herter congratulated me on my Asian trip. Mr. Nixon gave one of his false-looking smiles, and that was it.

We talked about the various receptions and outcomes in the countries visited. They thought everything went as they had predicted, and Australia was a big win. They attributed that to my and my team's efforts. I made certain to give the State Department group plenty of credit for their help and guidance.

I never could get that gentleman's name to stick. Once again, I learned his name was William Battle. I wondered if I would remember it.

They then got to the real reason for the meeting. China. The United States wanted to open China for trade. It was potentially one of the biggest markets in the world. The president thought it would take twenty or thirty years to open them up, but he was thinking of the future.

Capitalism is great as long as there are growing markets. He saw the day when we would saturate our current markets and raise everyone's standard of living as high as it could go. After that, things would stagnate. India was a possibility, but for some reason, they just went in circles and never broke out of their caste system, which was holding them back.

The Soviet Bloc wouldn't trade with us, and we didn't want them. Meanwhile, Ike thought they would collapse under their weight, given the time. He didn't want to extend that by boosting their economies. This all made sense when he explained it, but I would have never put it together on my own.

It also gave me some dos and don'ts about where I should do business. We even discussed South America, but until stable governments arose and allowed a middle class to thrive, it would be throwing good money in to be nationalized later.

During this conversation, Mr. Nixon looked uncomfortable. I found out why. It hinged on my contact with the Chinese. He was against me following up on their request to drop a suit off at their dry cleaners. He wanted to put everything off until he was in office so the credit would go to his administration.

The president and Mr. Herter thought it should proceed as requested. I knew what I would do. As I was taking my leave, Ike cornered me and told me not to worry about Dick Nixon. He was a politician through and through and would go with the winners.

Also, time had been blocked out for me to go to the State Department. I was going somewhere else to be briefed on China.

Somewhere else was the US Navy Bureau of Medicine and Surgery. At least, that was what the sign said. Since I recognized a young man passing in the hall, I knew it was a CIA building. He was one of those that had been tailing me and burned by the Soviets. He would spend his career here rather than in the field since he had been burned.

I was given an extensive rundown on the state of affairs with China and its leaders. Their main concern was that by putting container systems in their main ports, China would be able to export more weapons to their satellite groups, such as the communists in Vietnam.

Providing them with these tools would be a double-edged sword. I left there not knowing what the right thing to do was but knowing I would do what the president wanted.

They took me back to The Willard where I spent the night, then caught an early flight back to California. It seemed like I had been gone a hundred years though it was only five weeks.

Chapter 16

It was Monday, March 7th when I landed in California mid-afternoon. I had been in England two days before, so I had quite a few time zones to make up for. All told I didn't feel that bad. A good night's sleep would do it. The only problem would be that I would probably have a good night's sleep in by 2 a.m.

A driver was waiting for me at the luggage carousel. I only had a small carry-on bag, but it was the most convenient place to meet. He dropped me off at home. Dad was still at work. My brothers and sister were home from school and busy with their chores.

No matter how much money we had, the youngsters would always have chores. This was part of our Bellefontaine upbringing. Of course, they weren't your normal chores. Mary was polishing silver. Her chores varied as she was learning all the tasks needed to run a large establishment.

She assured me that all princesses needed to know these things, or else the staff would become lazy, and the next thing you knew, a wicked stepmother would be running the place. It made sense to me.

Denny was doing chores but wasn't as happy about it. Jackson House was finally switching over from coalfired heating to gas. His job this week was to clean out the now-empty coal bin. He looked like what I imagined a Charles Dickens chimney sweep would have looked like.

Eddie's chore was filling all the flower vases with fresh water. It was easy to find him. All you had to do was follow the trail of spilled water. I suspect his chore was creating more work for the staff than helping.

They were all glad to see me and wanted to know what presents I had brought them. When I told them I hadn't picked anything up, they went back to work—so much for glad to see me.

One of the first things I did was check my mail. Dad had opened all of it with my permission to ensure nothing time-sensitive was missed. He hadn't told me, but my SAT scores were there. I had an overall score of 1580. That exceeded my expectations, considering that other candidates would have had twelve years of formal schooling while I only had nine, plus a year and a half of self-study.

The good news was that with this score and my A-Level results, any university would take me. That was all moot as I was registered at Trinity College in Oxford, but it was still nice to know. It would also help with any future education plans that I may have. I knew I would have to obtain at least an MBA with a solid finance background. Mary's thoughts about the staff and wicked stepmother weren't that far off.

When Dad got home, we discussed our trip around the world. We had feedback from South Korea that the Rhee administration was out and that we could now buy the steelworks without much corruption. Notice I didn't say any, just not a lot. It was now a good deal, so Jackson Enterprises was proceeding.

We also talked about China. It would be hard for Jackson Enterprises to do business there since Chinese markets were closed to the world. Their currency had no real exchange rate established. The only way we could do business was to accept and resell agricultural products, as this was their only export.

The drawback there was that most of their exports were sold to Russia. They did make shipments to Indonesia. We wondered if we could set up a trade where they sold grain to Indonesia in exchange for rubber. With Indonesia acting as a broker, the rubber would then be sold to Australia for Australian dollars.

This sounded complicated as all get out. Physically, an Indonesian-flagged ship would purchase and load grain in China, offload it at Tanjung Priok, the main port, and reload with rubber. The only transaction in Indonesia was the barter exchange of grain for rubber. The rubber would be taken to Australia, where it would be sold for Australian dollars.

Using the Australian dollars, Indonesia would then purchase equipment and consulting from Jackson Enterprises. They would buy the training and equipment needed for Indonesian engineers to go to China to supervise Chinese workers in constructing a container port. Indonesia would have enough Australian dollars left over to make a profit.

Australian trade would increase. Indonesia would have increased trade and the core of a trained engineering workforce. Some of those engineers who would go to China as advisors would be Jackson Enterprise engineers. They wouldn't interface with the Chinese, only the Indonesians would. That way, China wouldn't be seen as doing business with the West. It gave me a headache to think about it.

We would have to set up a separate company in Australia to handle this, but that was probably a good idea for that part of the world anyway. It would also increase our influence in Australia, which would be good.

Dad explained to me that Jackson Enterprises Management, the US State Department, and the Australian State Department had come up with this possibility. My role would be to present it to the Chinese. The Indonesians would go for it as there was no way they could lose. The benefit to the United States would be a complicated diplomatic backdoor to China. This backdoor would be imperative if relations were ever to become public and formal. Of course, my company would make a ton of money.

My only concern about the whole deal was that I didn't get kidnapped by the Russians on my way to the dry cleaner. The entire proposal had been typed up and placed into a thick envelope that would be inside the suit I dropped off.

That brought up another benefit. If successful, it would move the Chinese further from the Russian camp.

The Chinese had just asked for me to drop off a suit. The proposal was being proactive.

After that talk with Dad, which took three hours, I was exhausted and went to bed and to sleep. As I thought, I was awake at 3 a.m. That was better than 2, but it was still way too early. I crept down to the kitchen and had a bowl of cereal and toast. From there, I went back to bed and slept three more hours.

Running the trails in the park felt good after a long absence. Not wanting to put off my trip to the dry cleaner and let it grow into a monster, at least in my mind, I drove down to Chinatown. It was anticlimactic. On the way down, I replayed my run-in with the Russians and later betrayal by a rogue FBI agent.

I went into the dry cleaner to hand the suit to the same woman I had seen in Hong Kong. She went through it to make certain I hadn't left anything in the pockets. She didn't blink at the envelope, deftly placing it in a drawer behind the counter.

I thanked her for my "tickee," which drew a tight smile, and I had an uneventful trip home. I thought about calling Nancy but realized that it was a school day in the normal world.

Instead, I drove over to Riviera Country Club, and after checking to make certain I was signed up for the US Open qualifying rounds on the 19th and 27th. I played eighteen holes after warming up using the driving range and putting greens. John Jacobs was out on the course, so I drew a caddie from the pool. I had initially thought the sectional would be played over two days as it was thirty-six holes. I was wrong. It would all be on one long day.

Today, I didn't try anything fancy. I just played the course as I understood it. I was a bit rusty, so I only played two under par. I would have to tighten up before the sectional and regional rounds. To that end, I stopped at the clubhouse and signed up to play three rounds next week and two the week after.

There was another issue I had to settle while I was home. My movie agent Mr. Baxter was effectively retired. He was working with Mary, but that was more like a hobby for him as Mum had limits on what Mary could do. I noticed that the brat kept pushing those limits.

Keeping that in mind, I did call Mr. Baxter. Before I left on my trip, I had asked him if he had anyone he could recommend. He said he would give it some thought. He returned my call after dinner. He did have a recommendation. It was a small startup firm.

They were the children of agents he had dealt with for years. He had always been a one-man show but thought I would do better with an agency. He did offer to act as a consultant if I had any questions about what was being presented to me, for a fee, of course.

I had to laugh at that. It was his nature. It was a good idea. The contracts and money were only part of the equation. The films and parts were probably even more critical as to where my career, if any, went. He knew me as well as anyone in the industry and would know what would work.

After my morning workout and run on Thursday, I made a call that I had been putting off. I called Mr. Sinatra's agent and told him that I would consider doing another duet with Mr. Sinatra. I was told my timing was poor. Mr. Sinatra had other projects scheduled and couldn't work me in. I had waited too long.

I couldn't begin to say how disappointed I was. I had been taught not to lie, but it made my day. Well, half a day. After a good ride on George, who was a little frisky because of his long layoff, and then lunch, I received a phone call.

One may have guessed it would be Mr. Sinatra.

"Ricky, I just talked to my agent. I don't know what he was thinking. I have plans for another song. I want to redo the 'Coffee Song'. It was fun, and I think we could do better than my first time around with it."

There was nothing for me to do but say yes. I asked about the timing.

"Oh no hurry, if you could be in the studio sometime next week that would be great."

"Would Tuesday or Thursday work? I have golf the other days."

"Playing golf is more important than singing with me?"

"I have qualifying rounds for the US Open at the end of the month, so I have to get some practice in."

"Oh, that makes sense. Let's reserve both days and try to get it done in one. It is a simple song."

At dinner, Dad asked me if I had seen the new house in Oxford. I very cautiously said, "Yes."

"Coward, your Mum has told me all about it. What's your opinion?"

"It is very grand. It is the sort of house Viscountess Jackson would live in and the Queen would stay there when visiting."

"She told me how much she paid for it. That doesn't bother me. She gave up a lot to follow me to Bellefontaine and never complained. I was wondering how the rest of us would adjust."

I told him how Mr. Hamilton had firm control over the staff and how helpful they were, like unloading all my books and ordering all the suggested reading ones. How there was a billiards room with a full-size billiard table and two pool tables. That got Denny's attention.

I had inquired for Eddie, and there is a local Boy Scout Troop. This made him happy.

I deliberately ignored the young lady sitting at the table. Well, I tried to ignore her, but she wouldn't let me.

"Is there anything I might like there?"

"They have a real tea parlor. I did notice some little girls playing in the nearby village. Oh, they do have a stable that would hold a pony. Then I think we found Cinderella's lost coach in the stables."

This elicited a bunch of questions. The upshot was that Dad was going to have to pay for the refurbishment of a coach very much like the state coach used by Queen Elizabeth at her coronation. It would not be gilded gold, though.

I told Dad about all the books in the library and that we would probably replace all those bought at auctions by the yard. They had no purpose other than to fill the shelves. With titles like *Reminisces of a Yorkshire parson in 1840*, one couldn't wait to read them. Well, I had read the first chapter and could cheerfully wait for the rest of my life to finish it.

Friday morning, I checked on the addition being done to the garages at Jackson House. I would have an excellent workshop here. It would be a shame if I could never use it. The same went for the Beach House, which was almost done. It was going to be a great place. If I spent five days a year there, I would be lucky.

I stopped for lunch at a little sidewalk café. I was almost finished when I was recognized. I spent half an hour signing autographs and talking to people. They wanted to know why I was wearing an Oxford University T-shirt. Without thinking much about it, I replied that I had just signed up to go to school there.

It turned out that there was a reporter in the small group. She didn't let on what she was doing, and I was skillfully interviewed about how I had qualified to go to Oxford University as I had just graduated tenth grade. It had made all the LA papers not that long ago. That led to a discussion about the English O- and A-level exam system.

From there, I just had to brag about my SAT score of 1580. I guess I came off as more factual about it than I thought because the article she wrote treated me kindly.

After lunch, I stopped by my office for a business update. It was astonishing to hear the dollars that were passing through my company. Also astonishing were the numbers that were staying with the company. If I sold the company, I would be well on my way to being a billionaire. That made no sense to me. As they say in New Orleans, "Let the good times roll."

After that, I drove up to the Forestry Service airport. It was in full swing. I wish my plane were ready. By the time it would be ready, I would be in school in England. I planned to have it taken over there. It would have to be on a ship, as the plane wouldn't go that distance without refueling. I wondered if I could take delivery in England. I would have to check on that.

Dinner was fun as we had pizza. It was a seafood pizza, which I had never had before. Octopus, lobster, and shrimp just didn't seem right. It tasted good, and there was none left so I guess we all liked it no matter how many turned-up noses there were.

Chapter 17

The weekend was quiet. I called Nancy several times Saturday morning, but there was no answer at their house. They were out of town. I had read in *Popular Mechanics* about a new product on the market, a machine that answered the telephone and recorded messages. That would be a handy thing to have.

I drove over to the studio to see what was going on. Usually, something was happening, some production running out of time, so filming on the weekend. The stunt area was deserted. I got my archery equipment out and practiced for an hour, but it felt different, and I got bored.

As I was packing to leave, a studio runner found me. He was one of the many acting school kids on the lot, working weekends for experience, money, and the hope of being discovered. I thought these were all good reasons and may have gone that route if I had needed to.

"There is a small scene on set 20. Do you have time? They need a big guy."

Having nothing better to do, I said, "Sure."

Upon arrival on the closed set, there was little activity.

"I found someone, Mr. Dodge."

Ron Dodge looked up, shook his head, and said, "You sure did. Rick, are you up to a change of image role?"

"What image?"

"Thug."

"Thugee would be better, but yeah, what do you need?"

"It is a single scene with no dialog. You will attack the young lady, and our hero will knock you down and save the day."

"Sounds like fun. What about makeup and costume?"

"Just highlights and what you have on will work fine."

I was wearing a pair of chinos and a polo shirt.

"Okay, but if they get ruined, you have to pay. What about the paperwork? I don't work for free you know."

"Ah Rick, you're getting all mercenary on me. I'm over budget as it is."

I almost relented when I saw him break into a smile.

They had me made up in under half an hour, which had to be a record for me. There was a walkthrough of the scene. I would grab the girl by the arm, our hero would run up and jump on my back, bringing me to the ground, and they would run away.

The scrawny hero ran up and jumped on my back while I stood there. He moved me a couple of feet, but that was it.

"Cut. Damn it, Rick, you are supposed to fall."

"Oh, I thought he was going to knock me down."

The next time when I felt him hit, I fell over. They ran away. This was done three more times before Ron Dodge was satisfied. He thanked me. I got a copy of the paperwork giving me the standard day rate and headed out. I ask for the names of the girl, the hero, or the movie. I never had any feedback on my role, so it may not have been released. Or, more likely, my face was never on the screen, just my back.

After that interlude to my day, I returned to the stunt area, and still, no one had shown up. I left the studio and headed towards the beach. When in doubt, go to the beach. After an early lunch stop at a drive-through, I stopped by Katin's. The latest news on Corky was that things were going great. He had come in second in a tournament in Australia.

I wondered how I could tie his success to Jackson Enterprises. I had sponsored him anonymously, but maybe he wouldn't consider it charity if the corporation did it. With it being a corporate sponsorship, it wouldn't put me in the limelight any more than I was already.

I was thinking about the new relationship I had with the Australian government. Anything that made the company look good worked for me. Since Nancy Katin handled the arrangement with Corky, I asked her if there was anything else we could do for him.

"He called the other day. It has been more expensive than he planned. He is eating light and sleeping in rental cars or with friends he has made on the road."

"Do you think he would mind being sponsored publicly by my company, Jackson Enterprises?"

"I suspect if it got him a meal, he would welcome sponsorship from the Devil himself."

"We can't have that; do you have a contact number for him in Australia?"

"Yes, I do."

She gave me the number of the friend he was currently staying with. It was six in the morning there, so I didn't feel too guilty and had a good chance of catching him.

Someone answered the phone and got a very sleepy-sounding Corky for me.

"Corky, it's Rick Jackson."

"Rick who?

"Rick Jackson. Do you remember that movie that went bust?"

"Oh, hi Rick, what's up?"

"I'm with Nancy Katin. She was telling me things are tight financially on the tour."

"That they are."

"I have a company, Jackson Enterprises, and it would be willing to give you a full sponsorship. This includes expenses for food, travel, and lodging plus five hundred a month for incidentals. That does not interfere with what you are getting through the Katin sponsorship."

"Are you for real, man?"

"Yes, my company does a lot of business in places you travel to, so we want to have our name in front of the locals in a positive light."

"How do we start this?"

"Why don't I wire you a couple of thousand through Western Union today and then follow up with a formal contract and payment method?"

"Wow, that must be some company you have."

"It is a large business. Last month, I was with the prime minister of Australia, so this is the real deal. Because of that, the contract that you will be asked to sign will have a personal conduct clause. This will be like the one I have with Warner Brothers. Getting picked up for speeding is okay. Underage girls not okay."

"Got it, and I have no problem with that."

We chatted for a few more minutes while he grew ever more effusive about the sponsorship. I finally got him off the line.

I filled in Nancy on what was going on and how it would affect our silent arrangement. Then, I looked up the address of the nearest Western Union office in the Yellow Pages.

At Western Union, they weren't anxious to take a check. It took a phone call to my bank and giving my safety phrase to the bank before the bank would guarantee the check and Western Union would accept it.

On impulse, I upped it to five thousand dollars. I didn't know how long it would take to settle things at this distance. Even by airmail, it would take weeks. In the meantime, he would be off to Tahiti.

When that was done I headed home for dinner and an exciting night at Jackson House. Tonight, Professor Plum did the deed in the library with a knife. Mrs. Hernandez won.

I asked Mrs. Hernandez if she liked Mexicali Delight beer or just the people who made it. I think that was the only time I have ever seen her blush. She didn't answer me. Dad glared, so I shut up.

Sunday was a surfing day. Eddie was off on a camping trip, so Denny and I spent the day at the beach. It was a fun time, with us catching some rather good waves. We had lunch at the little hot dog stand across the road next to Katin's.

A couple of girls there looked to be Denny's age. They checked each other out. He went over and introduced himself. After half an hour of sweet-talking, one of the girls was sitting close to him and twirling the ends of her hair. Way to go little brother! Now if I could only meet girls that easily.

Of course, he didn't have to worry about them chasing him for his fame or fortune.

The next thing I knew, I was driving Denny and two girls to one of their homes. He had volunteered my services as a chauffeur. Both girls sat in the back seat with him.

When we got to the house where both girls were going, there was a father waiting outside. They had been gone past their time, and he was getting worried. He didn't look happy that his little girl of about fourteen was riding around in a car.

He came up to me, wanting to know who I was and why I had his daughter in my back seat. I told him to ask her. I had just given the two girls and my brother a ride. For some reason, he still thought it was my fault. He kept punching me with one finger. I put up with that for the first three punches, then got out of the car.

I have to say this for him, he was smart enough to know when he had a problem. He looked to be about five foot seven inches tall. When I opened the car door and stood up, he quit punching me with his finger.

Now, he yelled at the girls to get in the house. As they rushed to the door, I drove away. I asked Denny if he got her phone number. He had. I bet him that he wouldn't have the nerve to call her. He agreed and made no bet.

For some reason, it struck both of us as funny, and we laughed most of the way home. I did find out that Denny hadn't identified me, so the police probably wouldn't be waiting at home. We fortified ourselves with milkshakes to settle the excitement of the day. When we got home, Dad asked how it went. We told him, "Fine."

He shook his head and went back to the magazine he was reading.

On Monday, I had a tee time of 10 a.m. at Riviera. John Jacobs was to be my caddie for all the practice rounds. We were put in with a threesome of seniors. They couldn't hit the ball long, but they sure kept it in the fairway and were deadly on the greens.

They were nice guys. I was recognized as the club record holder. I told them that today wouldn't be a record-setting round. John and I had a plan. I would be hitting the gambling shots for the rest of the rounds this week. These would either leave me in a great position or be the knell of doom, at least for that hole.

The idea was to find which ones I had a good percentage chance of making. Could I cut that corner or roll it through that flat sand trap with no lip? There were seven opportunities like that on the course, and John had seen people who could consistently make them and others who couldn't.

If I even find one of those with a good percentage, it might make a big difference.

I didn't slow the group down, but I did mess up four of the seven. The other three looked possible. I would still try all of them on the next two rounds to see what worked or didn't, as the case may be.

It was a nice day, and I thanked the gentlemen and shook hands at the end. This is what golf should be like every day.

Tuesday was working out and riding George. That took up the morning. After lunch, I tried Nancy's house again. Her mom answered and told me to try after school.

I called back later, and she was glad to hear from me. We talked for almost an hour. I did find out she had been to her grandmother's for the weekend. As we were getting ready to hang up, she said she had something to tell me.

"Rick, I know you are going to school in England and will be gone most of the year. I like you, but I want to date. There is a boy I like who has asked me to go steady, and I think I will say yes to him."

What do you say to that?

"I understand. It isn't as if I could fly home every weekend to see you. It has been nice talking to you, and when I get back from England, I will give you a call. Maybe that guy will turn out to be a jerk."

"Please do, but I don't think he would ever be like that."

So ends another relationship before it even starts. I would have to settle down in one location long enough to meet and date a girl. I have tried in Argentina, England, Ohio, and California. Well, I guess you really couldn't count Argentina.

I did realize that she was entirely correct. It wouldn't work; she wanted to date, and I hoped to date someone in England. No idea who as I hadn't met her yet, or maybe I have, that girl who keeps giving me rude gestures.

On Wednesday, I met up with John Jacobs again at Riviera to practice for the US Open qualifying rounds. The one-day local qualifying round is on Saturday week on the 19th and then the sectional on the following Saturday and Sunday.

Once more, I had to play in a foursome as the course was busy with people practicing for the open. Again, I was lucky as my group had no one in it trying to qualify. They were the two doctors and the dentist I had played with once before. I informed them I was practicing, so don't expect a course record.

They were polite the entire round but watched me like a hawk. I did okay. On the seven-gambling shots, I was successful on four of them this time around. I split two others, and I missed the seventh twice.

This time, at the end of the round, I had to do autographs for the two doctors. The dentist had recognized me the first time we played and asked then. I had learned to always have studio pictures with me. This time, the supply was in my golf bag for occasions like this.

One of the doctors even had a Brownie camera with him, so John took pictures of all of us. I then had one of the doctors take a picture of John and me with the other three caddies. Doctor Welby, who had the camera, promised to get copies of the photos to everyone.

Mum called at dinner time to talk to all of us. Each had a turn. She told me that all my paperwork had been accepted at Trinity, and I was now officially a student. I needed to be back in England in time to start Trinity term, preferably a few days early. I told her I planned on it, as I had to buy a car. I would try to be back by Monday, April 4th.

Instead of Clue, we played Pick up Stix. For a change, I won. No matter what they say, I didn't cheat. I had to sneeze at a critical moment for Denny. It would have been more convincing if it hadn't been the only time I sneezed all night.

Chapter 18

I goofed off on Thursday, no other way to put it. A leisurely workout and run followed by a ride through the park on George. I did make it over to the Forest Service airstrip by using the new bridge over the ravine in the park. What had been a fifteen-minute drive by the main road would be five minutes by Jeep.

Of course, there were posted signs saying no vehicles other than Forest Service maintenance. Maybe that was why a Jeep with US Forest Service written on its side seemed to be permanently parked behind Jackson House.

The afternoon was spent going through my wardrobe to decide what would go to England and what would stay. I was halfway through and said the heck with it. Ship everything over and sort it out later.

I found a good book, went up to the top of the tower, and read for the rest of the afternoon. Later that evening, as I was about to pick up the winning stick, Eddie had a sneezing fit. Cheater!

Mary had tried to get me earlier, but her sneeze came out as a cute little achoo. Even Dad seemed out to get me as when I started to reach for the winning stick, he pulled out what must have been a pillowcase and put it to his face as though he was going to blow his nose. It had us all laughing so hard it took several minutes to calm down for my try. That's when Eddie got me.

On Friday, I showed up for my tee time. This time, I was in a foursome that included an older man and two guys in their early thirties. The older man was named Bernard Swartz. He told me he was trying to qualify for the first round of the US Open. He had never made it, and after thirty years of trying, this was his last effort.

The other two guys standing there laughed at this.

"Old man, you won't make it this time. It is for us young bucks to win."

The other thirty-something guy asked me how old I was. When I told him I was sixteen, he told me to keep playing, that someday I might even be able to play real golf. Now, he said that sincerely, but not in a nasty way.

My reply was, "Yes, sir."

John Jacobs gave me a startled look, but I returned it with a slight negative shake of my head. He got the message quickly and went over to whisper to the other caddies, who were all course regulars.

I didn't feel a need to try to show anyone up. I kept to my game plan of trying the high-risk, high-reward shots.

We went ahead and tossed tees in the air to see who would lead off. I was last.

When I took my shot, everyone had teed off and was collecting their gear to head out. It was one of the high-risk ones and the one that I had yet to make. I didn't make it this time either, ending up in the sand trap on the left side of the course.

The guy who told me to keep playing told me tough luck, but maybe I should back it down and not challenge the course. I never had the honors as they all were playing well, even Mr. Swartz.

I was able to confirm that I could make four of the high-risk shots, had an even chance on two others, and probably no chance on one, the first hole. That helped define how I would play the course. If everything went right, I would destroy the course record I had set. Of course, it never does.

When we were done, we all shook hands, the one middle-aged guy encouraging, the other not so much. As we were walking to the clubhouse, Mr. Swartz held back to talk to me.

"Sir Richard, I'm an admirer and am impressed with how you stuck to your plan and didn't try to show those guys up. I would avoid trying to drive the trap on the first hole, though. You are a long hitter, and if you made that shot you would be placed well no matter where the pin was on the green, but you seem to be about five yards short of doing it."

"My thoughts exactly, sir, and that was the third time I tried it this week. It is a no-go. I would only try in the actual play if I were desperate."

"Somehow I doubt if you ever will be that desperate."

"One never knows. I've been known to blow up on the course."

"When was the last time that happened?"

"It happened two years ago when I was on my high school golf team."

"I don't think it's a worry anymore. Good luck to you during the local playoff."

"Good luck to you also, sir."

John and I discussed my round. We both had come to the same conclusions about the higher-risk shots. I wouldn't try any of them if I were ahead of the field. The object was to qualify for the US Open, not set any course records. If I did, it would be incidental to my play.

After that, I spent another two hours on the putting green. John was with me the whole time. We discussed every putt as to how fast it should be, the lie of the grass, and the break of the green. It was much about us communicating what we saw as anything. Any pro will tell you the caddie is a team member. Acting as a second set of eyes, if you will.

A good caddie will help you with everything from reading the course, to the club needed, to keeping you centered on your game. If there is any outside information about the immediate shot, it is your caddie's job to know it and decide if it is worth breaking your concentration.

There is some truth to the old joke where the mushroom cloud is in the distance, and the caddie says, "You have time to putt out."

At dinner later, we decided on Monopoly as the game of the night. Eddie landed on Park Place, followed by Boardwalk in the first round. It was brutal. One of the shorter games we had played.

Saturday, I decided to go flying, so I drove out to Ontario and rented a twin-engine Cessna 310 like the one I had on order. I flew out towards San Bernardino. There was a large brush fire in the area. I wanted to see what it would look like from up above. Because of the unpredictable updrafts, I couldn't get too close as it was a no-fly zone.

As I approached the area, I noticed a branch of the fire that had headed away from the main blaze. Going as close as I dared, I saw something that chilled my blood.

A car was stopped between two foothills in the larger mountain range to the north. The road had a roaring fire in front of it and behind it. The only reason it wasn't engulfed in the flames was that the fire had farther to travel to go up and down the hill to their south.

Four people were standing outside of the car, two adults and two children. I dithered for a moment but decided I had to try something. There was no way to land on the road with a normal long glide in approach. If what I was about to try worked, I would owe Mr. McGarry a big thank you for teaching me various ways to strafe a runway.

One of those was to swoop almost directly down and pull out at the last second, then machine-gunning the aircraft on the ground. I, of course, didn't have a machine gun but it would let me land without going through the murderous updraft from the fire.

Heart in hand, I did just that. I dove down on the highway, pulling out at the last second, then made the shortest stop I could. It took me almost to the family. Leaving the port engine idle, I shut down the starboard and opened the door.

The family needed no urging as they had run the short distance down the road. The parents put the children on the wing and followed them up and through the door I opened.

I didn't wait for them to be seated and buckled in. I started the starboard engine back up and started taxiing down the road towards the furthest flame-free point. When I thought I would have enough room to take off, I gunned it down the runway. I can think of at least a hundred safety rules and regulations I broke, but we got safely into the air.

There was a lot of buffeting as we flew through the updraft, but since we were trying to climb, it generally worked in our favor. I say generally because the wind did cause the plane to nose down at one point. I was able to fight the controls to get us back up.

The whole incident, from me deciding to land to clearing the fire, couldn't have been five minutes, but in that five-minutes, flames had engulfed the car. Between crying children and parents trying to thank me, it took a while to get them settled and buckled in.

I flew back to Ontario, where I was going to have to explain how the aircraft would need a complete inspection for damage. I had stressed the heck out of the airframe with my stunt. I might be buying a replacement.

All of this didn't happen in a vacuum. When I got too close to the fire, ATC warned me that I was in a no-fly zone. When I landed and went off their radar, they went crazy, well, as crazy as they ever get in that flat business-as-usual voice they have.

When I came back up on the radar screen again, there were calls for me to report in. Once I had the family settled, I did that. Using my aircraft tail number, I reported that we were now headed to Ontario airport with five souls on board. I had learned that in the TWA incident.

They knew I had been alone since I had taken off from Ontario. That required clarification. When they found out I had landed and picked up people it became dead air or silence for a few seconds.

"Cessna 310, land and taxi to the main apron and turn off your engines. An FAA official, the medical team, and law enforcement will meet you. Well, I knew I had broken a lot of rules.

I greased the nice landing. A group was waiting for me at the main apron in front of the terminal. They even had brought out the fire engine. First out was the family whose name I hadn't even learned.

The medical team surrounded them. The law enforcement contingent turned out to be one deputy sheriff who had nothing else to do. I also recognized a stringer for one of Dad's newspapers.

The FAA guy immediately wanted to know who I was, my flying background, and what I was thinking. I answered, making certain that the reporter heard me.

"I was thinking that those people would die if I didn't help."

That took the FAA man, Mr. Thompson, back a little.

"Okay, I get that. However, I see you are not licensed to carry passengers yet, you landed in a no-fly-zone and certainly carried out maneuvers that aircraft wasn't built for."

"You are right on all counts except the aircraft maneuvers. The Cessna 310 is built for such stress, though it will need a complete inspection."

By that time, a savior, Mr. McGarry, walked up.

"Rick, what have you been up to?"

I described how I had landed and taken off. He nodded his head and told Mr. Thompson that it was within the airframe's capabilities and that he had taught me how to do that approach.

That helped somewhat.

"Well, his license is still suspended until there is a hearing on his going into a no-fly zone and hauling passengers."

As this was the normal procedure in any event like this, I wasn't too concerned.

The man whose family I had saved came over. He handed a business card to me and Mr. Thompson. It read Marshall F. McComb, Associate Justice of the State of California Supreme Court.

I don't think I had too many worries.

I introduced myself to the judge, who told me his kids, ages nine and twelve, had figured out who I was. He and his wife thanked me again and again for saving their family from certain death.

The reporter, by this time, had a camera out and was taking pictures of everyone. Oh well, I had been through this before.

Mr. Thompson, who had been professional every bit of the way, told me I would receive a notice in writing about the hearing but didn't think I had too much to worry about. I had acted within the scope of my training and the capabilities of the aircraft, so there was no reckless endangerment. Nothing succeeds like success.

Mr. McGarry and I talked for a while about what I had done.

"Rick, it was like combat; you did what had to be done. Rules at that point become guidelines. You shut the engine down so people don't fall into the prop. You don't worry about clearances from someone not involved. I would say you got it completely right. Of course, if you had died, you would be considered a stupid failure.

"Now, are you settled down enough to drive home?"

I had to stop and think for a moment.

"Yes, I am. That was what this conversation was about, giving me time to get the adrenaline out of my system."

"You're learning son, you're learning."

From there, I drove home. I had to shower and change clothes. I was stinking from sweat by the time I walked into the house. Enough that the cook shrank away from me as I went by her. I hadn't noticed at the time, but stress does make you sweat.

When I came back downstairs, Dad was walking in through the door.

"Rick, are you all right?"

"Yes, Dad. I guess you heard."

"I got a call from the San Bernardino paper. They are all over the story, and it is out on the AP wire. Sir Richard does it again. Of course, there will be Sir Richard is reckless again."

"Those don't even bother me that much anymore. What I hate is all the requests for interviews that will now be coming my way. That reminds me, I had better call Susan Wallace."

Susan hadn't heard anything about the latest, so I had to go into detail with her.

"Rick, let me get this straight. You landed that airplane using the same technique as strafing a runway?"

"Yes, I did."

"That is fantastic. Remember when you were in court taking your tenth-grade exam, a big deal was made about it, to the point Bill McGarry had separate stories written about him? This will give the publicity legs."

"Oh, Susan, you know how I feel about all those interviews."

"Okay, how about one press conference at the Ontario airport and an interview on KTLA?"

"I can do that."

"I will try to set them up for tomorrow."

"Sounds like a plan. Thanks, Susan."

That ended my day. I retreated to the tower and read.

Chapter 19

Monday was another practice day. The course was full of players for next Saturday. I met three others in my group, and they made no impression on me at all. I focused on playing the course as I would on Saturday. The only thing I couldn't plan for was the time of day I would tee off. This was important on this course as the sea breeze kicked up at about two in the afternoon.

I was hoping for an early tee time. I had seen what those "breezes" could do. Gale force, in my opinion, at least when they were affecting the golf ball.

I deliberately did nothing for the rest of the day. I wanted to be calm and centered, not for the coming golf match but to sing with Sinatra tomorrow. I had sung with him but had never been in the studio with him. I heard he could be demanding.

Tuesday, I woke up and realized I didn't know the words to the "Coffee Pot" song. I looked up music stores in the *Yellow Pages* and called around until I found one in Santa Anna that had the sheet music. By the time I drove there and back, it was time to go to the studio. Of course, the first thing they handed me when I walked in was the sheet music.

Mr. Sinatra hadn't shown up yet. He had left word that I was to learn the words and practice the song. There was one musician there with a guitar to keep me in time and on the tune, or was it on time and in tune? Either way, I thought I was pathetic.

I practiced most of the afternoon. I finally figured out Mr. Sinatra knew what he was doing. He had me work for the day, knowing I wouldn't be ready to try it.

Wednesday was another day at the country club. If nothing else, the staff was beginning to recognize me and so did many of the other members. We didn't talk but did say "Hello" to each other. They were all older than me. Since it was the school year, no kids my age were hanging out.

My practice round went okay. I played the course straight today to see how I would do. I had a sixty-nine, which was probably good enough to qualify, but I knew I could do better. My putting was my weak spot.

On Thursday, Mr. Sinatra, or as he told me, Frank, was at the studio. He had me do a run-through. I don't speak Italian, but I recognized some of his swear words. Then he surprised the heck out of me. He had us try the duet but in a very low-key manner. We sang it softly with the guitar for accompaniment. There was an ensemble there, but he had them sit it out. He made me sing it without the energy the song was supposed to have. We ran through it four or five times, then took a break.

If nothing else, I was learning the words and getting a little relaxed. He then had us pick up the tempo. Again, we repeated it several times. Finally, he brought in the full music group.

After six full run-throughs and many a stop, the man in the recording booth held up his hand. He then played back our last trial. Frank smiled and shook my hand.

"I think we have a winner here. It will be part of an album, but if it plays well, we'll put out a single."

"Could I ask a favor?"

"What do you need?"

"An autographed copy when it comes out. Mr. Norman, the head of the Queen's Messengers, is a huge fan. I don't know if you are aware, but I am one of those messengers."

"I'll sign one and send it to you. You can sign it, too, then present it to him."

"Thanks, I appreciate this."

I still can't believe that anyone thinks I can sing. I was impressed with what a recording studio can do to strengthen a weak voice and a professional like Mr. Sinatra could carry me through.

Friday was the big day I was waiting for. Today, I will win the local qualifying round of the US Open Golf Championship as an amateur. That may sound overconfident, but I know my skills and that of the rest of the field.

After a light workout and breakfast, I headed to the country club. The normal laid-back atmosphere of the club seemed charged today. People were everywhere as they came in to watch or play. The usually quiet locker room was buzzing. It was filled with strangers as they changed into their golfing outfits.

I saw the two thirty-year-olds and Mr. Swartz but didn't have an opportunity to say hello. I couldn't wait to see the look on the two guys' faces when they figured out who I was. The one guy was nice, and it would be fun to surprise him. The arrogant one I wanted to shock.

My tee time was 10:06, so I had some time to use the practice greens. This proved to be futile as they were almost trampled by the early birds and so many of us trying to use them. I gave it up and found a seat in a corner where I could watch people tee off. John Jacobs found me there and joined me.

The par 5 first hole is 503 yards and plays straight from the black tees. Most people were hitting their first shot anywhere from 210 to 240 yards in the middle of the fairway. It was the second shot that would make or break this hole. Very few would ever hit the green on their second shot. It would be dicey even if I got out to almost three hundred yards.

The pin on the first green was on the right side, tight against the front. This meant you had to lay-up in front of the sand trap in front of the green, chip it over the trap, and make it set down immediately. That or you could challenge the trap protecting the left side of the green, which would allow you to do a pitch and run-up to the hole. Depending on how close the ball was to the hole, it would set it up for a birdie or possibly an eagle.

Those who tried the left side invariably were hitting or rolling into the trap or flying over the trap and ending up in the rough to the back of the green.

That is why I would only try that shot if I were desperate and was almost 300 yards out in the center of the green.

When my tee time came, I was in with three people I had never met. We introduced ourselves and teed off. I was second. Not wanting to get in trouble on the first hole, I kept it in the middle and didn't go for distance. Instead, I hit it out about 240 yards. This left me in a good position for my second shot.

Instead of laying up in front of the trap, I angled to the left but didn't challenge the trap or go for the green. I landed on the fringe of the green with a long putt but was laying two.

I was able to get the ball close enough to the pin on my first putt that I had an easy in for a birdie. Nice start.

The second hole is a 471-yard par 4. Here, you are hitting directly into a constant sea breeze, which will blow your ball off course easily. There are trees on the right and the out-of-bounds driving range on the left. Here I hit the fairway's left side, keeping it shy of the deep trap. From there, a 5-iron put me on the elevated green where I two-putted for par.

The third is a 434-yard par 4. I carried the left side bunker to set up my approach. The trick then was not to go by the hole which sloped away from the fairway. I got lucky and hit the fringe, and the ball popped up in the air a little, which slowed it down and rolled within two feet of the pin for an easy birdie.

The fourth hole is a 236-yard par 4. I had to hit directly into the sea breeze. This was one of the high-risk shots I had been making, so I attempted and carried the 60-yard-long bunker in front of the green. I was close enough to the pin that the hard right-to-left slope didn't come into play. This gave me another birdie.

They are nasty on the fifth, which is a 419-yard par 4. The tee shot is semi-blind to the hole. However, I had practiced this enough that I had no problem staying to the right and landing in a nice position. From there, I was able to hit the large putting surface and go a little past the green. I thought it would be another birdie, but I choked and took a bogey. John was quick to remind me I was playing to win, not set a course record.

The sixth hole is a 169-yard par 3. The hole is unique in that it has a sand trap built into the back center of the green. The pin was placed to the back right. I suspect they were saving the more difficult back left for next week. I had a simple solution to this hole. I hit directly to the pin for an easy roll-in for a birdie.

The seventh hole is a 408-yard par 4. There is a long bunker up the left side of the fairway. The fairway narrows at the 270-yard marker. Most golfers will lay up just short of this. Here is another one of the risky shots. I was doing well enough that when I asked John for my driver, he nodded yes.

I went for it booming it out to the left 290 yards. This left me an easy layup to the green and another birdie. I came within inches of an eagle.

The eighth hole is weird; it has a split fairway. The hole is a 416-yard par 4. Today, the pin was set up that it would pay to stay to the right. This made the eighth play longer, and I was satisfied with a par.

Nine is 420 yards and a par 3. The trick to this one is to end up about 270 yards out, just short of the last bunker. Today, the pin was front right, and I was able to hit the green and roll up to the pin, leaving me in position for a par, which I made.

As we made the turn at nine, I managed to get a Coke and a hotdog to tide me over.

The 10th is a 315-yard par 4. Considering how short it is, one would have thought it should be a par 3. The green is angled and extremely narrow with a dangerous right-to-left slope. Though reachable, only a perfect drive will hold the green. I made the smart play here by hitting my 2-iron down the left side. This left me in position for the par, which I got. This was one of the high-risk holes I made about half the time. I would only go for the green if I were down a stroke.

Eleven, a par 5, is a straight shot of 581 yards. One has to keep it in the center of the fairway to avoid the trees. I managed to hit one of my longer drives of the day, which rolled to 310 yards. From there, it was easy to get over the barranca grass cutting across the fairway. After all that good work, I parred.

I was lucky to be playing hole 12 early in the day. The afternoon wind had not kicked up yet, so I didn't have to drive into it, making the 410-yard par 4 much easier. I was able to get over the deep bunker on the right with no problem, ending up close enough to the pin for another birdie.

The 13th is one of the most demanding holes on the course. It is a 438-yard par 4. What makes it tough is the fairway bending left around the barranca, and it is flanked on both sides by tall stands of trees. It took me a controlled long draw and then a five iron to the large green. Fortunately, the pin was not in the back left corner, which was the hardest position. Again, it was probably being saved for next week. I ended up at par.

Fourteen is 182-yard par 3. Again, the wind hadn't kicked up yet, so it was an easy birdie for me.

Fifteen is a nasty dogleg right par 4 at 443 yards. This was another one of the risky shots that I had been making. By this time, the wind had kicked up, and I paid for it. My drive was shortened enough that I ended up on the wrong side of the swale, which divides the green. This resulted in a bogey.

John and I both agreed that you win some and you lose some.

Sixteen was my favorite hole on the course. I seemed to have a knack for ending up on the green on this par 3 166-yard hole. You have an excellent chance of making a birdie when you make the small green. It held today.

I let it rip on the 17th, a 576-yard par 5 monster. With the roll, it went 340 yards. A 3-wood put me on in two. I then managed four putts for a six, giving me a bogey.

Eighteen, a 451-yard par 4 is a strong finishing hole. The trick is the tee shot. It is not difficult. All you have to do is hit it, without seeing the spot it will land which is hidden behind a rough grass-covered hillside. I had played this course enough that I was able to make the shot without stress. From there, it was a 6-iron to the green and two putts for the par.

At 67, I hadn't set another course record, but I did win the local qualifier. The only reason that happened was I didn't have to fight the wind. Also, it was a single round. Everything had broken my way; more rounds and the averages would have got me. I would have to practice my putting; it wasn't so hot today.

I was so focused on my game I didn't realize that my family, less Mum who was still in England, had followed me all day. Mary ran out to me after my last putt, and I guess there were several cute pictures of her jumping up to me and my catching her. I loved the picture title, "Ricky gets his girl." I wish.

I was glad to see Mr. Swartz was included in the qualifiers. Also, the nice guy of the two other guys from our foursome had made it. The arrogant one hadn't.

There was a very brief press conference as this was only a local tournament, so I was able to get out and head home quickly.

Chapter 20

John Jacobs asked if he could have some time with me on Saturday. He had some ideas on my putting that he would like to share with me. Since this was the weak part of my game, I would have been crazy to say no.

He asked that we meet over at the Calabasas Country Club. It certainly wouldn't be as busy as Riviera with all the US Open candidates trying to get in practice rounds.

It was a beautiful Southern California day as we met and sat on the patio. The hillsides were still brown. The spring rains hadn't come yet to turn everything green.

"What's up, John? You say you have some ideas?"

John was unusually nervous-looking today. He would have been tugging at the collar if he had a formal shirt on. He had a thick notebook with him.

"Rick, I have been noting where you have been landing on the greens at Riviera. Let me show this to you from the first hole."

He pulled out a sheet of paper with a diagram of the first green. It had a bunch of x's marked on it. They were bunched in a round pattern.

"As you can see, you are very consistent with where you are landing the ball. I have this pattern on every hole."

At that, he leafed through the book, showing me all the diagrams.

"My thought is those putts are what you really should be practicing. Now, the problem I see is that it would be impossible to do that at Riviera this week. Now come with me. I want to show you something."

He led me over to the enormous practice green. It had split levels, breaks, and just about any type of break or slope, you could imagine. He led me over to a position on the corner of the many-holed green.

"See, if you set up to putt here, it is the same as the first hole at Riviera. I have plotted out all eighteen holes. You can practice here all week. Yes, the grass will be a little different, but not that much. You can even vary the time of day to try to match your tee time. That way, the grass will be leaning the same way."

I remembered what Arnold Palmer had shown me about how the grass will turn to face the sun, which will speed up or slow down a shot.

"This is great, John. I was wondering how I could get enough practice this week. Not only will I have more attempts here, but the attempts will be better focused. By the way, in my statistics class, they call this a measles chart, as when it is finished, it looks like it has the measles."

"Thanks, Rick. I'm thinking of my future here. If you win the US Open, my future as a caddie will be secure no matter what you choose to do in the future."

"John, have you been keeping other notes on how this has gone from the first time you caddied for me?"

"Not the first time, but I do make notes after every round. My wife wants to know how things are going, so I have learned to write them down, so I have something to tell her."

"If we win big time, you have the beginnings of a book and a new method of golf instruction. Think about it."

"Wow, I will!"

"There is one more thing I want to show you, Rick."

"What's that?"

"See this putt on the seventeenth. You have bogeyed it several times. You are landing the ball where you want it, but it is a low percentage putt for you. Now, look at this."

He walked me over to another portion of the practice green. He showed me a putt that matched the putt I made frequently on the second green.

"This putt is longer than what you do on the seventeenth, but you make it more often. Now, look at this."

Referring to the diagram of the seventeenth, he showed me a different landing spot that left the same putt as the second. Yes, it was a longer putt, but there was a little less break, and it was right to left, which I did better with than left to right.

By changing the landing spot on the green, I would go from an average of two and a half putts on the hole to one and a half. This was a big deal.

"John, I am in awe of what you have come up with."

"Okay, now if they move the pin a lot, it will negate some of this. But I have the diagrams for every pin position they have historically used in tournaments, so you should practice that this week."

I did that for four hours every day for the next week. I varied the time of day, practicing for each hole to get different sun conditions. Altogether, each green had four basic pin locations they used: front, back, left, and right. This gave me seventy-two different pin placements to work on. I timed it. I could do six putts a minute if I laid out the golf balls in a line. John would have six balls at each hole lined up for me.

In theory, I could do all seventy-two variations in twelve minutes. It took the better part of half an hour to do each round, so I was doing eight rounds a day. So, six times eight, times seventy-two, I had stroked a golf ball over three thousand times in practice. Every one of those was very much like what I would face on the real course.

We went to the clubhouse and talked to the pros about what we were trying out in the next week. They had done similar things in the past, but nothing so studied and planned out. They were all for trying it and would cooperate with keeping other club members away. They still considered this my home course and wanted bragging rights.

If nothing else, it helped my frame of mind each day. I had to give thought to what I could do for John.

On Saturday afternoon, I went to the beach. I didn't even surf, just people-watched; okay, girl-watched.

Sunday was more of the same, putting practice in the morning. I also used the practice range, going through each of my clubs ten times to keep myself loose. Quite a few strangers wished me luck, but no one stopped me for an autograph, so my practice wasn't interrupted.

That did give me a thought. I asked the club pro if he wanted me to do an autograph session if I won the sectional next week. He thought that was a great idea. It would sort of pay back the people working around me as I hogged the practice green and tees.

The afternoon was back to the beach, but I did spend time on my board. Believe it or not, even girl-watching can get boring.

Monday, I went to the studio in the afternoon. That may not have been the best idea I have ever had. Mr. Monroe had left word at the gate that if I showed up to stop and see him,

He wanted to know if I had any plans for the rest of the week. I told him about my practice sessions for Saturday.

"Oh, good, your afternoons are free."

Boy, did I set myself up.

"Yes, what do you have in mind?

"There is this movie...."

"Not to be rude, but there is always a movie. That is your job."

I can't believe I said that to the head of the studio. A year ago, he was this mysterious, powerful, godlike figure I would never have talked back to.

He laughed, "I guess it is. Rick, we lost an actor. We need a teenager who could be funny in a clueless sort of way. I immediately thought of you for the part."

Should I be insulted? But then, I am a teenager and usually clueless, so this would just be character acting for me. Still, I think I'm insulted.

One problem was that I didn't yet have an agent.

"What are you thinking about pay?"

"No points, your role isn't that big."

"Fair enough."

"How does one hundred thousand sound?"

"How many scenes?"

"Three, and we do them all this week."

"Okay, let's seal it with a handshake until your people can come up with a contract. I will pass it by my lawyers, but if it is the same as my others have been, we have a deal."

We shook hands.

"Rick, you have taught me to be straightforward and upfront and never try to push you around. The early reports from the focus groups on *Over the Ohio* say it is going to be a blockbuster."

"What sound stage?"

"Studio B. Let me walk you over."

He took me over and introduced me to the director, a John Adams, no relation. The movie didn't have a fixed title yet, but they were using *Teenage Angst* as a working title. If I saw that on a billboard, I would walk right on by.

Its basic premise was a new boy in school trying to fit in. I would be a bit of a sideshow for laughs. I hadn't worked with the male and female leads before. They were nice, but again, enough older than me, they didn't socialize. They seemed to keep their socialization to her trailer.

I had to go to costuming and makeup. They had a bit of trouble finding an outfit that was in my size. The guy who had to drop out for whatever reason was much smaller than me. They finally had me wear the clothes I came in wearing. The movie was in modern times so my clothes were fine. Better quality than what they had for the previous guy.

In makeup, I had to shave as it was in the afternoon. My beard had come in dark and heavy, so the stubble was showing by the end of the day. I was getting used to shaving twice a day. It was too much to hope that stubble would ever be in fashion.

My lines were amazingly simple. For my part, it was all in the timing of the delivery. It took me fourteen takes before I got the first one right. By then, it was getting near dinner time, and the director called it a day. The rest of the movie was on schedule, so they could work with me.

Tuesday, I was up early. I exercised, ran, headed out to Calabasas, met John, and practiced golf. I did a lot of putting and spent some time on the driving range to keep loose. John had set out bushel baskets at various locations and angles on the range. These were to show the sort of drive or fairway shot I would have to make on the Riviera course.

A lot of my fellow golfers paid attention to this. They were still polite and left me alone as I practiced, for which I was thankful. I had a lot of work to do.

The afternoon was back to the studio to try to get the second scene in the can. As directed by the costumer, I had worn a more casual polo shirt and left off my sports coat. This was to be inside a classroom. In this scene, I had to talk to the male lead.

The director kept yelling cut as the scene didn't look right to him. Finally, someone pointed out that I was so much taller it was hard for the lead to be condescending to me when he had to look up so far. A wooden box put us at eye level, and it worked. Of course, it took another five extra takes because the lead and I both started laughing and couldn't stop.

At one point, he put his arms around me like he was going to kiss me. That broke us up. I thought the director was going to throw both of us off the set, but when I looked, he was laughing as hard as everyone else.

The director did say, "Now that you two clowns have gotten that out of your system, could we get down to work?"

We both could take a hint and took it seriously. It took three more takes because of my timing or lack of timing, but I finally got my line out correctly.

I shared my experience at dinner, and it didn't get the laughs I thought it would. I guess you had to be there.

I had been pushing myself for the last few days so went to bed and went to sleep early.

Wednesday was a rerun of Tuesday with the exception it was the female lead on a box. She didn't try to kiss me. My timing must be getting better for it only took seven takes, five of them because of me. It was a shame that I did the scene with Tuesday Weld on Wednesday.

Anyway, that was the three scenes I had agreed to do. I might be called back for a retake or extra scene, but I had let them know when I would be leaving for England.

My putting had improved dramatically. Even my work on the driving range was paying off.

I continued my golf practice on Thursday. I stopped by the studio to see if they needed me anymore. They didn't, but the film for my scenes had been developed. They showed me it. The way it came off, you would have thought I knew what I was doing; that is, I looked like a clueless teenager. That or I hadn't been acting. I knew the success was because of patient directing.

John Jacobs surprised me on Friday by cutting the entire workout in half. The rest of the morning, we sat and talked about what we thought the rounds would be like. There would be two rounds of eighteen holes back-to-back with a slight intermission between the two.

We both agreed that no matter the draw, I would be facing the sea breezes. One of the problems I faced playing just eighteen holes last week was that I got hungry! That and thirsty. Since my family would be there, I would ask them to have food and drink ready each time I returned to the clubhouse.

John also thought I might want to change socks as they would get sweaty during the day. He also had a sun visor for me. This one was different from what the pros wear. It had no advertising.

I spent the afternoon up on the tower reading. Mrs. Hernandez came up at one point to discuss what sort of food I would like at the turns. I settled on a Coke and ham sandwich after the first nine, then at the end of the first round, corned beef, followed by tuna fish at the turn on the second round of the course.

This may sound like overplanning, but I had a tremendous headache after last week's round. I was used to eating a lot more. That had to be due to my size, exercising, and maybe I was still growing. I hoped I wouldn't get any taller. Six foot-five made me stand out as it is.

As far as I know, we had done everything we could to get ready for the sectional qualification for the US Open.

Chapter 21

Saturday was my make-it-or-break day for the US Open sectional. I wanted to win and qualify cleanly for the main tournament in June.

The day started like last week. The first hole was a birdie. The second hole was where my practice began to pay off. Last week, I two-putted for par; today, it was a birdie.

I birdied three and four again. I had a bogey on five last week. Today, it was a birdie. This was due to all my practice. My putt was never in doubt. This was one of the greens where I chose a different landing spot. It was a longer putt, but I had a higher percentage chance of making it. I drained it in.

The par 3 sixth hole had me nervous. I was putting for a birdie, and I rimmed it. I swear it rolled around the cup rim at least a dozen times until it dropped. John later told me it dropped halfway around. He must need glasses.

The seventh hole about got me, and I was glad to get off with a par. A stray gust caught my ball and put it in the rough. It took one putt to save par.

Eight and nine were both pars. Nine was one of those I had practiced putting the most, but I still two-putted for the par.

At the turn, my family had me set up fine for food, so I wasn't about to fall over from hunger on the course. I only ate half my sandwich as I didn't want to carry a heavy lunch. I suspect there would be penalties for taking a nap on the green.

I started with a birdie on 10. I had a string of pars on 11 through 13. Fourteen, a par 3 was an easy birdie. At this point, I was eight under.

Fifteen was a bogey for me last week. I had changed my landing spot, again taking a longer putt but had a better chance of making it. I made it for another birdie.

Sixteen gave me its usual gift of a birdie.

Seventeen had been a bogey due to poor putting. Today, instead of taking four putts, I put it in with two for another birdie. I finished hole 18 with a par.

The golf gods had been kind. I was 10 under and killing the field.

Another sandwich and a quick trip to the men's room prepared me to start the next 18. I never paid attention to the other golfers in my foursome unless there was a question about who was farthest from the hole. I did take a look, and two of them looked a little worse for the wear. They didn't run four or five miles every morning.

While the golf gods smiled on the first 18, they frowned at me on the next set. It was not a disaster, and maybe I got overconfident. Not to drag a sordid story out, I finished the second 18 even. It still left me 10 under for the day, but I had my comeuppance.

The wind had kicked up. Normally, it was a constant breeze. For me, it was erratic and would carry my ball in strange directions. The only thing that saved me was my putting. I one-putted 11 greens, which should have put me way under.

In the end, it didn't matter. I ended up 10-under. My nearest opponent was six-under, so I didn't have to face a playoff.

I talked briefly to Mr. Swartz. He told me that the wind had favored him on every shot. His putting kept him out of contention. He laughed as he told me he would be back next year. I wished him luck.

The press conference was easy to do. When questioned about my improved putting, I had John Jacobs come up and describe what he had come up with for my previous week's practice. This caught the golf reporter's interest and got me off the hook from any hard questions. I hope John comes up with a business plan as I think he has a winner.

Dad and the kids were there. Today, Mary restrained herself from running out on the green. We had to hunt her down. She had slipped away and somehow come up with a short putter and was on the practice green. She wasn't doing too badly.

Dad and I watched her for a minute until she missed an easy putt. I don't know where she learned that word. Dad took charge and gave her a swat on the butt.

"Watch your language, young lady!"

"But Mum said it!"

"You can talk like your Mum when you are thirty."

I swear I saw her doing the math in her head.

She countered with, "How about twenty-five?"

My Dad is a saint.

"Twenty-seven, and that's my last word."

"Okay, thank you, Daddy. What does the word mean?"

"I will tell you when you are forty."

Even Mary knows a lost cause.

We went out for pizza at a restaurant on Sunset Boulevard. Mrs. Hernandez was at the course all day. She was escorted there and to the restaurant by a gentleman I hadn't met before. We were introduced, but his name didn't stick. It seems she is playing the field. Go, Mrs. Hernandez!

Sunday was a relaxed day doing nothing. Well, I went to the country club to check out my locker to ensure everything was returned and cleaned up. I know full well that John Jacobs takes care of that. Maybe I just wanted to bask in my glory.

Bask it was. I must have spent half an hour straight with people coming up to me with congratulations. I did spend some time with the pro. We talked about the Open being held in Cherry Hills outside of Denver. I knew nothing about the course.

He suggested he knew I could afford it. Move John Jacobs out there until the tournament so he could learn the course. I would have to try to get there and play it as much as possible. My being at school in England would make that kind of hard.

I still wanted to do this. John was in the clubhouse cleaning my gear, so I asked him if he and his wife would like to live in Colorado for a while. He shook his head at that. I told him all expenses would be covered. This would be all travel, food, and lodging. He told me he would talk it over with his wife.

They had no children, and she had time off work, so there was no reason not to do it. But he knew better than to make such a commitment without talking to her. Good to know.

We both went back to the pro. He told us he would make some phone calls and get John listed as an eligible caddie at Cherry Hills. They didn't have a reciprocal agreement with them, so I would have to be a guest of someone to get on the course. He had some ideas on that and would let me know.

When I got home, I told Dad what I was trying to put together. He also had some thoughts about Cherry Hills. It seems Jackson Enterprises was being courted by the Denver Development Authority to consider them as a manufacturing location. He would call on Monday to see if he could get an appointment with them next week. Maybe they could arrange for us to meet on the Cherry Hills course.

In a way, this seemed unfair to other people in the tournament, but many of them had played the course professionally and some as amateurs. I was trying to play catch up. I also realized this was a rationalization as some of the guys playing would have never seen the course before. C'est la guerre.

A nice long ride on George helped me calm down from the stress of yesterday's tournament, and I suppose, of the last several weeks. George and I crossed the bridge built over the gully to the Forest Service airport; it was posted for Forest Service use only, but I was allowed. Unlike the road to the front gate, there was no one at the entrance to ride around the area.

Besides reconditioning the buildings and runway, the Forest Service people knew how to landscape a large area. Not fancy gardens, but a nicely trimmed, controlled look about it. As I neared the Headquarters building, a Jeep came driving up to me.

A Park Ranger wanted to know what I was doing here and how I got on base. I introduced myself and told him I had ridden in the backway. There was a gate there that someone had forgotten to close. That raised the question in my mind of how my family was to get in if needed.

Of course, he had no idea. Since it was Sunday, no one was in the office, so I went home. I brought it up with Dad, who showed me where our key hung on a hook by the kitchen door. I suggested we make another one and hide it outside near the back gate. He thought this would be a good idea. Mrs. Hernandez, standing right there, volunteered to take care of it.

She also took the opportunity to bring up something that had been bothering her: if our family had to retreat to the subbasement, what about the staff? Dad thought for a moment.

"If that happened, we would not leave them up here in danger. They would come with us. Any event like that would make our secret moot at that point. That means I had better get some cots and additional food and drink down there. Thank you for bringing that up. It never occurred to me. We are not used to having staff."

On Monday, Dad went to work but called me to tell me we would fly to Denver on Wednesday to discuss building a plant in Denver while playing a golf round at Cherry Hills.

I wondered how that would go as Dad had taken to playing golf. He and Mum had taken the lessons I gave as Christmas presents, but I didn't know if they went out after that.

Dad had chartered a plane to take us there on Tuesday evening after work. It was a small jet that would have us there in three hours. We would come back on Wednesday after our business concluded.

Todd Goodson would meet us there. We needed a site to assemble containers for the airlines, so Denver would be as good as anywhere.

The question was what sort of tax breaks they would allow. I found out that cities, states, and even countries would bid to increase local employment and their tax base. Interestingly, we were selling a product, and we were selling increased income for an area.

Tuesday morning, I collected my golf gear from Riviera. John and I had discussed his accompanying me but decided that he would be pushing it with the Cherry Hills people. Later, I found out that wouldn't have been an issue, and the pros traveled with their caddies all the time.

John told me his wife thought living in Denver for a few months would be fun. It would be like an extended vacation. If they liked it, they might even stay there. I guess it wouldn't matter to me. If I did well in the US Open, I would be playing at different courses worldwide, so it didn't matter if he had to travel from there.

I couldn't try for a grand slam this year as the Masters would be in April, and I had no way of qualifying. Maybe next year, if I won the Open, I would be eligible for four of the tournaments.

The trip to Denver, the Mile High City, was uneventful. A limo took us downtown to the Brown Palace Hotel. I asked if it had any connection to the Unsinkable Molly Brown and was told no, but that she had stayed there after returning from the *Titanic*.

We had a late sandwich in the Ship Tavern and then turned in. I did my workout in my room, but upon looking outside, I decided not to run in downtown Denver. It didn't look very friendly.

Dad's and Todd Goodson's meetings were in a conference room at the hotel. I was taken out to the golf course. I found out how weird the weather is in Denver. There could be a snowstorm on the city's west side and sunshine on the east.

Well, there was no snowstorm today, and the sun was out. Considering it was late March, the golf course was in excellent shape.

However, they asked that I not use the fairways as they were wet, and we would tear the course up. There was no one else on the course and I realized that a lot of influence had been used to get me here today.

I asked if it would be okay if I just walked the course to see what it was like.

The pro about fell over himself agreeing to my doing a walk around and volunteered to accompany me. I was given a steno pad and pencil from the office to take notes.

This turned out much better than trying to play an out-of-season course. The pro Mr. Williams and I discussed my playing style and what would be the best positioning for me to get on the green.

From the eighteen holes, I had twenty-four pages of notes. I noticed that I was a little tired after walking all eighteen holes. I mentioned it to Mr. Williams who told me, "Welcome to the Mile High City." We have less atmospheric pressure, so you have to work harder to get oxygen.

I had known it, but reading about something and experiencing it are two different things. He told me I should try out the driving range. I would like the distance I would be getting.

I did, and it appeared I would get an extra ten percent in distance on every shot. I was warned that a high-flying ball would go farther than one hit low. Also, the weather had a lot to do with it. On a warm day, the ball would go farther. This was good information to have.

I told Mr. Williams about my plan to move my caddie out here to learn the course. He replied that he would be glad to have another professional caddie available. He also filled me in on the pros who brought their caddie and then hired a local caddie to teach their caddie the course. It is good that you could only have one caddie, or there would be up to a dozen people in a foursome.

All in all, I gained more information about the course than if I had played it. I would try to play it before the Open but didn't know how at this point.

We flew back to California later that afternoon. An agreement had been made in principle to manufacture air cargo containers at a local industrial park, so the trip was a success all the way around.

I planned to spend the rest of the week getting ready for my move to England. I didn't realize how much stuff I wanted over there with me. Maybe I should talk to Mum about getting a larger house.

Susan Wallace called me on Wednesday. I had planned to fly from LAX on Saturday evening and arrive in London the following morning. She asked if I could instead fly via New York and interview with the *Today Show* on Friday morning. They wanted to know about my forest fire rescue. It was a brush fire, but I wouldn't get wrapped in those details.

It worked out that I flew to New York on Thursday evening and interviewed on Friday. I spent Friday night in New York, then flew to London on Saturday evening, arriving in London as planned on Sunday morning.

The interview was a bit of a snooze. How long can you talk about how I swooped down, landed the plane, picked the family up, and took off? Of course, they had to have Justice McComb there, who told them what it looked like from his family's perspective. To them, I was an angel from Heaven. I would have been a fallen angel if I had misjudged that dive.

I was glad to be on the ground in England to get on with the next stage of my life.

Chapter 22

After clearing customs with my British Diplomatic passport, I caught a cab to my hotel. My new suite was complete and cleaned up after my cousins' wild parties. That would not happen again unless, of course, I was invited.

Even though it was mid-morning, I took a short nap. Then I took a shower and felt much better for clean clothes. I wore a suit and tie as I had some business to attend to after having coffee and a light lunch from room service. One could get used to this.

My business was buying a car. Specifically, I wanted an Aston Martin DB4 GT. I had read about it in several auto magazines. It would do over 150mph and go from 0-60 in six seconds. The fact it was used in the James Bond movies had nothing to do with it. Okay, a little. Well, maybe more than a little.

The dealer had one on the showroom floor. It was a beautiful pearl grey. The sticker price was 11,000 pounds.

Of course, I was approached by a salesman.

"May I help you, sir?"

Using my best Mayfair accent, I informed him I would like to purchase this vehicle.

"It is a showpiece. Customers view it and then order one. It is taking almost a year at this point."

"May I speak to the manager? I'm sure that we can come to an arrangement."

"Your name, sir?"

"Sir Richard Jackson."

That got a reaction. I may be famous for being an actor in the United States, but I saved the Queen in England.

"Sir, please follow me; I will introduce you."

Walking the fifty feet to the manager's office, I must have heard the word "sir" fifty times. The office door was open, so after a perfunctory knock, I was taken in and introduced.

The manager's reaction was the same as the salesman's. The car was a display piece and not for sale.

"You are asking 11,000 pounds. I have read that the retail price is between 11,000 and 13,500 US dollars. That would work out to 10,500 pounds."

"Yes, Sir Richard, there is a premium on this vehicle."

"Would you take fifteen thousand pounds for that car?"

You could see that I had his attention. His body language told me he wanted to do the deal but thought he could get more.

"If fifteen thousand won't get it, what will?"

Now I had the greedy bugger sweating. He needed the car to sell more cars, but at the same time, I was offering a profit that wouldn't be met unless he sold six or more of them. Given the predicted production rate I had read about, maybe fifty cars total this year, it would never happen. He had read the same magazine.

He slowly gave out a number like he was ready to take it back if I jumped at him.

"Twenty thousand pounds, and it is yours."

Almost double the suggested price.

"I will take it."

At times like this, it is nice to be rich.

"How will you be paying for it?"

"By check; I see there is a London branch of my bank around the corner."

I had looked it up before coming to the showroom.

The manager and I walked to the bank while the salesman arranged for the car to be prepped to drive away.

At the bank, all I had to do was write the check, show my British passport, and write down my secret password to show I was not under duress. They issued a cashier's check to the dealer.

The manager was a nice chap, and he had a mechanic show me the car's features. I was even given a test drive out on the highway, so they were certain I could handle it. I was careful about all my turns. I spoke which way I had to go out loud. I didn't want to enter a roundabout in the wrong direction.

At first, the mechanic thought that was funny but then nodded his head and told me he would recommend that to all American drivers that he dealt with. Considering the type of cars they sold, this would happen frequently.

He shared a little tidbit. The James Bond actor had tried to buy this car but wouldn't come up to a premium price. That's the Scots for you.

It took almost three hours, but I was able to drive away in my newly licensed Aston Martin. I was on pins and needles to get back to the hotel. I never jumped the gun, waiting until the amber went to green. This gained me a few honks, but I wasn't taking any chances.

I realized I was being a little too slow when a traffic warden signaled me to speed up! That was a first for me. Of course, when I stepped on it a little, I almost rear-ended a double-decker bus. I slowed back down. The traffic wardens could signal all they wanted.

At last, I had my new car in my private hotel parking spot. I took the time to pull the car cover out of the boot and cover the car. Wouldn't want it to get dirty or scratched, you know.

By the time I got to my room, I was exhausted. I had flown from New York to London, had a brief nap, and then bought a car and finished up with a nerve-racking drive. I changed into casual clothes and walked around the corner to Mr. Treacher's shop for dinner.

I read the owner's manual for my new car and fell asleep at about 300 bhp.

The next day, I went through my morning routine, cleaned up, and had breakfast in the swanky hotel dining room. The décor was too heavy for my taste, all teak and mahogany with red drapes and all the trimmings in gold. Even the silverware was gold. Would you call it goldware? It must have been flash-plated as the weight wasn't as much as real gold.

I then had a leisurely drive up to Oxford. I did get to step on it a little. That car could go. Fortunately, the only police car I saw was when I was obeying the speed limit. When I went past it, it followed me halfway to Oxford. The patrolman must have thought that I would speed if I could. It drove me crazy, keeping the speed within limits as we went through small towns. As we left High Wycombe, the patrol car finally turned off the main highway.

When I reached Oxford, I stopped and refreshed myself on the directions to our new house, The Meadows. I had to drive down the High Street, right at Turl, left at Broad, which is where Trinity is with my parking garage immediately across the street, and then keep going as the street names changed from Broad to Botley Road, then West Way and Eynsham Road with finally a left onto Nobles Lane.

That sounds complicated, but to get back to Trinity, all I had to do was turn right onto Eynsham and follow it into school.

The grounds of The Meadows were beautiful. Great care had been taken; I hadn't had a good look inside the house, but if it was that good, we had a nice residence. Residence. What do you call a place like this, a mansion? I later found out that the smart set would call it a country house.

I was never a member of the smart set—maybe a member of the moderately intelligent set, but not the smart set.

I parked on the gravel in front of the house. I wasn't certain about that as it could damage the paint job on my new car. I tried to kick some of the gravel up as I walked to the door. That stuff must have been put in place around 1860; it was going nowhere.

I didn't know if I should knock at the door or not, but Mr. Hamilton was there to open it. I wondered how he knew. He led me to a sitting room where Mum and Grandmum were ensconced, along with a lady I presumed to be Grandmum's companion. I must say Grandmum looked a lot better than the last time I saw her.

We all did the kissy-cheek thing, and I was introduced to Mrs. Booth, who was the new companion. There was something warm about her I liked at once. She was in between Mum and Grandmum's age and was probably a looker a long time ago. She was now comfortably settled into middle age.

A tea cart was wheeled in, and the quizzing started. I had to talk about picking the people out of the brush fire, my golf tournament, and, in general, how my travels had gone. The subject of a new car came up. Mum thought I had taken the train to Oxford and a cab to the house.

When I told her about what I had bought, she had to look at it at once. Upon seeing it, she held out her hand for the keys. All I can say is my Mum drives like a bat out of hell. She came back to the front of the house in a four-wheel drift. It never moved one bit of gravel. Her only comment was.

"It will do."

At least she gave me the keys back. Mr. Hamilton promptly held out his hand for them. I didn't know if he intended to take it for a spin or what, but I handed them to him. Instead, he handed them in turn to a young man standing there. He took the car for a spin. Well, he drove it somewhere behind the house.

Back inside, Mum was telling Grandmum that boys will be boys, and I had bought myself a toy. Grandmum nodded in agreement and told me I would be taking her for a ride later.

I could see it now, a slow grand parade around the town. One does what one must do.

After another round of conversation, Mum brought up that all the books I had requested had been obtained. This surprised me as it was over one hundred books, counting the suggested reading. I excused myself to go to the library to see my new treasure.

And treasure it was, all neatly labeled and put away on shelves. A good many of the books by the yard had disappeared. I asked the ever-present Mr. Hamilton how this had been accomplished so quickly.

"We hired a young lady who is studying at the Bodleian Library to become a librarian to take care of matters."

"Brilliant, absolutely brilliant."

I had learned a new bit of English slang; brilliant of me.

"At your Mum's direction, she is also obtaining copies of your American library, so you have a complete collection here. The copy machine will be here next week. You will find your typing machine in the corner under a cover. Supplies are in this closet.

As he said this, he opened an unobtrusive cupboard door. It was a walk into a full-sized room that held office supplies. It was probably better stocked than most supply stores.

"This is great, Mr. Hamilton. Thank you for seeing to this."

"Truly our pleasure, Sir Richard. After running with a stretched household budget, it has been a sheer delight to do things properly."

"The previous owners had money problems?"

"Skint, Sir Richard."

"You don't have to keep calling me Sir Richard."

"Your consequence is the household's consequence, Sir Richard."

It hit me then that the class system was still alive and well in England.

"As you know, I'm from a different background, so I will have to get used to my new life."

"It is understood, and we all wish you well."

I made a mental note to learn who all these "we" were.

"I think I know where my room is. Second floor, turn right, and is it the door at the end?"

"Correct, Sir Richard. Shall I show you the way?"

"I can do that on my own, thank you."

Man, this is going to take getting used to.

I managed to find and climb the main staircase, turned right, and then went to the end of the hall. My room was a small suite. You entered a nice sitting room with a sofa or divan in front of the fireplace. There was a leather wingback chair and footstool with a lamp on an end table. It just screamed, "Get a book and sit here."

In front of a large window overlooking the east side of the house was a small table with a chair at each corner. I knew which chair would be mine. There was a captain's chair set, so one could eat breakfast if one desired, facing the morning sun.

By the door, if one were leaving the room was a wall-mounted mirror with a stand below. The stand held a new telephone, with the box it came in left beside it.

A door to the left of the sitting room opened onto a small office. It had an empty set of bookshelves, an IBM typewriter, a filing cabinet, a wastebasket, and other office paraphernalia. The desk lamp was cool. It was like those I had seen in the New York City Library reading room.

Mr. Hamilton had certainly turned from being skint to free-spending once more.

On the other side of the sitting room was my bedroom. The bed was king-sized and an obvious new addition in a more modern style. A small fireplace graced the far wall. A chest of drawers, a floor-length mirror, and nightstands were on both sides of the bed. The nightstand had a lamp and a telephone. Again, the box had been left. What's with leaving the boxes?

There were two doors, one leading to an enormous walk-in closet with many shelves. Most of my clothes had been moved from the hotel in London to here. I loved the slanted shoe rack. My shoes looked great on them, both pairs.

Lastly, there was a bathroom with a tub and a separate shower. I had to see about getting the old-style showerhead changed to one of my models.

I started exploring the house but then realized there would be rooms for the staff, and I didn't want to disturb them. I called them staff because I was too American to call them servants.

Going downstairs, I ran into Mum. It was getting close to dinner time, and I had to change. Drat, we were expected to dress for dinner. I think Mum was taking this viscountess bit too seriously.

Chapter 23

Early the next morning, dressed in blue jeans for work, I drove into town to check out my garage. I walked to the nearby Woolworths and bought cleaning supplies. The place needed a dusting and wash. It took me several hours before I felt like I could put a single bed here without getting bugs and whatnot all over me. I had started with the ceiling and then worked my way down the walls.

I saved the floor for last. I was glad that the room was empty. If there had been furniture, I would have had to move it outside or at least downstairs. A sweeping, then a wet mop, and the room was livable.

There weren't any bugs, but I did find some old mouse droppings, so I put a mousetrap on my list to buy the next time I was out. One thing I noticed while I was out; there were people about my age everywhere. This was going to be fun.

I stopped at a local furniture store with a sign for student rooms furniture. I explained to them what I was looking for: a single bed with a mattress and box springs extra long, a small armoire, a chest of drawers, a small dining table and two chairs, a sitting chair with a footstool, and an end table.

The sales clerk asked me where it was going. When I told him up above a garage, he took me to an area and showed me what was available. The bed wasn't long enough for me, but they had a padded bench that would sit at the foot of the bed to act as an extension.

He told me I would need an electric fire, what we called a space heater, as there would be no heat in the garage. I was also given a list of basic supplies I should have on hand such as towels, dishes, and silverware, along with dish soap for the washing up. I would also need towels to dry the dishes and me, and most importantly, toilet paper.

I wasn't the first college student to walk in the door. I didn't tell him I had been through this when I moved out to California and had my list in my pocket.

I paid in cash. Pound notes took some getting used to. When it came to shillings and pence, I just held out my coins and let them take what they needed. It took a little while, but I was able to figure out what tuppence, threepenny, and farthings were and how much they were worth. I even knew a crown was five shillings and a florin two shillings. I was given a sovereign in change, which I immediately put away.

What was amazing was being given a penny in change and realizing it was minted in 1721 with George I on it. Old and almost worn to nothing but still in circulation. In the US, we hardly even saw Indian Head pennies.

After carrying a huge bundle of stuff to my garage with a promise of delivery of the rest later in the afternoon, I decided to take a bicycle ride around Oxford to get to know the town. The first thing I learned is that their car horns sound different than ours. I learned this by riding on the wrong side of the road.

When this happened, I pulled onto the sidewalk rather than try to cross traffic. Several students standing there commented on the dumb Yank. Since they were right, I didn't get upset. I was a dumb Yank, at least on the streets of Oxford.

I had to walk close to them to keep moving. That is when they realized how big I was. You could see them gulp.

"You're right. I'm a dumb Yank, a big dumb Yank."

I was smiling when I said that, and you could see the relief. I wondered what they were used to. Would I have to go around thumping every smart aleck to fit in?

"Maybe you aren't so dumb after all but watch the road. You have been on the wrong side all your life, now you need to do it correctly."

I guess that depends on your point of view. Of course, a ten-ton lorry's point of view counts more than mine.

"Thanks for the tip. I do have to learn and learn quickly."

"No problem. Do you go to school here?"

"Starting Monday at Trinity."

"Oh, we are at Balliol. Go join your fellow capitalists."

That is when I found out that the current Balliol student population was a bunch of leftists, socialists, and communists. I was glad to be at Trinity as I certainly was a capitalist.

I think they were kidding on the square about not liking my school.

Of course, if they were confirmed socialists, they weren't very smart about the real world. I mean, socialism is a wonderful idea. It is just a shame that it depends on all people living to an ideal. I had noticed that not all people lived up to ideals. The KGB came to mind. Oh well, their loss. They would get woken up one day to the real world.

I continued my bike journey around the City of Oxford. I couldn't believe how beautiful and well-maintained it was. Some buildings were over six hundred years old and looked like they would stand for another six hundred.

While Trinity was an all-boys school, plenty of girls were in town. I had read about the all-girls schools of Lady Margret Hall, Somerville, Saint Hilda's, and I knew there were others. I intended to learn about them all.

While girl-watching, I also made certain to watch the traffic and what lane I was in. I've had enough excitement for one day. I came across a café with seating outside, so I stopped and had coffee. This alone made me stand out; all the other customers were having tea.

Students were coming and going all over the place. Many of them were only a year or two older than me. They didn't look it to me. The boys looked like boys to me. When I looked into the mirror, especially on days I hadn't shaved and with my Atlantic and Pacific Ocean-weathered face, I thought I looked older than them.

I walked around some more, especially checking out where the lecture halls were at Trinity. Walking back to my garage, I saw an addition that made sense. I could use a rug to cover the rough wooden floors. Why didn't I think of that before?

I bought a rather large nine-by-twelve, but I could carry it, so rather than arrange for a delivery, I carried it on my shoulder the block and a half to the garage. I set the carpet down and unlocked the door when an elderly lady called to me.

"Young man, I say, young man, I could use some help here."

I walked over to her, thinking she needed something carried into the house.

"The front stoop needs painting. I will pay you five pounds and no more."

"I don't know if I have the time."

"Oh, stuff and feathers. You college students have too much time to get up to mischief, and you always need money."

She was certainly feisty. Still, I had no desire to paint a porch.

Then *she* walked out of the house.

"Well, that didn't take you long, Grandmamma. You said all you had to do was wave some money, and some young man would want the work."

I didn't need the money or want the work. I wanted to meet her.

"Ma'am, I would be delighted to paint your porch. Do you have the materials?"

"Yes, I do. It was just delivered by Marks and Sparks."

"Fine, then I will change clothes and start the job. By the way, my name is Richard Jackson."

"I'm Sandra Butler, and this is my granddaughter Iris."

"It is nice to meet you, Mrs. Butler and Miss Iris."

Iris said, "You're an American, aren't you?"

"Yes, I guess my accent gave me away."

Now, I had been speaking in my flat Ohio accent. The last was pure Mayfair.

Iris gave me an evil look.

"Now I'm confused."

"Nothing compares to the confusion that is going through my heart and mind right now, oh fair one."

"Iris, you have to watch this one. His tongue is way too smooth."

Have I mentioned that she was beautiful? Long blonde hair, blue eyes, pale complexion, and a slender figure; maybe not what I usually fell for, but I couldn't help it. My luck, and she would have goose feathers for a brain.

Iris asked, "Richard, what college are you attending?"

"I start at Trinity on Monday."

"That is unusual. Most students start at Michaelmas."

"I just passed my A-levels and took the SATs. An exception was made for my enrollment."

"That is why you live in a garage; no rooms to let."

"Well, the garage is for the car, but I decided the room up above would make a nice getaway during long breaks between classes."

"I noticed the auto. That Aston Martin must have cost a packet."

"A bit. Do you mind if I ask, do you go to school here?"

"I'm at Lady Margret Hall."

"You youngsters can flirt on your own time. I need the porch painted today, not next week."

"Sorry, Mrs. Butler, I will change clothes and get to work right away."

One thing I learned on the *Pride of Liberia* chipping paint is that it paid off to clean the old stuff off first. The porch wasn't that big and the last paint job not that old, so it didn't take long to scrape the loose paint off first.

I was just finishing when Iris came out with a can of Coke for me. I stopped and sat on the steps, and she joined me.

"You look like you know how to paint."

"I've done a few properties that were being updated, and I worked on a freighter last year."

"Oh, you are working your way through. The car confuses the issue."

Not wanting to sail under false colors with my newest love, I confessed that I didn't need the money. I didn't live in the garage, I lived in a place called The Meadows outside of town. The garage was for the car as parking was difficult to find.

"Then why did you tell Grandmamma that you would paint the porch?"

"It seemed the only way to get to know you."

Fair English girls really can blush.

"I'm glad you did."

"Well, I have made a commitment. I had better get back to work."

"Yes, you had, Sir Richard."

"You recognized me?"

"I thought I did when I first came out. Grandmamma has a magazine with your picture in it. I can't wait till after she pays you to tell her. She will be embarrassed to no end, but this will give her and her friends something to talk about for weeks."

"Well, I have been in the entertainment business, you know."

"Yes, I do know. Are you going to school here?"

"Yes. Would you be my native guide?"

"I would love to."

It took me two more hours to finish the job. Mrs. Butler paid me and even gave me a crown tip.

"As I walked away, I could hear Iris saying, "Oh, Grandmamma. Look at this picture; do you think?"

"Do you think that is him? What will your boyfriend say?"

"Oh, Grandmamma, I just met him. He is a nice person but not my type of guy."

I walked out of hearing but had heard enough to know my love was done. Maybe Dad was right. There is no sense in hunting for love. It will sneak up on you and hit you right in the heart.

Oh well, I had made five quid for an afternoon's work.

I changed clothes in the garage and headed back to The Meadows. I first asked Mr. Hamilton if we had any form of paint remover in the house. I hadn't any gloves to wear while painting so it left my hands a mess. He looked at me in a funny way and then led me around back to the garage.

In a little shop to the side of the garage were all the tools and materials needed to keep the place up. Of course, some of the paints were so old they were solid in the cans. Looking around, I realized some of these chemicals had been here while Victoria was Queen.

"Can we have the old paints and chemicals hauled to the tip? They are a safety hazard here."

"Now that we have the money, I will hire a firm to do so."

"Make a list of everything. That way, if we have to match an old color, we have a starting point."

"I think that has been taken care of, Sir Richard."

He then showed me a multi-drawer cabinet with drawings of every room in the house. With each room was a list of each paint color used and a swatch enclosed in cloth to reduce fading. Someone had been thinking.

I said as much.

"It was the original owner, I believe. He planned on a dynasty and wanted good records. In the basement is a file full of all expenditures made to improve and maintain the property. I believe he was of German descent."

No bias there, but then, Mr. Hamilton was probably in the war.

After cleaning up and getting dressed for dinner, I had a little time, so I browsed the library. Our librarian had done a first-rate job. What I loved was the new sign.

It read, "Please do not shelve the books. Please leave them on the cart."

What was odd was a notice that read, "No candles allowed."

At dinner, Mum and Grandmum wanted to know about my day. I told them everything, even the painting and falling in love. Grandmum asked me if I had ever read a story by Mark Twain called *Tom Sawyer*. I had, and I got her point immediately. I don't think that is what happened, but if it was, the joke was on me.

I had to laugh and tell her she was probably right, and I was a prat.

"You made five pounds?"

"Well, yes."

"A prat would have done it for free."

"That makes me feel so much better."

I hope she understands sarcasm.

She went on to tell a story, about how when she was young there was this greengrocer who pushed his cart down the back alley selling his veggies to the cooks. She talked him into lifting her so she could pick apples from a tree. That started a relationship that continued until his death five years ago, so all of Tom Sawyer's tricks weren't bad.

"How did you get the apples when he wasn't around?"

"Oh, we had a device on a long pole that would grasp the apple; then all you had to do was pull it down."

We men never stand a chance.

Chapter 24

I was up early on Monday, April 4th. It was my first day at a new school. I felt like a little kid. All excitement, looking forward to a new school mixed with some fear of the unknown.

I ran the road surrounding our property. I had to learn about the area and find the best places to run each day. I did my pushups and sit-ups. I had to buy a weight set and find a place for it. I would also like to have various punching bags for boxing.

There was enough land to set up an archery range. I didn't know about a rifle or pistol range. I don't know if you are allowed to shoot like that in England.

As my breakfast was being served, I saw Mr. Hamilton. I asked him if he knew where I could buy a set of weights.

"Aren't the ones in the gym satisfactory, Sir Richard?"

"I didn't know there was a gym."

"We call it the gymnasium, but it is a large room attached behind the garage."

I had time, so after getting cleaned up and ready for school, I checked out the gym. I had noticed the door in the back of the garage but must have thought it was an exit.

The gym wasn't like an American high school gym where you could play basketball. It was high enough that you could put a hoop on one wall. It was a combination weight room and ballet studio with bars and mirrors. It even had the various punching bags set up.

The weights were all free weights, but it looked like a complete set. I could see us kids using this room a lot. Mary would love the ballet setup; I wonder if a Princess Ballerina Flight Attendant costume exists. Oh yeah, all on roller skates.

I drove my new car into town and parked it in the rented garage. Students were out and moving around, and the Aston Martin got some attention. Parking the car, I grabbed my bicycle and rode over to my first lecture hall. I had a book bag on a strap over my shoulder filled with pencils, pens, and notebooks. I was ready for school.

I was surprised that none of the bikes parked outside the lecture hall had locks on them. There were bike racks, but they were hardly full. I had thought as it was the first day and all with the first lecture, they would be full to overflowing.

The room in the hall that was listed was a small one. It was set up for fifty students. I was only a few minutes early, so was surprised at how few people were in the room. I didn't count them, but it couldn't be more than fifteen.

I don't know what defines it, but most of them looked like they were new to this series of lectures like I was. The lecture was the first on the properties of various metals used in different types of construction. Everything from housing to aircraft was included.

As the syllabus read, it was to give the student an overview of metals used in various constructions, their benefits, and weaknesses, along with the process used to bring the metal from an ore to a usable product. I was looking forward to this.

What I was looking forward to and what I got were two different things. The professor, what they called dons, was an elderly Chinese man who spoke broken English very softly. I could only understand about half of what he said. He talked nonstop for forty-five minutes, walked off the podium, and left the room by a side door, giving no chance for questions.

I looked at the notes I had taken and realized they were worthless. Standing to leave the room, my attention was caught by a man a little too old to be a student but not that old, maybe thirty. He took the podium.

"All right, you lot, you see what you have to look forward to for the next few weeks. Old man Wang is considered to be the best in the field of metals, but he can't give a coherent lecture. I have for sale a complete set of lecture notes compiled over the last five years. He never varies the course, and unless there is a breakthrough in metals, they won't change. I am asking ten pounds for the complete course."

If there were fifteen of us in the room, he just made one hundred forty pounds because all but one of us bought a set. One young man had a gloomy look as he turned away. On a hunch, I bought a second set and hurried to catch him as he was leaving the hall.

"Wait up, I have something for you."

He turned and took the notes I handed him without looking at them. When he saw what I had given him, he shook his head no.

"I can't afford these. It takes everything I have to be here. Until I find a job, I have to make do."

I understood that I was looking at pride.

"Consider them a long-term loan. I can afford them, and there is no way you can learn anything listening to that don. When you can pay me back, do so, but I'm in no hurry."

At that, I held out my hand to shake and introduced myself.

"My name is Rick Jackson. What is yours?"

"William Benton, call me Bill. I'm from Yorkshire."

That explained the heavy accent.

"Where about in Yorkshire?"

"Farsley, near Pudsey, which is next to Leeds. Where are you from? Your accent is Mayfair, but I hear something else in it."

"Darn, I was hoping it was pure Mayfair."

I then dropped into my normal American midwestern accent.

"I'm from Ohio in the United States but now live in California."

His face lit up.

"Are you the actor chap who saved the Queen?"

"Guilty as charged."

"Well, I don't feel too bad about accepting a loan; I know you can afford it. Where are you off to now?"

"I have no real plans. I'm free for the next hour. How about you?"

He didn't have any, so I invited him to my garage rooms. He had a funny look.

"Oh, I have rented a garage with a room up top; it has a kitchenette with tea and coffee pots."

"You scared me for a moment. I have read about the strange habits of some American actors, and I'm not like that."

I stuttered a little as I told him, "Neither am I."

After that, we both gave a nervous laugh, went to the garage, and settled down with our hot drinks.

Bill turned out to be exactly what I thought: a wicked smart young man here on a scholarship and barely able to make ends meet. He was desperately trying to find a job.

Our conversation and the events of the day made me realize something. I thought I was special because the college allowed me to start at a different term than the official first term in the fall. They did this for a lot of people, as demonstrated by my first class this morning.

I told Bill I had a contact who might know about jobs. He wanted to go talk to the man right now! It was a lady, Mrs. Butler, for whom I had done the painting.

We knocked on her door. Iris answered and called for her grandmother to come to the door. When I posed the question to Mrs. Butler, she told Bill and me that there were all sorts of jobs open around town with various merchants.

The sticking point was that so many college students were rude to customers or didn't care to do the job correctly that they didn't like hiring them. Bill got a very discouraged look. Mrs. Butler said if he could promise to be polite and work hard, she would put in a word for him.

He said he was desperate for work and would be on his best behavior. She told us to wait a minute. She came back and told Bill to go to Blackwell's Bookstore. They were expecting him.

He asked if he was dressed okay or if he should run to his apartment and put on a suit and tie. Mrs. Butler told him he was fine. Bill took off down the street like his pants were on fire. It was only a block, but he wasn't going to miss out on a job.

I thanked Mrs. Butler and told her if I could do anything for her, I would, other than being out of the painting business. She got a thoughtful look and told me her garage needed a good cleaning.

I must have gotten a stricken look because she had a good laugh.

"If you would be kind enough to autograph this magazine of Iris's, that would be enough."

I did it quickly and bailed out before she did have me clean out her garage. That woman was a force of nature.

It was time for me to head out to my next lecture. It had more people in attendance than my first class. There must have been fifty people waiting. This one was much better. I could understand the don; he spoke clear, concise English when he spoke up. Unfortunately, he spoke softly and turned his back to us to write on the blackboard.

Then you couldn't hear him. After he left, I didn't wait for the sales pitch for the course notes. I was waiting with money in hand. So were five other people. I asked the guy selling the notes if I could buy them all at once.

He gave me the name of a little sidewalk café down the street. He was a runner for the group selling the notes. I rode my bike to the café and saw a short line at one of the tables.

I got in line and when my turn came, I was asked what lectures. I showed him my written list and for a mere thirty more pounds, I had all the course notes. I had been the last one in line, so I felt free to take the time to ask a question.

"How do the colleges react to these notes?"

"They don't. We have solved a problem for them, so they ignore us."

"I gather the problem is instructors who can't instruct."

"Yes, they are all brilliant names in their fields and have done exceptional work to prove it. They give prestige to the colleges, but that doesn't mean they are good presenters."

"What is the best way to use these notes to prepare for any examinations?"

"See the red star in the upper right-hand corner of the front page. They are for courses where the questions are taken from the notes. A blue star is for the textbook. Some have both red and blue. Just hope you never see a green star."

"What does a green star mean?"

"It means we have no bloody idea where the questions came from or what will be on the exam. If I were you, I would buy or at least check out the course notes for any course you might take and avoid any green. There are only a few, so you can work around them for most degrees."

"Why are dons kept on staff if they are that bad?"

"Dons with Nobel or Field prizes."

"I could see that."

"Now, if you are a graduate student in those areas, you want to work for them to look good on your resume. A couple of them will even share credit where it is due, but most of them are credit hogs. It must go with the territory."

"Thanks for your time. I will be seeing you on every course I take to avoid the greens."

"Good luck, Sir Richard, and thank you for saving our Queen."

I could see that I wouldn't be anonymous on campus for very long. I told him I was surprised that so many people in town recognized me.

He pointed behind me. There was a movie theater with posters all over the front. The largest was for the current movie *Bandits of Sherwood*. I was front and center in the poster.

"I guess that answers that."

"Tell me, did you do any of those archery shots, or were they all done by stuntmen?"

"I made them all. Last year, I took a bronze in the event at Sherwood Forest."

"I forgot about that; I saw a picture of you in the paper in those silly tights."

"I will never live that one down. Thanks for all your help; I have another lecture in a few."

"Piece of advice: never fall asleep in class. It ticks them off."

"Good advice, see you around, and thanks again."

At that, I returned to my garage space to drop off the extra notes and rode my bike to my next lecture. I had forgotten how handy a bike could be.

After the lecture, which was amazingly straightforward, and easy to hear and understand, I started back to my garage to go home for the night. Walking down a path, I heard singing.

A group of students was standing beside a wall adjoining Balliol College. I was curious about what they were singing and why. I realized it was a scurrilous song about Balliol as I approached them. As I got closer, I realized a competing song was coming from the other side.

Several people were standing there, so I asked what the event was. It was a Gordouli, which was the two schools singing nasty songs about each other to demonstrate their traditional dislike of the other. I asked if it was a long-standing tradition. The answer was that the school had been here since 1555, so who knew? All he could tell me was that Balliol was full of a bunch of socialist slackers.

I guess the answer is we hate them. We've always hated them and always will. Don't know why we hate them, but we just do. Hmm, I wonder if that could fit into a song.

When I got home, I changed into jeans and a sports shirt with a button-down collar and started reading the notes on the lectures I attended today. I now understood why attendance was so low. I had spent time in the lecture hall and had nothing to show for it. Now, I had to read the notes to get the information. It was like double time for each course.

I would have to attend each course lecture at least once. If the don were unintelligible, I would skip future ones and depend on the course notes or books depending on if it had a red or blue star.

A strange thought crossed my mind: how had the star color system come into being, and in what century did it occur? This was going to be interesting.

Chapter 25

While talking to Dad on one of our frequent transatlantic phone calls, he informed me that my workshop addition to the garage at Jackson House was now completed. Also, the deck addition at the beach had been inspected, and the house was now ready for occupancy.

A fat lot of good the house or workshop would do me here in England for the foreseeable future. My timing on projects and girls was terrible. I had a penthouse suite in London I would seldom use. Now, a beach house in California and my dream workshop would sit idle.

Having money and using it wisely seemed to be two different objects. I could afford all that but to my Ohio upbringing, it seemed such a waste.

There was nothing I could do about any of it other than whine, so I would shut up and soldier on, as Mum would say. It was odd; Dad was the one in the military, but Mum was the one with all the sayings. I bet there was more to her war than she ever let on.

My school life was settling in. I had learned to attend most of the lectures and read the specific lecture notes following along. At the end of each session, I ended up with a series of notes which needed further research. I accidentally found the best way to go about that.

I had retreated to the student lounge in the basement to avoid going out in the miserable cold English rain. A group of fellow students from the same lecture had entered at the same time as I. Only one large table was available as no one wanted to go out in the weather. We all sat at that table. Someone said they didn't understand one point that was brought up.

That unleashed the dam. None of us understood everything in the lecture, but we understood it all between the group and the course notes. We spent the next hour going over our questions. I found myself writing feverishly as all my questions were answered.

That started a study method that held for the entire term. We would gather after the lecture and review what we had missed or were confused about. I tried to get others to do it after other classes, but advanced calculus was the only one where there appeared to be universal pain.

One nice thing about that first session was that when we were finished, the rain had stopped. It was still damp and chilly outside, but at least we wouldn't get wet. On the way out, one chap said it would soon be golfing weather. Well, maybe a month from now in May.

I asked him if he played, and he told me he was a member of the Oxford University Golf Club. I didn't even know they had a golf club. This could be interesting.

"What does one have to do to join the club?"

"It's only for a select few exceptionally good golfers. Most of us have plus one or two handicaps."

He said this in a dismissive tone as though I, a stranger, could never play that well.

He went on about how they played other schools, culminating in a match against archrival Cambridge in July. I asked him when in July. He gave me the dates of the 6th-8th. I didn't have anything planned, but I would have to join the team and play the full schedule before that. I just didn't have the time.

I thought about the many smartass things I could say at this point but decided that the weather was gloomy enough that I didn't need to further ruin his day.

Back at my garage hideaway, or as I thought of it, my Hernando's Hideaway, I also read the official textbook and worked on calculus problems. This was probably the hardest course I had ever taken.

An exam would be available at the end of the term to see if I had mastered the subject.

This way of learning aligned well with my study methods for the last several years. Accidentally going to that student orientation at Berkeley two summers ago had been a godsend.

As I sat in my warm garage listening to the rain, which had started again, I realized that half of the reason I was here was to be with people my age. Where were they? Even though it was advancing my education, sitting in this garage wasn't helping my socialization.

I only knew Bill Benton here at school. He was probably at work, so I walked over to Blackwells. He was in and glad to see me. Though the bookstore had a lot of browsers, they weren't buying. Most probably just wanted to keep out of the rain.

I asked him what he was doing after dinner tonight. He invited me to join him and some of his fellow workers at the Dog and Crown Pub to have a pint and play darts. I told him I wasn't much of a drinker but would love to join them.

I attended another lecture where the lecturer was as dreary as the day, then headed home. I complained about the weather at dinner in answer to Mum and Grandmum's inquiries about my day. They told me welcome to England. April showers bring May flowers.

Mum brought me up to date on Mary's clothing line. It was going very well. This had come out of nowhere in the last month. It started with her being teased at school about having a brown thumb. Mum had started a greenhouse, and they had silver bells, cockle shells, and pretty maids all in a row. From there, somehow puppies got involved. I would love to hear the complete story one day.

The long and short of it is that I had better watch my back; my mercenary little sister may out-earn me. Good for her if she did.

When I told Mum I was going out for the evening, she only commented that if I had anything to drink, spend the night in town, and please call her if I did. Now I know why she insisted on a telephone line in the garage.

I met Bill at the Dog and Crown right after dinner. It was an easy two-block walk from the garage, so I wasn't worried about drinking too much, nor did I intend to do so.

One thing that can be said about English pubs is that they take care of their appearance. The façade was black with the name in red letters. There was gold trim around the façade and windows. Green plants were located on each side of the door. It was posh-looking. Inside, it was clean and well-lit.

There were tables and booths. The booths had tall backs, so each was well separated. One thing that I found interesting was that a coat hanger hook was between each booth on the divider. Many were full. It must rain a lot around here.

Like all bars, the smoke was hanging low. I would have to send my clothes to the dry cleaners after tonight.

Bill was already there with two other guys, Tom Weston and Steve Stewart. They seemed like nice guys. Bill introduced me informally as Rick Jackson, saying nothing about my background. We dressed alike, each in chino pants and a shirt with a sweater over.

We all went to the bar and ordered a pint. I did it to fit in. In America, they had waiters; in England, you had to go to the bar and order. The Watney Brewery owned the pub, so they served Red Barrel. It was cheap, and it was bad!

After a sip, that was the end of my beer drinking for the night. The guys all laughed at the face I made. They didn't give me any grief about not drinking with them, so I had an enjoyable evening after I traded that swill for a Coke.

The bartender tried to get me to taste a different brew, but once burned twice shy. Besides, I didn't want to take up drinking because of our family history.

None of the guys got staggering drunk, but you could tell they were drinking. We played darts. I lost every game. It looked like they would have to be falling drunk for it to be a fair handicap.

They exchanged stories about their hometowns. Tom Weston is from Liverpool, and he told us we should visit. A new band had been playing locally, and he thought they would do well. They wrote songs with a different sound than American Rock and Roll. We agreed that it could be interesting.

Steve Stewart came from Edinburgh, which was no surprise with a name like Stewart. He was a member of the Stewart clan but not of direct descent.

They wanted to know me. They were genuinely surprised when I told them I had just arrived in England from California. My accent was really good tonight, or they had too much to drink.

I switched to Ohioan, and Tom said, "That is bloody marvelous. You ought to be an actor."

This cracked Bill up. It got the attention of several other tables.

"Tom, you twit. He is an actor. His movie *Bandits of Sherwood* is playing at the Odeon right now."

That started the inquisition. It all boiled down to what famous people I knew, whether I made a lot of money, and then the big one about being a star and all those girls.

I admitted to John Wayne, Sharon Bronson, and Anna Romanov as I had been in movies with them, plus Frank Sinatra and the Beach Boys because I had made records with them.

Bill's laughter, which had gotten other tables' attention, brought questions from them. I answered everything that I could politely. On the issue of beautiful women that flocked to the stars, I commented that one had to be careful about the gold diggers, other than that a gentleman never kisses and tells.

I didn't want anyone to know what a loser I was in the female department.

Since I kept my answers short and polite, the questions soon disappeared, and everyone but me went back to the serious business of drinking and tossing darts.

One young lady approached me and asked, "How can one break into the movies?"

I told her about central casting in Hollywood, and I imagined there was something like that in the English industry. She thanked me and returned to her group.

Other than that, we just talked about the dons and how difficult some of them were to understand. We also checked out the girls in the bar, but all of them were in groups or couples, so all we did was speculate on what each of them might do if approached properly.

After listening to their ideas, I began to think I might not be such a disaster with girls after all. Or at least all guys my age were disasters. Somehow, that felt right. We broke up before the eleven o'clock closing time. We did have classes and work tomorrow.

They planned to meet back at the Dog and Crown tomorrow night at the same time. I declined. I had no studying this evening. I couldn't do two nights in a row like this and maintain my grades. Well, I guess it wasn't maintaining grades but passing the examinations.

I walked back to the garage and drove home. I don't think a sip of beer four hours ago would cause any problems. It was a good thing I didn't drink because I got a speeding ticket on the way home. The panda car was waiting in a parking lot. I was doing forty-two mph in a thirty-mph zone.

The bobbies were nice. They gave me a warning. What they wanted was to see the inside of my Aston Martin. Not being a complete fool, I invited them to sit inside it while I gave them a tour of the car and its performance statistics.

They let me proceed after establishing that I had a valid driver's license and insurance. I had used my American accent since I had an

American driver's license. I was reminded to obtain an English one if I would be here for a while. When I told them I was enrolled at Oxford, one of the policemen joked that I would have gotten a ticket had they known. Students were a pain!

I had publicity photos in my satchel. Never leave home without them. I pulled them out and autographed them to each of them specifically. I used Sir Richard, and that got their attention. I had saved the Queen. Please keep it under one hundred and be on your way!

I didn't plan to abuse it but knowing it might get me out of a hole someday was nice.

Mum was still up when I got home. She was waiting for my call. When I walked in, she walked right up and smelled my breath. Nothing was shy about Mum.

She wanted to know all about my evening. When I told her it was nothing; it was just a group of guys talking guy talk.

"How about the girls there? Any interesting ones?"

"Not really; they were in groups, and we never talked to them."

"How did you guys rate them?"

"Mum!"

"All guys rate girls just like girls rate guys."

Did she mean I had just sat in a bar, and a bunch of women rated me? How demeaning.

"Rick, this was exactly the sort of evening I was hoping you would have; you enjoyed the company of your peers, and nothing exceptional happened."

I decided not to tell her about being stopped for speeding. Knowing Mum, MI6 would soon notify her after calling 10 Downing Street.

I went on up to bed. While getting ready for bed, I thought about the evening and realized that I looked forward to doing it again, certainly not every night, but it was fun and relaxing. No work, no studying. How unusual. People lived like this. No wonder many did not get ahead. Their lives were in a pleasant rut.

I would have to watch that I didn't fall into it permanently, but it was a nice place to visit.

With that, I turned out my light to go to sleep. There was another change in my life. I seldom read before I went to sleep. I was so tired when I went to bed that I didn't even try anymore. I didn't consider this to be a good thing. I would have to make time to read when I wasn't tired.

I had always read fiction. Maybe it was time I started reading newspapers and magazines on current events. Not the tabloids, but serious journals.

Chapter 26

The next several weeks were the same: go to lectures, Thursday nights spent at the pub with the guys. I did get better at darts, but I was still about five years behind the group in experience.

One thing began to stand out. In college, they didn't care if you attended a class or if you learned anything or not. They had your money; the rest was up to you. I thought of the kids my age in Bellefontaine sitting at their desks in the tenth grade. They would be spoon-fed information at the rate of the slowest learners.

If they were failing, extra counseling would be given and their parents brought into the picture. Here, it wasn't even noted. You would just get a letter saying you had been sent down.

I did find out there is an entire support system available if you elected to use it. They had what they called laboratories or workshops. You could attend these for hands-on experience in science or class exercises in any subject. There were tutors available at a price—group, or individual. Then there were the students getting together and working as a team to self-teach.

I wondered how the Blackwell gang, as I thought of them, could have so much time that they could do the pub three or four nights a week. When I asked, I was surprised. They hadn't come to Oxford to learn anything, well, except how to socialize with their peers and make a double twenty.

They were all taking the minimum number of the easiest courses they could. Even Bill, who I thought was trying to learn, was coasting, maybe not as much as the others, but to my mind coasting. I found out that he had been desperate for a job because his dad wouldn't fund a party life.

The more I learned, the more I realized how fortunate I was that I had internalized that message at Berkeley.

My toughest course was Calculus. I had to hire an individual tutor. I could almost grasp single-variable calculus, but as soon as the word multivariable was mentioned, my mind turned off.

The idea of instantaneous change or derivative of various functions being a process called *differentiation* is like a dim light in the distance. I could almost see it. Of course, every time I felt like I was getting close, it receded into the distance.

My don was enthusiastic about using derivatives to solve various kinds of problems. He seemed to miss the fact that half the people sitting in the room still didn't understand how to find this apparition called a derivative.

Then, after assuming that we could find this elusive thing called a derivative, we could go back from the derivative of a function to the function itself. He called it *integration*. It was nothing like George Wallace trying to stand off the United States Army.

It was like wading in mud, but I was getting there. Without the tutor, a nice guy named Charles Erich, I would have floundered. I mean, I can plot x, y coordinates, and draw a curved line to join them smoothly. It was calculating a point on that curve without the equation that stumped me. Then, when I knew the point to be able to describe the equations that gave the coordinates, it became black magic.

Chuck was the most patient guy I had ever met. He worked with me, trying different methods to get it through my thick head. It finally dawned on me that calculus is seeing the relationship of patterns in equations. If I have an equation for a circle, I can see the relation to the volume of a sphere. One thing that will always be true is *pie is not square,* no matter the equation. Chuck about lost his cool when I brought that up.

I don't think I will ever win a prize in mathematics, but I can follow the tune.

One evening, when I got home from school, there was a message from Dad. I was to call Cessna in London. They had called Jackson House for me to tell me about a model 310 that had become available in England. If I could take delivery there, I would end up getting it almost two months early.

It was too late to call the Cessna business office in London, so I had to wait until the morning. I didn't call until I got to the garage at school. I had been up since 5:00, wondering if it was too early to call, so I thought I did fairly well waiting until 8:02.

I was put through to the sales manager. When I had placed the order for my plane, I left word with Cessna that if that model became available early anywhere in the world, I would consider it. You could tell the sales manager was happy to hear I was already in England.

As much as I wanted to drop everything and rush to London, I arranged a Saturday appointment. That bloody calculus.

On Saturday, I pulled into the Cessna office parking lot on the private side of Heathrow in my Aston Martin. I was glad the price was fixed because one look at my car, and it would probably double.

When I settled into the sales manager's office after a round of Sir Richard this and Sir Richard that, I asked how this aircraft became available. It seemed a company had ordered them with a good down payment and then gone out of business overnight. The manager didn't say it, but it sounded like something dodgy had been going on.

They had ordered three aircraft, which were now sitting in the hangar. With half a laugh I was asked if I wanted to buy three airplanes for a good price. Without thinking, I asked how much off for the lot. He quoted me a number that would get me three airplanes for the price of two.

I shook my head and asked how that could be.

"Sir Richard, we have a cash flow problem. We are a Cessna franchise, and they want their money. Unless we move these soon, we may be out of business ourselves. Remember, there was a good down payment, so we are giving up our profit and breaking even just to move these off our books."

Now, I needed three aircraft like an extra hole in my head, so I promptly told him, "Let's take a look."

As we were going to the hangar, the manager diverted us to introduce me to the owner and told him I had an interest in all three. If I had asked them to carry me, they probably would have.

In the hangar were three brand-new Cessna 310s in standard colors. I hummed and hawed around, looking at the brand-new logbooks with the first maintenance performed outside the factory noted. I tried to look like I knew what I was doing. I even opened the cowling on several engines to see if they were clean.

The truth is the wings might be ready to fall off, and if they weren't in the normal walk-around mode, I wouldn't know it. I will never know why I said yes, I will buy them.

The only extra I asked for was that one of them be repainted in the colors I had ordered. They had no problem with that. The next question was how I would pay for these and when my parents would be there to finalize the deal. That was getting a little old, but I don't think I would let some kid come off the street and take my aircraft, no matter what type of car he was driving. I explained that I was emancipated, so I could make a purchase like this on my own. I had been through this enough that I brought an extra copy of my emancipation decree with me.

As to how I was paying, would they take a check? Again, the deer in the headlights look. They gave me the total amount with VAT added in, and I wrote the check, then called my bank and gave the name, account number, and the current magic word.

The word would have to be changed after this. Every time I made a purchase that required using the safe word to indicate I was not under duress, it was changed. While I was on the line, I was given the next word on the list. If I forgot it, it would be a nuisance. I would have to go to the bank in person with my ID to start over.

They would have the aircraft ready for delivery by next Saturday. It takes time for the paint to dry and all the paperwork to go through. Now, I had to get back to Oxford and find hangar space for my little fleet. I also had to figure out what I was going to tell Mum. Unfortunately, she was the one on this side of the pond. Dad would understand boys and their toys, at least, I thought he would.

I had a moment of genius before I left the Cessna shop. I called Mr. Norman of the Queen's Messengers. He had asked me to let him know when my plane was in England as it would be handy to have a messenger with a plane.

It was Saturday, but I don't think the man ever left Buck House. Maybe he had a suite there, for all I knew. Anyway, thinking that I would be leaving a message, I was surprised to catch him at his desk.

I told him I now had a plane in England.

His response was, "Capital. Remind me of its specifications."

I did that, giving him the range and passenger capability.

"When will the plane be in service?"

"They promised all three would be ready by next Saturday."

"Three?"

"They had a sale going on, buy two, get one free."

Hey, I'm still sixteen going on seventeen. That sounds like it belongs in a song.

"Seriously, I got them at a good price because of a company going out of business. I will probably be reselling two of them. They are still factory new."

"Would you be willing to rent one out on a long-term lease?"

"Certainly, what do you have in mind?"

"Our budget this year would allow us to have a plane in our livery. If we did one of yours up, we could lease it, and you could fly it for us. You are the only one on staff with a license who lives in England."

"I checked, and the UK is the same as the US. I have to be seventeen before I haul passengers."

"Not if you are in the Royal Air Force as a flying officer. You can join the RAF at fifteen with a parent's consent."

"If you remember, I am emancipated, so I don't need that. But wouldn't I have to go to special schools?"

"Normally, yes, but we will have you listed as a Queen's Messenger seconded to the RAF. That way we are responsible for your training. There will be training on proper behavior, ranks, uniforms, and odds and ends like that, but it will be on our schedule, which will be at your convenience."

"The idea is to allow me to fly one of my aircraft as a Queen's Messenger and pick up passengers?"

"You got it, my lad."

"Would my flying officer status allow me to fly nonduty passengers?"

"Absolutely."

"Sign me up. Now I have to tell the Cessna people they have two planes to paint. Will they have the livery?"

"I believe so. If not, have Cessna give me a ring."

"Okay, when shall this happen?"

"You mentioned you will be back next Saturday to take delivery. Why don't you pop in."

"Okay, I will do that. I'll call from Cessna before I head over."

I went back to the sales manager and explained that one of the aircraft was to be painted as a Queen's Messenger, greyhound, and all. He took me right at my word. Not so bloody likely.

He called the number for Buckingham Palace and asked to be put through to the head of the Messengers. As expected, he talked to

Mr. Norman, who confirmed the request and thanked him for being cautious. Who knows what teenagers would get up to?

The sales manager brought up something we hadn't addressed. How would we get three planes to Oxford and end up with my car in Oxford after I come in for a final inspection and signing of the paperwork?

We finally decided that I would pay for three pilots to fly them to Oxford. We would all return to London in one plane, and then I would drop them off and return home in that plane. This would do away with needing my car that day. I could take a cab to the Palace.

The sales manager, of course, wanted to know all about the Queen's Messenger bit. He knew about my saving the Queen but hadn't learned anything else. I had to show him my greyhound pin, which I also had with me, in this case, attached to the inside of my sports coat.

He then came up with the idea that they take pictures of me taking delivery. I think I have heard that one before. Ford Motor Company was still probably mad at me. I think they would buy Aston Martin if they could, just to spite me and keep me in a Ford.

I explained that as an actor, I charged for personal appearances. He quickly dropped that thought.

As I was driving home, I realized that I had solved one problem, the one about buying three airplanes. When I told Mum I was joining the RAF, the planes would be ignored in the explosion. Clever me.

When I got home, it was time to get cleaned up for dinner, so I didn't have to face the music until I was at the table. I decided I would make a clean breast of it, so I asked Mum to let me tell the complete story of the day before getting excited. I thought I had better warn her she would be getting excited.

I hoped it might act as a safety valve like on a steam boiler.

When I said three airplanes, her body language got tightly closed. When I mentioned the prices and my original intention was to sell the other two, and good news, I had already leased one to the Queen's Messenger service.

Of course, I would be using it some of the time to carry people for them. All I had to do to be legal was to be seconded to the RAF as a Flying Officer.

I finally ran out of words and braced myself. From the look on her face, it would be tremendous, horrible, momentous, loud, long, and never to be forgotten. However, before she let loose, Grandmum said, "And what were you doing at his age, Olive?"

Grandmum always used Mum's real name. Mum had taken a deep breath to start on me but let it out with a scream of "Arrgh.

"We will talk about this later."

I knew what she was saying was, we will talk about this when my mother is not around to remind me how stupid I was when I was your age.

Now, all I had to do was hide in my room for the rest of the evening, get up early, leave for school, and hope she had cooled down by dinner. Oops, I forgot tomorrow is Sunday. Well, I could take a long run around the countryside, maybe a double marathon.

Chapter 27

As Robert Burns put it, "The best-laid schemes o' Mice and Men, Gang aft agley." Mum was waiting for me in the morning. At least she didn't have that tear your head off and pull your heart out look that she had last night.

"Richard, now that we have both slept on it will you please explain to me what you were thinking."

Maybe I will live. I proceeded to break it down, starting with the opportunity to take delivery of my plane early in England rather than wait another month or more and then have to have it ferried from LA to Oxford. That made sense to her.

"Now, how did three aircraft enter the equation?"

I explained how a local business went broke and had to default on the purchase, leaving the local dealer in a bind. They were willing to sell me three airplanes for the price of two. I had already paid upfront for one. So, I was getting two for the price of one. I know, poor logic, but it hit the female shopping nerve.

"You get to live so far. Now, why did you leave your mind and join the RAF?"

"I haven't joined the RAF. I'm a Queen's Messenger who has been seconded to the RAF with the rank of Flying Officer so that I can ferry passengers for the Messenger service. I will also be able to carry private passengers on my own time."

"When you put it that way, it almost makes sense. What you are missing is that the Messenger service can be directed to deliver almost anything around the world."

I had an image of being told to deliver a nuclear weapon. What Mum said next was almost as bad.

"This includes MI6 personnel and defectors."

Jackson, Richard Jackson.

"That may sound romantic right now, but remember your run-ins with the KGB? It's that world that has me frightened for you. I have been there; and trust me, you haven't seen the bad side yet."

Now, that was disconcerting. I had helped kill KGB agents and transported their severed heads, and I hadn't seen the bad side?

"What course do you suggest I take?"

"You have told Mr. Norman that you will do it, so don't back down on your word. Staying safe will depend on your common sense, which I don't feel as strongly about now as I did yesterday morning."

"Mum, to have full flying rights, I didn't think things through."

Mum sighed as she told me she well remembered how she kept her mum up at night with her antics.

"Can you share what those antics were when you were my age?"

"It involved French cognac and unpaid taxes. That is as much as I'm going to say. My being on the wrong side of the channel at the war's outbreak led to everything else."

My mum was a smuggler!

"I will try to think things through before I accept any missions moving people around."

"I'm glad that's settled. Now, you have to call your father and tell him."

Crikey, I thought I had gotten away clean! With the time difference, it was way too early to call Dad, so I had the rest of the day to stew about it.

I did end up going for a long run. I had to use up energy, or I would go nuts. After running and showering, I drove to the Oxford airfield. It's a private airfield owned by the City of Oxford. It was in the small village of Kidlington and had been an RAF station during the war.

Now, it was a center for private aviation and pilot training. It also had major maintenance shops. I was used to small airfields in

California, excluding LAX. This was the second busiest airport in England after Heathrow.

I wondered if there would be any hangar space available. I went to the private aviation center and found their business office. Even on a weekend, it was staffed. I could see why. Looking out the window, you could see at all times at least three aircraft in some form of movement, taxiing, landing, or taking off.

I inquired if there was any hangar space to let. I was told no; all their single aircraft buildings were rented out. I replied that I was hunting for space for three aircraft, Cessna 310s. That got the man's attention. He called another employee over and asked him to man the desk while he, Mr. Morton, showed me what was available.

Mr. Morton took me to a hangar that could have held twenty of mine. His attitude was that this was the only open space on the airfield, take it or leave it. Since I needed space starting next Saturday, I told him I would take it.

"Oh, I thought you were inquiring for someone else."

By now, I had had enough of these discovery conversations, so I went to the heart of the matter: I'm Sir Richard Jackson; I'm emancipated, so I can legally make my own decisions, and I have the money in the bank to pay cash.

I delivered this factually, trying not to seem arrogant or nasty. He took it well.

When I asked about the leasing fee, he told me it was a lot better than I would think. The RAF owned it, and they wanted to get it off their books. This made me think of possibilities. Either I could buy it outright, or better yet since the RAF owned it, have it assigned by them for my aircraft.

I explained my connection as a Queen's Messenger to Mr. Morton and how I was being seconded to the RAF so I could carry passengers.

His only comment was, "Make a decision fast; it has only been sitting empty for five years."

What a dry sense of humor the British have. I told him I would call London on Monday and see what could be arranged. One way or the other, I would be using this space. At least if nothing else, I could leave my car inside when on trips.

On the way home, I had a thought and stopped at Blackwell's. Unfortunately, they were not open. I had forgotten it was Sunday and like in the US, most stores were closed on Sunday.

I went home and worked on that pesky calculus. It was now reduced from being a nightmare to pesky. Things were looking up.

Monday, after my normal routine, I arrived at school with enough time to stop at Blackwell's. Bill was there, so I explained that I needed anything they had on the RAF.

"Have you been disowned, sent down, and are now joining the RAF to get away from it all?"

"Not quite. You know I'm a Queen's Messenger. They are seconding me to the RAF as a Flight Officer. The Cessna I told you about became available here in England, and the Silver Greyhounds want me to have one of them painted in their livery so I can fly people around. The only way I can legally fly people while still under the age of seventeen is to be in the RAF, which you can join when you are fifteen."

"Slow down, mate. One of them—how many airplanes did you buy, and how old are you if you aren't seventeen?"

"I bought three planes, all Cessna 310s, and I'm sixteen years old."

"Why would you buy three planes? You can only fly one at a time."

"They had a sale."

That cracked him up.

"Right, the wealthy Yank sees three aircraft for sale and buys them all to get a better price. Pull the other one."

"Bill, it's true. I bought them, figuring that I could sell the other two to get my money back for the first one. Now the Service wants to lease one from me and have me pick up some passengers. They are seconding me to the RAF so I can legally do that. I want to buy some books to see what I'm getting into."

"Okay, that makes sense. Now tell me about being sixteen and going to Oxford."

"That is a long story, and I will share it at the pub. I need to buy the books and get to class."

"I'm holding you to that."

At that, he led me to a section with a dozen books on the RAF, some of them manuals. I bought one of each without looking. I was running close on time.

The morning tutorial on metals was as unintelligible as the first day. I had my course notes out and followed the don on those. Luckily for me, he was one of those teachers who never varied their lesson plans, so I could follow by using the notes.

Most of the other guys present were doing the same. One guy was reading a novel, and another was sound asleep. Why are they here? Not my monkey, not my circus.

I returned to my garage hideaway and went through the books I had just bought. No thanks to looking at what I was buying, I had made several good choices or at least grabbed good books off the shelf.

The most important was the "Handbook for the New Officer." It was written in 1959 and from its printing history it was only updated about every five years, so it probably was the current edition in use.

It had everything that I could see a new officer needing to know. It had uniform types and insignia, plus all ranks and ratings and where they fit, job titles, and descriptions. There was a listing of all types of aircraft in service, plus all the bases in the UK.

Another book was about the specifics of each aircraft including speed, range, armament, flight crew, and type of missions flown. They even had Cessna 310s in service listed as executive aircraft. I wondered if I would end up flying any air marshals around. They were the same as generals.

I spent every spare minute left from schoolwork studying about the RAF. Its history and pilots like Roy Brown and Douglas Bader fascinated me.

I even practiced standing at attention and saluting in front of a mirror. I wanted to do this right. The more of a head start I got, the better.

On Wednesday, Mr. Norman called. The RAF was giving notice to the airport that I had free use of the hangar for the Queen's Messenger Service and any private equipment I owned. They would not be making any improvements to the facility. I was welcome to do so, but at my own expense.

Once I had the keys, I did a walkthrough. Just like in the Forest Service hangar in California, there was a basement. I went down the steps, wondering what I would find. I found an empty room. A careful check revealed no hidden doors or spaces.

I arranged with the airport for their cleaning crew to come in at my expense and give the large hangar a good trash pickup and sweep. That included the many cobwebs on the rafters. I saw no need to spend a lot of money on improvements but eventually did break down for a desk and chairs for the office, and a coffee pot.

There were toilets with running water, so it was set there. Other than that, I was in business. On Saturday, the three airplanes landed and were directed to the hangar.

The three aircraft were so cool. One in the Queen's Messengers livery, greyhound painted on the side. My plane was British racing green with my coat of arms on the doors. The third one was in factory colors. I guess if I wanted to fly incognito, I could use that one.

Somewhere along the line, my mind had accepted the fact that I owned three planes and was keeping them. Precious, my precious, I loved those stories.

One of the pilots told me the hangar would look good with the Messenger service logo on the side of the hangar. I would have to think about that. Another one of the three gave me his card and told me he was available to ferry any of them around at need.

The other two then produced their cards. It looked like I might have the start of my air force. After a bathroom break, I gave a quick tour of the hangar, not much to see.

The question arose if I would have any maintenance done here or if I would fly them back to London. I told them since all services were available here, I would probably have it done locally. I didn't want to get involved with having to go through this all the time.

We took my plane back to Heathrow. It was neat getting re-familiar with the aircraft type whilst other pilots were on board. We discussed the strengths and shortcomings on the trip back to London. It only took forty-five minutes from gate to gate.

I then took a black cab to the palace. I had worn a suit along with my tie with its greyhounds. The driver never blinked when I told him my destination. They were even getting to know me at the palace security entrance. I was on the list and had no luggage of any sort, so it was a quick pass-through.

Mr. Norman was ready for me. He wanted to know if getting the planes in place had gone okay. I told him that there were no problems. He then brought up the RAF.

"It has been made clear to me that you will not be involved with any operations from MI6. Your mum spoke to the Queen, the Queen spoke to me and the head of MI6. I must say it cut back on several plans."

"Mum was not happy when I broke the news about being in the RAF."

"I know her displeasure was felt through the system. Something about severed heads was mentioned. I have no idea what that was about, but C took it very seriously and personally.

"Now that that is out of the way, I would like to introduce you to someone."

He had a wing commander brought in who proceeded to take me through the paperwork to second me to the Royal Air Force. Once that was taken care of, he told me that I would be contacted in Oxford by Flight Lieutenant Smyth, who would start teaching me the basics of being with the RAF. The flight lieutenant was on limited duty due to an injury and lived in Oxford, so this worked out well.

The wing commander was all business, and I didn't get a positive or negative feeling from our interaction. He also told me to get a full kit of uniforms. At that, he left before I could ask what a full kit consisted of or where I could obtain it.

Mr. Norman recommended G.D. Golding. He called them for me. It seems that a phone call from Buckingham Palace will get you special treatment. I was told to come right over.

Taking another cab, I made it to the tailor in twenty minutes. I explained I was being seconded to the RAF as a flying officer and had been told to obtain a full kit. Little did I know but eventually it came to light that I was supposed to buy a set of daily working uniforms.

They spent a good hour taking all my measurements. I was asked how I was going to be paying. I would be paying on delivery, but they would like to know if my check would be honored upfront.

They didn't use those words, but that was the message. I didn't know you could dance around a subject like that. The guy was even better than the mayor of LA, who was a professional at using a lot of words to say nothing.

I would take a final fitting in a week, and then it would all be available after that. They could arrange for it all to be delivered to The Meadows. I made an appointment for the following Saturday, left for the airport, and flew home. It was quite a day.

Chapter 28

On Sunday, Mum wanted to get Grandmum out of the house, so we took a drive out to the airport to check out my new planes. They both oohed and awed over my planes but immediately got into plans for redecorating my very plain-looking office.

I started to say something when Mum shook her head. Then I figured it out: she wanted Grandmum involved in a project that would get her out and about, which would be good for her health.

To redeem myself from my almost faux pas, I asked if a budget of a thousand pounds would be enough.

Grandmum replied, "Oh heavens, yes. Olive and I can find things at the thrift shops this week."

Mum's smile said everything.

On Monday after school, I had a phone call in the evening from Flight Lieutenant Smyth. He wanted to know if I could come to his house as getting around was still a bother. Of course, I could. We set up a meeting for Tuesday evening after dinner.

I swotted up on the "Officers Handbook," as I expected that to be the basis of my training. I was correct.

Tuesday, I knocked on the door of Flight Lieutenant Smyth's house. It was answered by a pert young lady, his wife Priscilla. She led me to the kitchen of the small cottage. Bill was at the table, and I was relieved to see a copy of the handbook in front of him.

Priscilla excused herself while Bill and I got to know each other. He explained that he had been in a motorcar accident. The bonnet had collapsed like it was supposed to, or he would have lost his head. However, the engine block did move back far enough to break his legs. He was in the middle of a year-long recovery.

He was on duty at the time and was not judged at fault, as the other driver was on the wrong side of the road and drunk. It was an

American officer who was visiting the base, so right now, the Yanks didn't rate remarkably high with the Smyths.

I had been using my Mayfair accent, so he didn't twig about me right away. When he asked about me, I was open and honest, describing myself as a Queen's Messenger being seconded to the RAF so I could legally fly.

"You are licensed, aren't you?"

"Yes, but under civilian rules, I have to be seventeen to carry passengers."

He stopped and stared at me for a moment.

"You don't look that young. I would have guessed nineteen or twenty."

"I am, and I have a shameful secret to share. I'm half a Yankee."

I changed my accent with the last sentence. It was worth it seeing the confused look on his face. I guess it was the final clue for him.

"Rick Jackson, would that be Sir Richard Jackson?"

"Guilty as charged."

He half-shouted, "Priscilla, get in here."

She quickly returned to the kitchen to see what the fuss was about.

"Prue, this is Sir Richard Jackson, the actor who saved the Queen."

"Oh my!"

That led to a half-hour conversation on my career and attending Oxford. They were nice people and polite about it, so it went well. Prue made us tea, and we enjoyed our time. When it wound down, it was time to go to work.

Bill gave me a copy of the handbook and told me to start memorizing the first four chapters, as there would be a quiz the next time we were together. That would be next Tuesday evening. I knew an order when I heard it, so I replied, "Yes, sir."

"Would you like to get the first four out of the way now? I bought a copy last week and have been going through it."

"Let's give it a try.

He then opened a three-ring binder with pages of what I assumed were the exam questions. They were, as he started to question me. There were also pictures of various uniforms and ranks, which I had to identify.

I even had to stand at attention and salute. He told me my salute was sloppy. I thought it was sharp, and my face must have given me away as he started laughing.

"All drill instructors tell you your first salutes are sloppy. Welcome to the RAF."

"Rick, I'm pleasantly surprised at where you are. It is obvious how you got to this point in life. I was also supposed to do an estimate of your fitness. You look fine to me; do you work out at all?"

I told him about my exercise routine and running regime, and he about had a kitten.

"You may be the fittest person in the RAF. Most of us are chair-bound sods."

I told him I doubted that, but I had to keep in shape for my movie roles, and it had become my way of life.

He went on to tell me that I had a good understanding of the basics required and to keep it up.

As we were finishing up, his wife returned and asked a question. "When you come back next, do you mind if I bring a few friends over to meet you? They won't believe me otherwise."

"No problem. Anyone with a camera is welcome to take pictures with me."

Susan Wallace would be proud of me. I wondered how she was doing. As I had backed off from pictures for at least a while, she had taken on several other clients.

She was also working with Mr. Baxter on learning the agent trade. She had a real monster of a client to start with. My sister Mary was transitioning from Mr. Baxter to Susan. I wondered if they would survive the experience. They were both strong-willed. Susan was bigger; Mary was more stubborn.

I made a mental note to be sure to bring publicity photos and said good evening.

The next two days passed quickly between lectures and studying the RAF handbook. I could never think of the lectures as classes. They were too dry, and there was no interaction between a student and the teacher.

This worked well for me as I was used to it. It was how I had been learning for the last two years. I pitied those who were facing this for the first time. Maybe that was why, while I had to study, none of it seemed impossible. Even calculus was not impossible, just improbable.

I was getting calculus, painfully, but I was getting it. Chuck Erich was very patient and kept coming up with new ways to explain things that I didn't understand. When I didn't get what he was saying, he would try another approach. As a teacher, he was fabulous, and as a private tutor, he was almost priceless. I say almost because I had to pay him ten pounds in cash every session. I bet the taxman was pleased.

Thursday night came around, and I had to face my reckoning with complete disclosure of my age and past. It took me a whole pint and most of the evening to tell my story. The guys kept interrupting with questions.

Besides the movies and songs, I told them about my inventions. I ran down after a while because I felt like I was bragging. I mentioned this to Bill, who reminded me if I did it, it wasn't bragging.

Most of their questions were about the girls in my life. They couldn't understand why I didn't have Hollywood starlets hanging all over me. I explained that I had too many run-ins with gold diggers and girls who wanted to use my fame for their purposes. This had made me twice shy.

Tom Weston put it best. "Guys, remember he is just a kid. He has a lot to learn yet."

Yeah, at nineteen, he knew everything, but he was entirely correct; I had a lot to learn. They all agreed that my problems were unique as they involved fame and fortune.

Bill asked me, "Rick, you come across as pretty levelheaded and aren't full of yourself. Why is that?"

"You haven't met my parents. My father is a tough ex-military police officer, and Mum is plain scary."

"Your Mum is scary?"

"Ask MI6. They sit up and behave themselves when the viscountess gets on them."

"Wow, she knows people in MI6?"

"She was and probably still is a member."

Tom Weston said, "I think I would behave myself if my Mum could kill people with her bare hands, though she has threatened to strangle me in my sleep several times."

We all laughed at that; all Mums made that threat.

Steve asked, "Have you had any spy-type training?"

It took until closing time to relate my experience with the CIA in evading a tail and the involvement of the KGB.

Tom Weston asked if they should be afraid to be around me. I told them I was in hiding, that Oxford had me attending under another name. Unless the people at the next table were agents, they were probably safe.

Of course, they had to look over at the next table. The guys at that table either couldn't have cared less about us or knew their tradecraft.

Questions arose about my movies and the different stunts. When I told them I did my sword work, Steve got excited. He was a member of the Oxford Fencing Club; would I like to attend with him and get some practice in? I told him I would be delighted. They met on Monday nights, which I had clear, so we planned to meet at his club the following Monday.

He asked the other guys if they wanted to attend, but they passed.

I didn't get into archery, unarmed combat, or the fact that I was a US Marshal. Being a Queen's Messenger put me over the top with them. No sense in gilding the lily, as Mum would say.

The next morning, I could tell I had drunk more beer than I ever had before. I didn't have a hangover, but I never peed so much in my life. I also drank about a gallon of water. Well, it seemed like it. I don't think I like to drink, which is not a bad thing. I would have to learn to say no or nurse one all night long.

Saturday morning, I flew the plane in the Queen's livery down to London and, from there, got a cab to G. D. Goldings for my final fitting. They had me try on mess, dress, and daily wear, and I don't know what all. There were many shirts and pants, formal jackets, and, oh, my, lions and tigers. Then, all the shoes, socks, hats, ties, and badges.

It came out to over a thousand pounds, which I paid in full. I had seen the pay rate for a flight officer. At less than ten thousand pounds a year, there was no way they could afford it.

I mentioned this to the man at Goldings, the head fitter, or whatever they called him. I think Bandit Chief would be a good title.

"Well, Sir was very explicit in ordering a complete set of uniforms. Normally, we only have orders for one set of dress uniforms and several working sets from flight officers."

Ah, the English language is a wonderful thing. Yet the wing commander was specific in telling me to order a complete set. Maybe he knew something I didn't, not that it was hard to do.

The cab was full of my purchases. There were so many clothes that I would have had a weight problem on the Cessna if I had five passengers on board.

Of course, when I got home, the clothes wouldn't all fit in the Aston Martin. I had to pack in as much as I could and then make another trip. That was even with unpacking everything from the cartons and stacking them on the seats and in the small boot.

As I drove home on the second trip, I saw a panda car beside the road. One of the officers waved at me. It's nice to be recognized favorably, especially by the police. Of course, it was the car that was recognized. How do they know it wasn't stolen?

At home, Mum and Grandmum had to see all my new clothes. I even had to put on the Mess Dress uniform. It was really neat looking. The jacket I liked best was a double-breasted uniform jacket. Go figure, there is even a uniform for being out of uniform.

It was a nice-looking dark blue like my blazers, but as I said, double-breasted. The buttons looked like they could be real gold. I know I paid enough for them to be real.

Monday came around fast enough. I showed up at the fencing salle a little early. There were two club instructors there. I introduced myself, and when they asked, I told them what training I had. They were most interested in what was taught in Hollywood vs. the real world.

I told them I had worked little with fencing epees, and that most of my work had been with broadswords, rapiers, or dueling sabers. They didn't use broadswords at all and did little with rapiers but used the saber a lot.

About this time, other people started showing up. I had been talked into a demonstration bout with the saber first thing. They were outfitting me with one of their fencing outfits, masks, and all. I thought this was effete as we didn't use them in Hollywood. We couldn't use them on the screen, so we didn't bother off-screen either.

I was introduced to the best saberman in the club. They told me it would be safest for me if there was someone who knew what they were doing involved with the bout.

I felt insulted by that but chose to act as though they had my safety in mind.

We went to the main mat, and everyone closed in around us. No leaving the mat. What if I decided to jump up on a table as we did in Hollywood? Steve Stewart was there. I noticed he was talking to a lot of people and writing something in a notebook.

We saluted each other with our sabers, and it was on. We both were a little tentative, but then I saw an opening and took it. His sword went flying. Someone said best two out of three. So, we went at it again.

This time, I didn't mess around. I went high as though I was going to slash him, and then used a kick from the other side to knock him down. He was enraged.

One of the instructors told me, "That's not fair, old boy. In a real match, you would be disqualified."

"In a real match, he would be dead. I wasn't taught a stylized showpiece; I was taught how to kill."

"You fight to the death in those movies?"

"The movies are choreographed to the ninth degree like a ballroom dance. I'm talking about the training I received off the set."

"How did you do with that crowd?"

"I fought Basil Rathbone to a draw."

This wasn't quite true, but they didn't have to know that Mr. Rathbone said I was good and with additional experience, could fight with the best of them.

"Well, you would have to play by our rules here."

"Okay, when I come back, I will."

Not that I will. If the guy I fought was their best, there was nothing here for me.

Steve came over with a great smile on his face.

"I made over a hundred quid betting on you."

"That was a lot to risk."

"Not when you described your training last week, and I know what the all-Oxford champion can do, so it was easy money for me."

"He's the champion?"

"Yes, if you follow the rules. You Yanks don't seem to have any."

I shook my head and left. Thus, my Oxford sword-fighting career ended. They didn't play rough enough for me. I think I will call the people at the Tower of London to arrange some real training.

Chapter 29

One thing I hadn't taken care of was finding a place to get some golf practice in. I had asked around at the pub and was told the Huntercombe was the nicest course around. It had a high world ranking. It was located about fifteen minutes from The Meadows at Nuffield, Henley-on-Thames.

I rang them up and talked to the golf pro. It is a public course but will only allow visitors with a known handicap. I identified myself and was told I would be very welcome to use the driving range and practice green, but they still wanted to see my handicap card.

Maybe he didn't believe that I was carrying a two-under handicap.

I drove over Monday morning. Yes, I cut some lectures. When I identified myself by showing my handicap card and diplomatic passport, I was made very welcome. I knew that this passport was good for something.

I explained that I needed to keep up with my game as I was playing in the US Open in June. When he heard that, he picked up a magazine he had been reading. I didn't know that *Golf Digest* had included me in an article along with a fairly good picture of me driving.

Well, I could have had the keys to the course if they had any.

Since I didn't have any clubs with me, I was offered a loaner set. I took them up on that for today but ordered a set of my favorite clubs with extended shafts. Then there was all the other gear, from balls to shoes and all else.

The pro Mr. Simpson told me that if I applied for a membership, there was a one hundred percent chance I would be accepted. I was going to be in the area, and this was the closest course, so I filled out the paperwork right then.

This took me a good hour. From there, the pro showed me the practice green and driving range. I think he was excited to have me there.

I spent an hour practicing putting. I hadn't completely lost my edge, but it was rusty. From there, it was to the driving range. I didn't push it, starting with the short irons and working my way up to the woods. By the time I was to the driver, I had loosened up, so I let a couple of swings rip. By the time the roll was finished, I think one of them passed the four-hundred-yard sign.

Unbeknownst to me at the time, a gentleman was watching me. He introduced himself as the coach of the Oxford University Golf Club. He asked if, by any chance, I was attending Oxford.

When I told him yes, he asked if I would like to join the university club. He was impressed with my capabilities and thought I could add to their team, especially in their upcoming match with archrival Cambridge in July.

I told him I couldn't make that date as I would be back in the States. He wondered if I could delay my trip.

"I'm playing as an amateur in the US Open in June, and I don't have time to play all the other golf dates before the Cambridge match."

"Are you Sir Richard Jackson?"

"Yes, I am."

"It is nice to meet you. I would love to introduce you to our team. They are cheering for you as the only Brit in the tournament."

"When will they be here next?"

"Our next meeting here is next Sunday morning."

"That works well for me. I can come out and practice and meet them."

We settled on 10 a.m. the following Sunday.

When I got home Monday evening after attending my afternoon lectures, there was a package waiting for me. It was all my mail that had accumulated at Jackson House for the last month. There was also a stack of business reports to go through.

There were even a couple of movie scripts that Mr. Baxter thought I might be interested in. That poor guy kept trying to retire, and my family kept dragging him back in. Now, it was Mary. I gave the scripts a cursory look but neither of them grabbed my attention. I had pretty well decided to stay out of the movies, at least this year.

Next, I went through the business reports. There were expansions recommended based on the amount of work coming to us. None of them out-stripped our capital reserve, so I initialed them as approved and set them aside to return to the States.

A financial statement was included. It was a high-level overview. The basic message was that I could spend as much money as I wanted for the rest of my life and never outspend it. Not quite true. I could spend it all if I wanted to buy a small South American country.

The amounts of money being projected were obscene to my worldview. I would like to meet Mr. Getty and ask him, "What is the end game of having all that money?"

I had heard the saying that he who dies with the most toys wins. What about having the most toy factories? Oh well, that is why I have a staff of accountants, investment counselors, and tax lawyers to keep it all straight. Thank goodness I don't have to deal with them, or they would see how lost I am at this level of finance.

There was one personal letter postmarked Columbus, Ohio. It was from Judy King. She wrote that she was sorry about the way it had ended, but she and her family couldn't stand the pressure of her dating me. They would have no personal life, so she had to end it.

She gave no hint that she would like to get back together, just regretted that we couldn't go on with a normal life. I thought about it and decided to write back my regrets that we couldn't date and learn more about each other. I gave no hint that I would like to get back to her. We both were keeping our lines of communication open without raising any hopes for the future. I found it all sad.

Tuesday, as I was wheeling my bike out of the garage to ride to my early lecture, I was waylaid by Iris Butler.

"Rick, could you give me a minute? I have a favor to ask."

"For you, my dear, all the minutes you need."

Where did that come from? It certainly caused her to pause for a heartbeat.

With a short stutter, she brought up, "There is this formal dance next Friday, and there is a girl in our house at the university who doesn't have a date. Her duenna is strict, and because of her social rank in Spain, she only lets her go out with people of 'Quality.' With this old bat that means a title. We have checked, and a Knight of the Garter is acceptable."

"I have no plans. You say it is formal. How formal, morning suits?"

"That and the military can wear formal mess dress."

How fortunate that I had just purchased such an outfit and had no idea when, if ever, I would be able to wear it.

I was told to promptly present myself to the porters' lodge at her school this evening at 5 p.m., where I was to meet the young lady and ask her out. Her *duenna* would supervise it so be on my best behavior."

"As My Lady wills it."

What is going on?

"Rick, you know I have a serious boyfriend."

"I know, you just bring out. Well, you bring out something in me."

"Five o'clock, don't be late; a suit would be appropriate."

"Yes, My..., sure thing, Iris."

"That's better."

Hmm, Spanish girl with a *duenna*. No, it couldn't be.

I had to rush home after my last lecture and change clothes, but I made it on time. I checked in at the porters' lodge, and my name was on the expected visitor's list, so I was escorted to a sitting room.

It was.

There sat the girl and her *duenna*, the one who snubbed me and then made me miss my flight to London. The *duenna*, not the girl, who had been shy and reserved during the whole event.

Iris was there and performed the introduction. Elena, may I present Sir Richard Jackson, Knight of the Garter; Richard, may I introduce the Contessa María Isabel Dominica de Silos de Borbón y de Grecia.

Not certain what to say, I gave a simple nod and said, "It is nice to see you again. I trust you have recovered from your trip here."

Since that trip was last summer, I think she probably had.

She gave a demure smile and told me she had.

In the meantime, I had an eye on the gorgon. I was waiting to be turned to stone.

She did give me a steely-eyed look and then asked me a question.

"I understand that in America, you are an actor.

"Yes, ma'am."

"That explains your dress and appearance when we first met. You were in practice for a role, no?"

My thought was no, I had just worked as a deckhand on an ocean freighter for the prior months.

My words were, "You see things."

We talked for a few minutes, mostly establishing that I was fit company for a Spanish Duchess. Halfway through the conversation, I switched to Spanish as soon as the *duenna*, said in Spanish, "He will do."

I thought she was going to have a heart attack. I didn't wish it on her, but....

We talked through the details of the dance at St Anne's. It was a sort of coming out, homecoming thing, but I wasn't certain what they were coming home to or even from, for that matter.

All that was important was that I pick up the young lady here at 7 p.m. sharp on Friday with a corsage to go with a red dress. My RAF formal mess dress would be acceptable.

I had to rush from there to my Tuesday meeting with Flight Lieutenant Smyth. He had wanted me to bring my uniforms with me so he could make certain I had all the correct pieces. When I arrived without them, he questioned me as to why not.

I informed him they wouldn't all fit in the car. He had a hard time accepting that. I offered to drive him over to my house and show him. I think he suspected that I hadn't bought anything.

His first surprise was when we pulled up to the front door of The Meadows. He had no idea that my family had a place like this in England. The next surprise was when Mr. Hamilton answered the door and told me that one of the spare bedrooms had been converted into a closet for me.

He led us to the room. My clothes from the US had arrived along with all my uniforms, so there were my civilian formal clothes and my RAF uniforms, a ton of them.

The lieutenant looked them over and told me he had never seen a complete set of RAF uniforms before. I even had various outdoor coats. On the way out, I had the pleasure of introducing Flight Lieutenant Smyth to Viscountess Jackson. Mum handled the event coolly. I normally didn't try to put on the dog, but the lieutenant's previous mistrust had gained him a little.

Thursday, I met the guys at the Dog and Crown. Early on, I told them about my aircraft, so the next thing you know, we made a trip to the hangar to show off my acquisitions. They waxed enthusiastic about the possibilities. We could do Paris on some Sunday for brunch, Munich for a beer, and Pamplona to run with the bulls in July.

That all sounded good to me, as I had those types of thoughts. I'm not certain about the bull run. I'm not that fast of a runner.

We came up with a tentative plan to fly to Paris for brunch the first Sunday after I had my RAF papers and official permission to fly.

The paper part came on Saturday in the form of orders to report to RAF Barkston Heath for a check ride on my Cessna 310. The tail number for the Queen's Messenger Service was specified the following Sunday at ten hundred hours.

I loved it. I had to fly to them so I could take a flying test to prove I could fly the aircraft. I couldn't wait to tell Mum and Dad; they both had their share of stories about absurdities that could occur in the military. I now had my own.

Friday was the day of the dance, so I cut my last lecture of the day to go home to get ready. Mr. Hamilton insisted on helping with my mess dress. I won't be a hypocrite; I needed his help.

He seemed to know his way around the uniform quite well. I asked about that, and he replied that he had some experience from the war. What could he have done in the war that would have made him familiar with the formal RAF dress? It wasn't my place to ask. I would bring it up with Mum and see if she could dig it out of him. She was good at the inquisitor role.

The only badge I had on my uniform, other than the service buttons, was a silver greyhound. I was hoping to get a set of wings soon. Mr. Hamilton showed me how to quickly turn the sword and its scabbard so I could ride in the backseat of Mum's Bentley. Yes, she had bought a Bentley.

There was a man in the local village who drove for her. It was a good thing as she had already collected two speeding tickets. He was my driver for the evening. The sword couldn't fit into the Aston Martin. Besides, this was a formal dance, so I had to have a formal car.

Mum had been kind enough to take care of the flowers. She insisted as she pictured me picking a bouquet of dandelions. I told her not to be silly; the yellow would never go with the red dress, but I would keep the thought in mind for future events.

Mum and Grandmum saw me off with cameras clicking. I admit I must have been a sight. I had worn many movie costumes, but I must say this was the grandest of them all. I told Mum she should send copies to Susan Wallace for the publicity value. She told me she already had thought of that.

The Duchess María Isabel Dominica de Silos de Borbón y de Grecia must have had someone on the lookout for me because as soon as I was escorted from the porters' lodge, she made an appearance.

We went through the formal greetings in front of her *duenna*. The room had grown quite full as we did this. I think every girl in the hall was taking a look at us. The duchess, who never went anywhere, was making her first trip a grand one.

To my dismay, the *duenna* (I wondered if she had a name, or it was just a title) was going to the dance with us. Not that I thought anything could or would happen, but still.

In the backseat of the car, it quickly became Rick, Maria, and Aunt Inez!

The dance itself was a mixture of high society put-on and high school prom. In other words, the girls wore designer dresses but acted like any other high school group I had known. We sat with Iris and her boyfriend David, who was okay. The girls gossiped about all the others there. Inez the Gorgon (so nice to have a name for the face) kept a beady eye on me all night as though she expected me to try something with her charge.

There were many young men in regimental mess dress present. There was even a hoity-toity lifeguard. I was the only representative of the RAF. Those in uniform would get close enough to see the silver greyhound on my breast, but no one asked about it. You could tell some were puzzled.

The ride home was quiet. Maria asked if there were other events, would I please escort her? There were so few that she would be allowed to attend. Of course, I had to tell her it would be my pleasure. The real fact of the matter, there was no chemistry between me and Maria at all. She was nice, but I had no desire to get to know her better. And that ended the ball.

Chapter 30

Saturday was a nasty day with wet cold rain. Not enough to prevent flying, but it wouldn't be an enjoyable experience. Face it, as a California flier, I hadn't much training in bad weather. I was up early and did my short version of my exercises.

I liked the exercise room off the garage. The house had a portico in the back, so you didn't have to cross over in the rain. Now, if the wind were blowing the rain sidewise, you could get soaked. Of course, if it were raining that heavily, I would think twice about going out.

I drove over to the hangar. I did get a little wet opening the hangar door. I had read about an electric door opener in *Popular Mechanics*, so maybe I should look into getting one. Of course, the doors on the hangar were side sliding or man doors.

Or maybe I should learn to use my umbrella.

Anyway, I went in through a man door and slid the larger doors open so I could get my car in and an aircraft out.

I checked out the Greyhound Cessna to a fare thee well. I made certain that all liquids were present and no water was in the fuel tank. I had filled it after its last use so there wouldn't be much room for water to condense in the tank.

I made certain all safety devices were current, like charges on fire extinguishers. They were all done at the factory, but I wanted no surprises. All checklists and logs were present. My flight log was current. I was pleased to see I had over five hundred hours in this type of aircraft and approached a thousand hours altogether.

The literature said I had just passed the danger zone of new pilots having enough experience to be overconfident and getting themselves in trouble. Mr. McGarry told me that was a load of bull, that it took more than three thousand hours to get your head out of your—well you get it.

I finally had to acknowledge that I was as ready as I was going to be. I went over to the flight office and filed my flight plan to Barkston Heath. It was only 105 miles north by northeast of Oxford, so it was an easy half-hour flight. By delaying as much as I had, the weather had abated, so it wasn't a bad trip. A little bumpy, but I could handle that.

I used very proper flight procedures when announcing my arrival at the Barkston Heath RAF air station, making certain they knew it was a Queen's Messenger Service aircraft. It wouldn't do to get chased away by jets or even forced down. I managed that without embarrassing myself.

I parked on the apron in front of the flight center. Two crewmen rushed out and tied the aircraft down. I could get used to that service. I was wearing an RAF work uniform. I left the greyhound pin off as I didn't know if it would be allowed.

I was welcomed at the doorway by a gentleman in flight clothes. He introduced himself as Flight Instructor Ed Tracey. His rank was squadron leader, so I presented him with my first official salute as a member of the RAF.

I told him that, and he called an airman over and told him to salute me. He did, and now I owed the airman a pound as that was the first salute I had taken. It was a nice tradition.

Squadron Leader Tracey told me to call him Ed, as it was too cumbersome to go with the rank and name on this type of mission.

I replied, "Yes, sir."

"Good answer."

We went to the flight operations area, got a weather briefing, and generated a flight plan and local pilot examination. The squadron leader asked me how this all had come about. I told him that I was a Queen's Messenger.

He knew all about that, as my saving the Queen was big news. He laughed when I explained how I was the only Messenger with a license, but they had to second me to the RAF so I could carry passengers. I thought he was going to laugh himself silly when I told him how I ended up buying three Cessnas.

"Rick, this story will get me free beer for a month at the club."

He then turned serious, and we went out to the aircraft. I went through the preflight checks thoroughly. Everything checked out, so we got into the plane. The squadron leader told me to take off. I went through the standard radio communication with the tower to start taxiing. As we took off, I mentioned that I could feel the wet runway and that I had better remember it would take a longer run out when landing. I only said that so he knew what was going through my mind.

One thing I learned was that when one was being observed, the observer had no way of knowing what was going through your mind, so it didn't hurt to talk, even if you only talked to a wall. They would know what was going through your mind. It helped in situations where you decided not to do something.

As I had noticed on the way up to Barkston Heath, the plane's performance was a little slow as the rain disturbed the airflow over the wings. It wasn't anywhere near enough to cause concern, but I mentioned it, so he knew I was aware.

It was pretty decent flying once we were above the low cloud cover. I was put through all the same paces as I had been when I did my check ride back in the States for both visual and instrument flying. He had brought a hood for the front windscreen. I think they used the same manual for their tests.

I'm proud to say everything went smoothly, and the squadron leader never once looked like he wanted to grab the controls. After he had given me the standard verbal quiz, he asked where I learned to fly.

I told him about the aviation school in LA but that my first instruction was from Mr. Bill McGarry.

"Did he teach you how to strafe an airfield?"

"Yes, sir, both a long low approach and a diving one."

"He is one of the more famous pilots in the world. I read about his teaching methods, and they sound fun but not very useful."

I was quick to correct him. I related how I used the diving approach to rescue people trapped in a brush fire in California. That started another round of questions about how the plane handled with the firestorm around it, and was I bloody crazy?

I told him school was out on the crazy part, but the plane handled well. The trick was to fly over the wall of fire with its updraft while taking off.

"This story will be worth another month of beers. I may keep you around for a while."

He then had me return to the field, where I managed to land without bouncing it more than once. He didn't seem perturbed with that. The wind had kicked up, and a crosswind had started, so I felt like I was landing sideways.

Back inside the flight center, he signed off on my logbook as having passed both visual and instrument requirements. He then took me to the base wing commander's office, where, with a photographer present, I was given my wings.

My grin would have done in a chuckle lion.

We shook hands all around and went to the Officer's Club for lunch. The club was busy on this rainy day, and a lot of people came up to congratulate me. I had fame in certain circles. I was proud to be well known by this group of professional airmen.

As always, I had publicity photographs in my Jepsen case, so I had put a stack in my jacket pocket. I had enough to go around, but it was close. The wing commander was taken aback at first but then realized that it was a way of life for a Hollywood actor.

On the whole, he must have thought I was a strange bird. He was too polite to say so, but from some of his questions, you could see he didn't know what to make of me. He did tell me he had met Viscountess Jackson during the war and could see where I had come from.

As I was taking my leave, he came up with a statement out of the blue. Pass the word to your superior at the Messengers that if they want you to start jet training after your term at Oxford ends, they have to get the request in soon. The summer class will fill up quickly. People like to fly in the sunshine.

I could relate to the sunshine comment. I also made a note to call Mr. Norman to see if he would nominate me for the training. I have had it on my mind for some time now, but if I could get the RAF to pay for it, that would be great. Also, they would have better toys to play with. I'm into better toys.

The flight home went like a dream. I took a leaf out of my driving on the wrong side of the road practice and talked myself through it. If there was ever a time that I could let my mind wander, this was it. I felt like I was flying without the airplane. I had a real set of pilot's wings!

Mr. Hamilton met me at the door. I don't know how he knew when I was arriving, but he was always there. He quickly congratulated me on my wings.

Mum and Grandmum were in a sitting room watching TV and knitting. They both were quick to give me a hug and congratulations. It was great to be around people who were happy for me. Dad was usually at home at this time, so I called and let him know. He also gave his congratulations.

I didn't mention the jet training to either parent. It wasn't a done deal, and of course, it was better if I was told by the Messenger service that I was scheduled for the training. It was always easier to ask for forgiveness than permission.

We talked for a while. Mum told me she had a request for me. Now that Grandmum was all settled, she was heading back to the

States. Could I fly her to London Heathrow next Wednesday? Of course, I could.

Sunday, I was on the practice green at the golf course when the Oxford coach showed up with his players. I noticed one guy who hung back. I was sure he was the one who had made the comments about how good they were, and I shouldn't waste my time by trying out for the club.

I didn't hold it against him, so I just introduced myself and pretended I had never seen him before. He played it the same way. No sense in having bad blood where it isn't needed.

They asked if I was going to play. I told them I hadn't planned on it. They finally talked me into playing against their coach. It was done nicely. My only problem was that I hadn't even walked the course. Surprisingly, the guy who had talked down to me volunteered to caddie for me.

The rest of them were going to follow as a gallery. Unlike the American courses with foursomes, this course only allowed twosomes, with an occasional threesome with special permission.

I must say I was given good advice on every shot. The golf gods smiled on me that day, and I avoided the obvious problems, well, except that bunker protecting the green on the 12th hole. That made me bogey. Other than that, it was a fine round, ending up one under par.

I think the gallery was suitably impressed. The coach asked me if I would reconsider joining the team so they could use me at Cambridge. From the supportive comments, I realized that one of them would gladly surrender their position on the team just to beat Cambridge.

I declined their offer and wished them luck. I joined them for a late lunch in the clubhouse. That gave me a chance to mention that I had received my RAF pilot's wings the day before. As they say, it's not bragging if you have done it.

That opened the floodgates. The guys started asking questions about my career and any other honors I had received. After a while, I realized it might not be bragging, but it can become embarrassing. I finally pled another commitment and tried to flee. I say tried to flee because I had forgotten one small detail. My golf clubs wouldn't fit in my Aston Martin. The Oxford coach was kind enough to set me up with a team locker. He may have been planning for next year.

I had no sooner walked into the house, somehow evading the ever-present Mr. Hamilton, than Mum told me I was to return Mr. Norman's call. When I called him, I received my first assignment. I was to fly a gentleman from London to Paris tomorrow.

It meant I would have to skip another lecture series. They didn't take attendance, so that wouldn't be a problem. I had taken to using each lecture period by following the notes and the lecture or just going over the notes if the lecture was indecipherable, like the Chinese gentleman's.

I would have to make up the study time for those missed lectures, as long as it didn't mess up my pub night. It was the highlight of my week. My circle of acquaintances there had widened. I came to know most of them by playing darts against other tables.

Not that I was getting better, but I had found out that not all Englishmen were natural-born dart players, so I wasn't considered too much of a handicap, just a minor one. As I would stop to talk to the person I had met, I would be introduced around the table.

It was an ever-changing crowd, mostly from Trinity. I didn't become close friends with any, but it was nice when someone would greet you when going to class.

Anyway, I had my first assignment. While on the phone with Mr. Norman, I told him about the opportunity to take training to fly jets.

"Are you ready to buy one?"

"If you get me into the class, I will research the market and see what can be done."

"I will make a few phone calls and let you know."

I hadn't thought that far ahead, and that raised another issue. Most jets required a crew. How would that be handled?

Chapter 31

On Monday, I flew to London Heathrow. Waiting there was Mr. Norman with a gentleman I had never met before. As I started to introduce myself, Mr. Norman told me it wasn't necessary, Mr. Smith wouldn't be talking on the flight, and the only thing I needed to know was his last name for the flight manifest.

It is less than 300 miles from London to Paris, so it was only about two hours from gate to gate. During that time, I gave some instructions to my passenger, like buckle up, but that was it. I had no idea why he was going to Paris. What I thought most telling was that he didn't have a Queen's Messenger tie, pin, or satchel.

After landing, taxiing to the private passenger area, and exiting, he gave me a curt "Thank you."

I nodded my head in return. With my "Buckle up" and his "Thank you," the honors were even. I wasn't giving him another word. While my craft was being refueled, I went over to flight operations to ensure there were no weather changes and to file my return flight plan.

There was a commotion at the window, looking out at the runway. I wandered over to check it out. A passenger jet aircraft I was unfamiliar with had just landed and was taxiing to a large hangar. One of the pilots there told me it was a Tupolev Tu-114, a Soviet Union passenger jet. Chairman Khrushchev was visiting President De Gaulle.

I wondered if my recent passenger had anything to do with that.

After the Tu-114 was in the hangar, we were allowed to go out to our planes and get in the queue to take off. I was something like the fifteenth plane in line and had to wait for half an hour. I was really glad I hadn't had that Coke I had thought about.

I flew right back to Oxford and then called Mr. Norman to let him know that the flight went as planned. I also mentioned seeing Khrushchev's plane come in. His only comment on that was, "Interesting."

I suspect he was as in the dark about my passenger as I was. Well, our job is to deliver the mail, not read it.

After that, I returned to school. Well, I got as far as my comfy garage and spent the afternoon between lectures catching up or trying to keep ahead of what I had missed. This was not as easy as high school. The information dump was about twice as much, twice as fast.

I told Mum about my flight to Paris and what I had observed. She wanted to know what my passenger had said, so I related our conversations one hundred percent verbatim. She asked me for a physical description, which I gave: medium height, brown hair and eyes, in general, nondescript. She got a small smile and changed the subject.

I spent the rest of the week getting ready for mock examinations. These were designed to help the student prepare to sit exams by sharing advice on revision, time management, and regulations whilst enabling one to become familiar with the exam venues. That was the official description. They were telling us how to prepare for and take the test.

The final exams were not specifically by subject but rather by degree, except at the mock test stage, where each subject had an exam. What blew my mind was the fact these weren't required. Oxford's version of college was that you could miss every class and laboratory, sit for the final exam, and if you passed, you received your degree. Bellefontaine High, it wasn't.

Oxford had to have some sort of policy about being admitted as a student paying for the full courses, or they wouldn't make any money. It was just after you paid your way in, they didn't care how you prepared for the test. They had offerings, but if you could pass without them, that was fine.

I didn't understand all their arcane rules, and I hadn't investigated them at all. Maybe I was completely wrong about how it all worked. Since it didn't affect my plans, I wasn't going to worry about it.

Thursday night was spent celebrating my new wings and planning a return trip to Paris. They were interested in hearing about Khrushchev's visit. I only told them I had to deliver an official package. It didn't seem wise to say more.

I also told them that I had my mock exams coming up, and I wanted to have a fair shot to see how I stood, so we would have to put our Paris flight back a bit. My celebration didn't extend to drinking any alcohol. I had previously told the guys that it just didn't agree with me, so I wasn't going to touch it.

They could drink all they wanted, and it wouldn't bother me just as long as I didn't have to join them. I put away the Cokes like there was no tomorrow. Was I turning into a lush for caffeine? I guess we all have our vices.

The next couple of days were a whirl; I had classes to attend, and on Friday, I had that series of mock exams. I had taken enough exams in my time to know that I did okay. These weren't going to be all A's, but I felt like I had passed everything, so if I kept on this course of action, I would be able to pass the true exam for my degree. Of course, that would be some years in the future, so I would have to spend a tremendous amount of time revising.

I even managed to go through the suggested reading books I ordered for The Meadows. I wasn't way ahead of the course, but I was keeping even with everything. Considering all, I thought I was doing okay. I also decided to hire a tutor for every course I took. It worked so well with calculus it was a no-brainer.

Saturday and Sunday were down days for me. I had just completed a whirlwind of a week and needed to recharge. I read, exercised, and took naps. By Monday, when I got up, I was ready for another week. I hoped it wasn't like the last seven days.

Fortunately, it wasn't. I was able to attend every lecture and felt like I was getting my studies back in line. On Friday, I was asked by Mr. Norman to make a flight from London to Brussels on Saturday, this time to deliver a package. The trip was uneventful.

On the way back across the channel, I was sightseeing on one of the busiest shipping lanes in the world. Because I was rubbernecking, I saw a small boat in distress. I knew it was in distress because it was upside down. I reported my sighting to the ATC. British ATC seemed more fragmented than the US. I had read in an aviation magazine studies were being performed to make it more like the US model.

People were clinging to the upside-down hull.

ATC told me they would notify the Coast Guard. My fuel state was excellent, so they asked me to loiter as long as possible to make it easy for them to find. I was just beginning to think I would have to leave when a Coast Guard cutter hove into sight. It seemed to grow out of the ocean as it came around the curve of the earth, but I loved the word hove.

I flew towards the ship, waggling my wings. My radio came on with a message from the ship. They asked me to fly directly back to the distressed vessel so they could get a direct bearing.

As I came close enough to the ship for them to get a good look at my aircraft, I was asked, "When did the Queens Messenger Service start flying their aircraft?"

"This is the only one. It has been in service about three weeks now."

"This is Captain Edwards of Her Majesty's Coast Guard ship *Hotspur*. To whom am I speaking?"

"This is Sir Richard Jackson of the Queen's Messengers Service, seconded to the RAF as a flight officer."

I might as well get all my cards on the table at once.

"Well, Sir Richard, good job here today. How is your fuel status?"

"On the low side, not bingo but getting close."

"How far are we from the ship?"

"About three miles, you should be able to see it soon; I will start circling it until I have to leave."

It was only another ten minutes and they told me they had spotted the vessel and that I was free to continue. I did but didn't try to make it to Oxford as my fuel was getting low. I landed at Dover and refueled before returning home.

I didn't give the events of the day another thought until the phone rang at The Meadows. It was a reporter wanting to know how I felt about rescuing Brigitte Bardot. My reply was it was the crew of Her Majesty's Coast Guard cutter *Hotspur* who had rescued her. I had only pointed out the sailboat to them.

I hadn't even known it was a sailboat until the reporter told me. As far as Brigitte Bardot, I was glad she and others were rescued, but I was so high up that I could barely tell there were people there, much less their sex.

That didn't stop the headlines in the scandal sheets, "Ricky saves Brigitte," was the headline theme. I wonder when she will be having my baby.

Once it started, the phone kept ringing. Mr. Hamilton kept answering it politely with, "There is no comment at this time."

Grandmum finally pushed him aside and answered the phone.

"The Meadows. Ricky and Brigitte are too busy to come to the phone right now."

Then she would hang up. I now know where Mary's telephone answering technique came from. She repeated this more than a dozen times, and they all went away. I guess they had what they needed for a headline.

The next morning, I called Mr. Norman and reported that I had made the delivery to Brussels. He told me he figured that out since I had time to stop and pick up Brigitte Bardot. Ouch.

I related the events, and he laughed saying he thought it would be something like that. I told him what Grandmum had said to the reporters. He got a kick out of that. I then asked if he had anything else coming up. He didn't but the nature of the beast never gave much warning.

He had the grace to bring up that he realized that I had been made a Queen's Messenger as a reward and that they had never intended to put me to work. However, the convenience of having an airplane available was too good to pass up. He would have to look into getting one put into their budget next year.

I reminded him that the cost of the aircraft over some time was not the major share of the cost. It was maintenance, fuel, facility, and aircrew that ran up the costs.

He told me he understood and maybe he would leave things as they were. The RAF was providing aircraft hangar space and maintenance. I was flying for free using my airplane and fuel.

When he put it that way, I informed him I would have my accountants come up with a cost package to submit for payment. He quit laughing at that point.

I had to do some research at the university's main library, the Bodleian Library. Before they would let me go to the study area, I had to swear an oath:

"I hereby undertake not to remove from the Library, nor to mark, deface, or injure in any way, any volume, document or other object belonging to it or in its custody; not to bring into the Library, or kindle therein, any fire or flame, and not to smoke in the Library; and I promise to obey all rules of the Library."

I now see why I had to swear that I wouldn't bring a lighted candle into the library at The Meadows.

It worked like the Library of Congress in that you would request a book, and it would be brought to you. When done with the tome, you left it on a cart for restacking. Maybe the Library of Congress got this from the Bodleian as it was several hundred years older. Not having been in the Library of Congress, I didn't know if you could bring a lighted candle.

I swear the place even smelled old, probably books slowly rotting over the centuries. The main hall was at least three stories tall and lined with bookcases; above that, there were rows of windows. The place was well-lit with lamps on all the tables. There were two rows of worktables going the length of the hall. I imagined several hundred people could work in the main room at one time.

Large oil paintings were hanging on the walls above the bookshelves. I didn't recognize any of them. They must be famous old librarians. How does one get to be a famous librarian? I bet they were the ones who could afford to have their picture painted, using late fines I figured. Though you couldn't check books out, so it must be something else.

That thought made me laugh out loud. It was brief, but now I can add being shushed at a world-famous library to my list of things that made me a bad boy. I had to let Susan Wallace know. I'm sure she would let all the tabloids know.

I was hunting for a report by a geologist named Robert Rich Sharp, who in 1915 found uranium deposits in the Belgian Congo, which had proved to be the richest ever found. I had the bright idea from a side comment made by one of the dons that there might be others like it in the world. I wanted to know what geological features defined this motherlode and see what might match it in the known world.

I say the known world; it might lie on the ground under the Antarctica icecap, and we would never know. Right now, the United States had a lock on the minerals from this mine, but it would have to play out someday. I'm certain other people are working harder at this than I am, but that was the glory of an Oxford education. As they said, you could follow your nose. It wasn't a regimented regime like most schools.

I would have to limit these side diversions from my studies, but they were fun.

Chapter 32

When I got home from school the following Monday, there was a phone message from France. It was Brigitte Bardot's publicity agent. I returned the call, very curious about it. In a very professional manner, he explained that they wanted to use the boat incident for publicity.

Unlike others who wanted to use me in their efforts, he understood exactly where I would be coming from. After a brief discussion, I gave him Susan Wallace's number. He could call her and work out the details. My fee would be considered payment in kind. In other words, I would get free publicity from the event.

The best part is that I would get to meet Brigitte Bardot. Heck, if he had asked, I probably would have paid them.

I called Mr. Norman and told him about my publicity opportunity. My question was whether he wanted the Queen's Messenger Plane in the pictures or if I should take one of the others.

"Take the Greyhound, Rick."

That is how the plane got its name from that day forward. I even had painted in small letters on the door, Sir Richard Jackson, pilot.

Anyway, Mr. Norman thought it would look good for the Messenger Service to be recognized in that manner.

We got a call from Mum in the evening. She told me that Jane Wyman had a little girl, Emily, all in good health. She also gave me the baby's length and weight. That went in one ear and out the other. It must be a woman thing, like fishermen on how much it weighed or what size. The only difference was the fisherman could throw it back.

I was smart enough not to share that opinion. She told me my gift to them was a one-year diaper service. Who knew there was such a thing? I thanked her for taking care of that. I liked Dick and Jane and wished them the best. They certainly looked out for me when I first moved to California.

I was waylaid coming out of my garage on my way to class the following day. Iris Butler was waiting for me. She had a message from the duchess. The duchess's family had investigated my background and decided I would be a good match for her due to my title and wealth.

She wanted no part of it. There was a young man back in Spain for whom she had set her cap. I was to be careful around her as her *duenna* was not above leaving her alone and then claiming something happened and we had to marry.

Gulp.

I thanked Iris for the message and went to class. I know darn well the don delivered a lecture, but when I left the room, I had no idea what was said. I spent the whole time imagining myself trying to run from the *duenna*, but I couldn't run faster than her. She was holding her long skirt up and gaining on me.

Would I have to drop out of school and move?

After school, I had a phone call from Susan. She had talked to Bardot's people, and all had agreed that it would be positive publicity for both of us, so there would be a photo shoot on Saturday at Orly airport near Paris. I was to fly in, bringing changes of clothes varying from formal to informal. Susan suggested I take my steamer trunk along.

The steamer trunk was a large metal trunk left over from the heyday of steamships. It contained a selection of costumes I had worn in my movies. There was Western, Robin Hood, and Frontiersman, along with associated props.

I also planned to take Oxford informal shirts, an Oxford sports coat, a suit, morning clothes, and my RAF uniforms, both daily and mess dress. It's a shame I didn't have my Boy Scout uniform or Civil War uniform, or I would have taken those.

I had no idea what they wanted to see me in, so I intended to bring a little of everything. Ostensibly, Miss Bardot was thanking me for my part in her rescue. The reality was a publicity shoot. A plain thank you would take half an hour, maybe. This was planned for the better part of the day.

They wanted to do it at the airport to show the airplane.

It took me an entire evening with Mr. Hamilton's help packing everything.

On Thursday night, I met the guys at the Dog and Crown. None of them had read the small article in the *Times* about a sailboat tipping over and the crew and passengers needing rescue. When I asked if they knew anything about it, they knew nothing about it.

When asked why I brought that up, I told them I just thought it would be scary as all get out and was interested in the story. Tom changed the subject and fell right into my trap.

"Rick, you have promised us an overnight trip to Paris. When can we go?"

"How about this Saturday? I have some stuff to deliver."

The gang, Steve, Bill, and Tom were all for it. We agreed to meet at the airport at 7 a.m. on Saturday.

Using the Bentley, I hauled all my clothes in garment bags and the steamer trunk and loaded the airplane on Friday night.

The guys were all on time Saturday morning. I had gotten there a little early, performed the walk around, and had the plane fueled.

The flight was easy. None of the guys had flown in a light plane before, so they followed all the sights below. Navigation was easy to get out of England; all I had to do was follow the Thames. Once over the channel, I had to look at the compass.

Other than all the rubbernecking going on, it was an uneventful flight. At Orly, when I identified the flight as Queen's Messenger 001, the tower gave me instructions to follow after landing. I was to taxi to a hangar on the edge of the field.

The doors of the hangar were open, and I taxied right up and into it. There was a crowd of people waiting. I had idled the engines way down so the prop wash didn't blow the people or all their equipment away.

Of course, by this time, the guys wanted to know what was going on. Tom started sputtering as he looked out the window.

"That's Brigitte Bardot."

"Oh good, we are in the right spot."

I had been hunting for the right phrase to use for days, and that was the best I could come up with.

I shut down the engines, and we piled out. Miss Bardot's publicity agent introduced me to Miss Bardot. She came up and hugged me and laid a kiss on me that curled my toes.

"Thank you. We could have died out there."

"You're welcome. I'm glad I could be of service."

I was speaking like an idiot!

After that, things settled down. I had a chance to explain to the guys what was going on. They were as tongue-tied as I was when introduced to them. We must have come off like a right bunch of prats.

When asked if I had brought changes of clothes as requested, I asked for the plane to be unloaded. A clothes bar on wheels was brought over, and my wardrobe hung up. They had survived the trip thanks to Mr. Hamilton's packing.

When I opened the steamer trunk and revealed the costumes, I thought the photographer was going to have a cow. He had been in rapture about having a Queen's Messenger plane as a backdrop. Now, he was in heaven. Maybe I overpacked.

They had set up a refreshment table with a continental breakfast and plenty of coffee, so Miss Bardot and I exchanged stories while things were being set up. I must say she looked fantastic, considering she'd had a child this past January. She was ten years older than me and about a hundred years more world-weary.

Despite that, we had a pleasant conversation. She was even sexier in person than on the screen.

The guys had been set up with a table and chairs to view the proceedings. It turned out to be like any other day on the set: makeup and costume, pose for the cameras, change, redo makeup, and repeat.

I had the college look, casual and formal, business attire, military work, and formal, then Cowboy and Robin Hood. It was only really interesting when they wanted me in the frontiersman outfit with my long rifle and tomahawk.

I had been going along with the makeup people all day. For this layout, I had them do me dark and evil as in my Lewis Wetzel-Deathwind character from *Over the Ohio*.

That got their attention on the set. I had to explain this was a look from my upcoming movie. Miss Bardot loved it. At least, from the way she clung to me in the photographs, I think she loved the look.

It took us up to dinner time to finish the shoot. Lunch had been catered, but we were getting hungry again.

Brigitte invited us to dinner at one of her favorite restaurants, Le-Train-Bleu. We accepted immediately. Fortunately, the guys had traveled in their Oxford sports coats with the Oxford University emblem, so we would be admitted.

The Le-Train-Bleu was built as part of a train station in 1901. It overlooked the tracks. Inside, it was the grandest building that I had ever been in as far as decoration went. It was ornate beyond belief. The food was wonderful. I now knew what escargot tasted like, and I loved them. The other guys, not so much.

It was a pleasant meal with quiet conversation. No one approached Miss Bardot until we left, and then there was a line of people waiting. She graciously signed autographs for a few minutes, and we moved on.

The Bardot party dropped us off at our hotel, The Clement. It was a small place, but the travel agent in Oxford assured me it was excellent. The only problem was they had put us on the top floor in the garret. The walls sloped, and I couldn't stand up straight in half the room. It was okay for one night, but I won't be back.

The next morning, we met for breakfast. I learned that the French do make the best croissants in the world and that espresso will wake you up. I had to stop later at the British Embassy and pick up a package to return to London. Since this was paying for the fuel for the trip, I was fine with it.

I wore my daily RAF uniform since I was going to the embassy as a Messenger. I had permission to wear my greyhound pin on my right breast to avoid confusing it with an award.

The guys all looked good in their Oxford sports coats. We had a ball going to the top of the Eiffel Tower, and then we took a bus tour of the city going through the Arc de Triomphe and then up to Montmartre to see the painting district. We even got to walk down Rue Morgue.

Along the way, we stopped at the British Embassy and picked up my package. It turned out to be a sealed envelope that fit nicely in my satchel.

The highlight of the day was an almost quick trip through the Louvre. I say almost because there was an event. We were in the line approaching the Mona Lisa. This was such a popular attraction you could only stand and look at it for a minute or less.

We were to be the next up when this man came charging through the line with something in his hand. He had just passed me when he raised his arm to throw the object at the painting.

I was in a position to grab his arm and, in doing so, overbalance him. He fell backward, and his container of what proved later to be battery acid spilled all over me. Thank goodness it didn't hit me in the face. It soaked my pants and shirt. From the way the fabric reacted, I knew I had a problem.

The museum guards wrestled the guy to the floor and kept him there until the gendarmes showed up. In the meantime, I had removed my shirt and undershirt. I have no modesty when I'm being eaten by acid.

One of the guards led me to a toilet, where he liberally soaked me in water. It was quick enough that I didn't receive any acid burns.

The gendarmes interviewed me. My passport didn't get soaked as it was in the small satchel I carried. Denny called it a man bag when he first saw it, but it was convenient for trips like this. Of course, the reporters showed up and got pictures of me without a shirt.

After that, we returned to the hotel where we had left our luggage in the luggage room while we were on our tour. There I put on a new shirt. The old one was yellowed and had holes eaten into it. I was lucky not to be burned by the acid.

The flight home was uneventful. The guys were bubbling over about the outing. They wanted to know when we could do it again. I told them I was up for it but couldn't promise Brigitte Bardot.

That was okay; they wanted Rome and Sophia Loren next.

I was very tired by the time we got home. Grandmum wanted to know how the trip and photo shoot went. I told her fine and that I would give her the details in the morning.

At breakfast, Grandmum had the *Times* folded open to a page with my shirtless picture.

"Your trip was fine? You are just as bad as your mum."

There was an accompanying article. I was described as a hero of France, saving the great artwork of the Mona Lisa and Brigitte Bardot. I'm not certain which one they thought was the great artwork.

I told her how events had unfolded. She sniffed and said, "That is like the French. They make a big deal out of the littlest things."

I don't think Grandmum is a fan of the French.

At school, a couple of the dons, who I didn't even think were aware I was in their class, recognized me and my recent heroics. That was embarrassing.

I just thought that was embarrassing. I received a call from Mr. Norman after school.

"Rick, saving the Mona Lisa means a great deal to the French. I received a phone call. They are awarding you the Legion of Honor in the rank of Chevalier. Since you were in uniform, it is an Award for Service. It is to be presented on behalf of France next Saturday by President Charles de Gaulle."

"Wow!"

I come up with the most brilliant words at times like this.

"It brings up another situation. The Minister of Defense does not like its officers to receive foreign awards without the British equivalent. So, you will receive the MBE, or Order of the British Empire. This is considered a knighthood in its own right."

"Double wow."

Well, what could I say? So now I was Sir Richard Jackson, KG, MBE, LOH. Some things in this world just don't make sense, but why try to fight it? I hadn't put my KG ribbon on my uniform as it would look very lonely. Now I had three of them. Soon, I would look like an American Boy Scout.

Chapter 33

Of course, the guys all picked up on the fact all my awards were knighthoods, so that made me:

> Sir, Sir, Sir Richard, the stuttering knight,
> He flew his airplane to a great height,
> He got so high he had a great fright,
> Sir, Sir, Sir Richard, the stuttering knight.

It only took them three pints apiece on a Thursday night to come up with that doggerel, this from people attending Oxford University.

Other than the creation of that masterpiece, it was a quiet week at school. More people seemed to recognize me as I went around the campus, but no one approached me or was a nuisance.

I was approached by a group from the Bullingdon Dining Club and asked to join. I heard enough about it that I wanted no part of it. Its reputation was terrible. It was considered a reflection of the worst in the British ruling class. When I declined, the snide comment was made that I probably couldn't afford it.

Later, I found out their club costume cost over three thousand pounds. Yes, I could afford it, but that was plain stupid.

I mentioned it to Mum on a phone call. She told me I had made the right call and saved her a trip to twist my ears. Ouch.

I spent most of my days either in the lecture halls listening and studying or with my tutors. I would attend the lecture and, while half-listening, read through the lecture notes. I would then immediately note anything I didn't understand and ask for clarification from my tutor.

This made my tutoring sessions very efficient as I set the learning pace. At first, the tutors wanted to plod through the materials at their rate. That would have driven me crazy. They all came in line as they realized that I was learning the material in depth as a student.

Well, all but calculus, in-depth was not the true description; learning enough to get by the skin of my teeth was more like it. Whenever I thought I had a handle on it, a new thought came up, and I was back to deer in the headlights. I spent at least twice as much time on it as anything else. Fortunately, Chuck Erich needed the money, or he would have run screaming by now.

My tutoring sessions mostly occurred in my garage loft. It was my private getaway and study area. It was snug in the damp English winter and convenient to the school. Tom, Steve, and Bill would join me at irregular times. It took strong words to make them understand that I was here to learn, not play. They came around.

I would also go to the driving range every other evening after school. I needed to keep loose for the US Open. I was looking forward to it as a real break from the school routine.

On the second Saturday after the infamous trip to Paris, I returned to receive my award. I first stopped in London to pick up Mr. Norman, who was there to represent the Queen's Messengers.

It was at the Élysée Palace, the residence and office of the President of France. Charles de Gaulle made the presentation. He kissed me on both cheeks. Yuck.

It was much better when Brigitte Bardot kissed me on the lips. It was just a kiss in passing, but oh my. Talk about bragging rights.

Pictures were taken, and a truly short speech of thanks was made by the president. The medal of the Legion of Honor Chevalier class was pinned to my uniform, and it was done. Several other presentations were made for fire and police rescues and even for military action in Algiers. Each was more heroic sounding than mine.

I did learn that the man trying to deface the Mona Lisa had recently been released from a mental institution, which appeared to be a big mistake. He wouldn't see the outside for a long time, if ever. As far as helping rescue Miss Bardot, not enough good could be said. The French took their art and women seriously.

From there, I flew us back to London. I was getting to be an old hand at flying the London-Paris route. Also, I was comfortable flying the Cessna. It was nice to know I had two engines when looking down at that cold water in the channel. There was never a hiccup, but still.

A limo took us from the airport to the palace. There, a similar ceremony was held with me receiving the Order of the British Empire from the Queen. She did not kiss me.

I had worn my RAF dress uniform as ordered, and it now had three medals that clanked when I walked. More like a clink, but they did jingle. I also had five sets of ribbons for each of the orders to be sewn on my working uniforms.

My Tuesday night introduction to the RAF continued at Lieutenant Smyth's. He was getting around a lot better and would soon be returning to active duty. He told me this would be our last session as I had the basic knowledge one would expect of a flight officer. I now knew enough to be dangerous!

I saw Iris Butler one morning. She told me that my Spanish problem was over. Maria had managed to get herself sent down. Girls were known to drink too much at school, but girls didn't drink too much and vomit all over the headmistress. I expressed disbelief that the prim and proper duchess would do such a thing.

Well, she did, and it was to a plan, according to Iris. Maria wanted to go home to her boyfriend so badly that she deliberately drank too much at a house party and then stuck her fingers down her throat and projectile vomited all over the headmistress.

I had to admire the audacity of the plan but not the execution.

Things settled down for the next several weeks. I had time on my hands in the evening as my daytime studying kept me ahead of the game. I took advantage of the time by exploring The Meadows.

Mr. Hamilton joined me. He had been hired to run the estate just before we bought it. A lot of it was a mystery to him also.

The first thing we did was explore the coach house. There were several old horse-drawn vehicles there. The most interesting were an open landau as they used on tours in New York City and what I thought of as a princess carriage. It was a full-scale replica of the Queen's state coach. Interestingly, the landau and the state coach had a little plaque, "Body by Fisher".

Both coaches were in good enough condition that they would be worth saving. I wondered who I could talk to at the palace. They had to have someone knowledgeable about such things. I would ask Mr. Norman the next time I talked to him.

The house wasn't old enough that it would have a priest hole, and it was too far inland for a smuggler's hidden room, but I had hope of an interesting find. There was an interesting find, and it was in a place I would have never thought of. The books by the yard that had been in the library were now in the coach house waiting to be disposed of.

I idly picked one up, *Memories of an Essex Minister*, and it opened to a page with an envelope. What stood out immediately was the octagon-shaped stamp. I had never seen one like that before.

I showed it to Mr. Hamilton, who turned pale, and his hands shook as he took the envelope for a closer look.

"Sir Richard, this appears to be a British Guiana 1c magenta stamp. Until now, it was thought that only one existed in the world. That is in the royal collection."

He handed it back to me. I could tell there was a letter inside the envelope, but it appeared that the envelope had never been opened. We went to the house and, using a knife-sharp letter opener, cut it open without coming near the stamp.

There was a folded letter inside. When I opened it, a stamp fell out. It was the same stamp as on the envelope, but it had never been used. It looked like the day it had come from the post office. The stamp had fallen to the table, so I left it until I could get gloves. There was no way I was going to touch it. If it was authentic, there was no way to value it.

The letter was from a British Embassy employee to his stamp collector nephew. The letter was dated 1856. How it had arrived at its current location would probably never be known.

After gathering the envelope, stamp, and letter in a folder using white cotton gloves loaned to me by Mr. Hamilton, I put them in the small safe in the estate office. It would take a safecracker to break it open, but a thief could just walk away with the safe and cut it open at their leisure.

I called Mum and Dad in the US since it was still daytime there. They thought it was amazing, and they recommended asking the Queen through Mr. Norman to have the two stamps authenticated.

That made sense to me. The next morning, after having woken up twice during the night and checking that the safe was still there, I called Mr. Norman. He was glad to hear from me as I was on his list to call about a flight to Oslo if I could cut classes the next day, which was Wednesday.

As I had been acclimated to the Oxford culture by my friends, I immediately jumped at a chance to cut school. That seemed to be the pastime of most students at Oxford.

When that was arranged, I told him I had two questions for him. Who would I talk to about having a State Coach refurbished, and who would I see about getting stamps authenticated?

He told me a man at the palace was in charge of the Queen's Coach, so he probably would know who to contact. As far as the stamps, if they were rare, the Head of the Philatelic Collection at the

British Museum would be the person as they were in charge of the Royal Collection.

He did ask me what the stamps were. He, like Mr. Hamilton, was a stamp collector from his reaction.

There was a very weak "Oh my" at the other end of the line.

He asked me if I could bring them with me tomorrow when I picked up the package for Oslo. Of course, I could.

I arrived at Heathrow around ten o'clock the next morning. Mr. Norman met me with a limo waiting on the tarmac in the visiting aircraft area. After shutting and tying down the aircraft, we went to the British Museum.

Two gentlemen, a Mr. Haes and a Mr. Van Noorden, were waiting to examine the stamps. We all donned white cotton gloves, and I opened the folder. Magnifying glasses, rulers, and a solution for watermark testing were employed. They had the one known stamp there as a comparison.

After half an hour of looking at the stamps and then referring to a list of Embassy employees of that time, they concluded the stamps were real. We agreed that it would be safest if I left them in their care. I was given a receipt. Photographs had been taken, and copies would be provided to me as soon as they were developed.

I couldn't help but wonder what had happened to the nephew to whom the stamps were sent. It was wonderful being in one of the world's largest museums and book collections. A simple search of the name and address led us to the young man, Samuel Thomas. He had lived a good life as a baker.

His obituary noted that he had been an avid stamp collector from childhood and that his collection was donated to the British Library at the time of his death. Further research on the donated items showed that he had many from British Guiana.

The museum people thought this gave an ironclad provenance for the two stamps. Mr. Haes wondered what I was going to do with the stamps. If they hadn't been set aside, they would have ended up in this collection. I took that as a very broad hint.

Continuing about the family, I learned there was only one child from his marriage. The family moved to America and opened a bakery in New York City. The poor, unfortunate son was killed in World War I, thus ending the family line.

I was returned to the airport and flew on to Oslo. I overnighted there because I didn't want to fly over the North Sea after dark. There are rocks in those clouds.

Back home, I called Mum and Dad and told them about the stamps and the fact they were potentially worth millions. Dad asked me if I wanted the cash. I dithered for a moment and realized I probably could never spend what I already had, much less what was coming in.

When I relayed that, he suggested I donate them to the British Museum on behalf of Jackson Enterprises. My company would have a hefty tax bill, and the donation could go a long way to offset it. That sounded good to me. I had pictured buying a stamp album and putting a hinge on the back of the mint stamp. Donating it sounded much saner.

I called Mr. Norman on Thursday morning and told him of my decision. He thought that was wonderful. I thought it would be a good deed that would go unnoticed.

It was not to be. In the Sunday edition of the *Times*, an article and pictures of the rare find appeared. They used the picture of me receiving the Legion of Honor from President De Gaulle. Knowing I would be chastised for not letting her know in advance, I called my publicity agent and told her the latest.

She laughed at me.

"When are you going to run for public office, Rick?"

"Now that is downright nasty. Take it back!"

"Okay, seriously though, you have all this wonderful publicity going to waste."

"What about *Over the Ohio?* Is it close to release yet?"

"Right now, it looks like a summer release in July."

"My school term ends at the last of June, so I will be back in the States. Maybe you could arrange a tour for me. You know I own most of that movie."

"Yes, I do. Sam Monroe reminds me every time I see him. He has forgiven you, but he will never forget.

Chapter 34

Dad let me know that construction had been completed on my garage workshop at Jackson House. I wanted a chance to see it and tinker around but wouldn't get home for some weeks. Even then, I didn't think I would have much time.

Mr. Hamilton and I did go through the rest of those books that had been destined for the tip. Over a thousand more, and we found nothing except some pressed flowers. Why or who had pressed them was long forgotten.

Linn's Stamp News wrote me a letter asking for an article on the finding of the stamps. I asked Mr. Hamilton if he would enjoy doing that as he was the stamp collector. He took on the job with great enthusiasm. He even knew all the technical terms to use in describing the find and its authentication. By this time, I had decided, with my parents' input, to donate them to the Royal Collection at the British Museum.

In the notes that would appear on its display, I made certain that Mr. Hamilton's name appeared as being present during the find. He chortled at that, saying it would give him bragging rights and a few pints at his stamp club. Here, I thought stamp collectors were a dry bunch.

The school term continued. During April, I only made two more flights for the Messenger service. I think the novelty of it had worn off, and now Mr. Norman was considering the expense of each trip.

I did have a call from the London Cessna representative. They had an immediate offer for a Cessna 310. Would I be interested in selling one of mine? Since the third plane had never been out of the hangar since it was delivered, it was an easy decision.

The price offered effectively offset the low purchase price of the other two planes. In effect, I had been given two aircraft for free. Well, until you count in the ground maintenance cost. Don't ever let anyone tell you it is cheap to own an aircraft. Whatever the purchase price is, double that for the upkeep. I suspect the new jet aircraft would be even higher.

That made me wonder about the Boeing 707 Mum and Dad had on order. It hadn't been talked about in a while. On our next call, I found out why. They had gotten into the Boeing build queue. Their place in line had just come up when an Arab prince offered to buy it.

They sold it to him and were now at the back of the line and wouldn't expect one until this time next year.

As Dad put it, "We've lived without one this long and can do without some more. If we can give up our place in line two more times, we will get the aircraft for less than half price."

I could see buying and selling aircraft could be an interesting but risky business. During my last call, I learned that my sister Mary now had her clothing line, and it was doing exceptionally well. The world had better watch out! Dad sent me a Feed the Puppies T-shirt, but I didn't have the nerve to wear it. Maybe I could find some young lady who would be interested.

Right now, there were no girls in my life, and that wasn't right. I understood hormones and all that, but really, I just wanted some female companionship, and maybe some cuddling and a few kisses, and maybe..., well, you get it.

The guys and I did a London outing one weekend. We stayed at my suite in the Plaza and went to several pubs that were known in Oxford circles as being filled with willing girls.

The result was a huge taxi bill and hangovers for the other guys. All I had was the taxi bill. I think I got the better of the deal.

The results of my mock exams came back. I had the equivalent of all A's and one B. The B was in Calculus, and I was prouder of that than any of the others. The grades did validate my study methods and time spent. Now, all I had to do was continue the process and keep revising the previous work until the end-of-term exams.

I was taking a light load as it was my first term. The more I thought about it, I decided to continue the practice. It wasn't as though I had to hurry through school to earn a living.

I went to Tom's home one weekend. He's from Liverpool. He lived in what I considered a normal house, with three beds and a bath. His parents reminded me of Ozzie and Harriet Nelson, both in how they looked and acted. They were plain nice. They made me feel at home immediately. I wish there were more people like them. I hope Ozzie and Harriet were as nice in real life.

Tom had to drag me to see his favorite band, The Beatles. They were okay. Tom knew John well enough that they joined us at a break. They asked Tom if he would be interested in investing in their band.

They had a chance to play in Germany but needed seed money to get started. Tom told them he didn't have the cash but then looked at me. No dummies, they asked if I had a couple thousand quid to spare.

I hate being put on the spot like that, but gave in. We wrote up a contract on a table napkin where I was a five percent owner of the Beatles and would receive my money back from the first income and then five percent of future net profit. I had my checkbook with me and wrote it out on the spot. I just knew I would live to regret this and never see a dime or a farthing back.

They knew of my songs and, while they were too polite to say so, weren't impressed with my singing. I agreed with them, so that didn't hurt anything. The drummer didn't seem to fit in with the group, and I wondered if he would last.

That was the highlight or lowlight of my trip to Liverpool. The only neat thing on the trip was watching the great ocean liners leave their docks with all the horns blaring. You could already see that air travel was doing away with this type of crossing. Just like the railroads, a golden age was dying.

However, across the Mersey was a new golden age starting. A container port was going into place. On Saturday, I ferried Tom over for a tour. They were reluctant to let me in at the gate to the terminal, but a call to the office brought two people down. One I assumed was the directing manager and the other Popeye.

With a shout, I ran up and picked up Popeye in a hug. He beat on me, telling me to put him down, you big galoot. I remembered my manners, introduced Tom, and told them we had stopped by for a tour.

We got the gold-plated tour of the facility. Whilst we were walking around Popeye also updated me on other terminals around the world. He told me our Australian projects were going much better than we thought. I took this to include the Chinese project. Some things were better not discussed in public.

Popeye did hit me with some news: our shipping line, The Scottish Line, had bought out another line, and we now had sixteen ships in the fleet, and it was growing. While we were talking back and forth, Tom paid close attention.

I asked Popeye if Aunt Sybil was along, but she was on her way to The Meadows to see her mum. I would just miss her all the way around. He told me about our family and its happenings. Did I know Mary now had a clothing line? I did.

Tom finally couldn't hold it in anymore. Rick, how does this all include you?

Popeye replied for me, "Just like Rick not to tell you. He owns all of this, the shipping line, and the factories that build the containers, you see."

Tom looked gobsmacked.

"I knew you had money, but you must be rich!"

I had to jump in before Popeye could answer that, "You might say comfortable."

Unfortunately, the managing director had heard all of this and put in his two shillings worth.

"He is working on being the richest person in the world."

I gave him a nasty look, but it was too late.

"Tom. I have a lot of money, but these projects cost a lot of money, so it isn't like I can throw it around."

Not that I was going to throw it around. No matter, I had watched my Uncle Wally ruin himself with a slightly better-than-average salary. I could put Tommy Manville to shame if I tried. No way was that going to happen.

"Well, it does mean you have the next shout at the Dog and Crown."

"That I can do."

"And what is this about a sister and a clothing line? Is she a model, and can I meet her?"

"She is a model, and she is five years old, and no, you can't meet her."

"Crikey, that is some family you come from."

"That it is."

I wasn't about to mention the KGB and my relationship with them. He just thought we were some family.

He held me to the drinks later in the week, but at least he didn't say anything to the others.

I made one small error. I left home without a handkerchief. That was no big deal. I sneezed and had to blow my nose. I felt a bar napkin in my pocket and used it. That was the end of my part ownership of the Beatles. They later sent me my money back, along with an offer to buy me out.

I replied that I had accidentally destroyed my copy, but they still made the offer to buy me out at the same amount I loaned them. I agreed, and we had real paperwork made out, so it was legal. I would have a story of my own in future years. They also all signed a copy of their first album for me.

Another weekend I spent at Bill Benton's house in Yorkshire. The way he had first described where he lived, I thought of a dreary suburb of an industrial town. His parents' estate was larger than The Meadows.

The house was about the same age as The Meadows and had been updated with modern amenities. That meant a shower and flush toilets. An electric refrigerator had just been installed and was the wonder of the town. I guess the local butcher was right put out about it.

I don't know why. They would eat the same amount they always had. When I saw the kitchen maid who went to the butcher, it was all clear. I would have been put out, too. She was too old for me, but what a looker.

I talked to her at one point and found out that looks were all she had going for her. She was as dumb as the mounting block at the front gate.

Earlier, Bill had taken me aside and told me, "My dad will probably approach you for money for one of his hair-brained schemes. Whatever you do, don't commit to giving him any. He has been swindled so many times. Yet he always falls for the next one. The only reason we aren't in the poor house is that Mum is the one who brought money to the marriage, and she keeps control of it."

"Thanks for the heads up. I will be careful."

"Dad's not a bad sort; he is just the eternal optimist, and he feels he can take a shortcut to get rich. I think it is because Mum brought a fortune to the family, he thinks that he has to do the same. Yet it would never occur to him to go into business or work."

His father reminded me of David Niven. His mother had a unique look that reminded me of Anna Romanov. Not that she looked at all like her, but she had class. A tall blonde with blue eyes, a

Scandinavian background. She looked like class and acted like it, but not over the top or better than you. She was pleasant and showed a direct interest in me as a person. It was not just me; she was like that with everyone.

Within half an hour of arriving at the house, Bill's dad asked if he could have a word. Bracing myself, I accompanied him to his office. He started with a name, *Andrea Doria*. This was a famous Italian cruise ship that sank around 1956. I remember a little about it, but not much.

"Sir Richard, we have a wonderful opportunity. A method has been developed to raise *Andrea Doria*. The safe in first class will have over a hundred million pounds worth of jewelry alone. Who knows what it may be worth?"

"May I ask how this will be done?"

"In brief, cables run under the ship attached to flotation devices."

In my mind, a bunch of problems prevented this. Getting cables passed under the wreck. How many cables would be required? How large would the flotation devices have to be? I had read about this method in *Popular Mechanics*.

They concluded that while theoretically possible, it would not be practical as it would take hundreds of cables to support the 29,000-ton ship without it breaking up. Not to mention the danger of that many dives at that depth.

"I have read about this method before, and it was concluded that it was not possible."

"Come, boy, where is your sense of adventure? Prove that it can be done and become fabulously rich in the process. Why, for every pound invested, you will receive a thousand back."

"I could use five thousand pounds."

"You only have five pounds to spare?"

"Yes, sir. I have an allowance till the end of term, and I'm afraid it will run out."

"Never mind. I thought you had access to real money."

"I'm sorry, sir."

At that, he pulled out his wallet and insisted that I take twenty pounds!"

Now I felt bad, I had lied to him, and now he was giving me money. I didn't know how to handle that, so I thanked him and hunted Bill up. I told him what happened, and he shook his head.

"That's my Dad."

I tried to hand him the twenty pounds, but he wouldn't take the money which was gifted to me.

We went out in Leeds on Saturday night with several of Bill's friends. I insisted on paying for drinks until the twenty pounds was spent. They were a fun group, and there were several girls in the mix.

The pub was crowded so some of the girls chose to sit on the boys' laps. Stella sat on mine. Having her close like that was a wonderful feeling. She may not have been the best-looking girl in the room, but she felt the best. I had to do multiplication tables several times during the evening.

I did get a steamy goodnight kiss, but that was it. While not exciting, I will always have kind thoughts about Leeds.

Another weekend I spent in Scotland with Steve Stewart. I hadn't thought about what his house would look like. I must have had a highland castle in mind, so the three-bedroom bungalow was a surprise. His parents were nice, ordinary people, and we had a good time.

Steve and I went to a pub in Edinburgh with some of his friends on Saturday night. Since they were from his rugby club, I didn't let any of them sit on my lap. Not that they would have. It was drink up, play darts, and get pissed. I once again proved that being born in England did not make you a great darts player. I had one pint and switched to Coke, so I was able to get us back to Steve's place.

His Dad was waiting up, and I thought we were going to get it now. Instead, he just helped me pour Steve into bed. I guess the Scots like their drink and don't mind the consequences.

Chapter 35

School and life went on. I was enjoying the routine. Even calculus was coming under control. It would never be my favorite subject, but I could now sing the tune. Heh, it was about the only tune I could sing no matter what people thought.

And people did have weird thoughts. Mr. Sinatra released our duet of the "Coffee Pot" song, and it became a hit. It rose to number two in three weeks but never made number one on the American side. For some reason, the Brits liked it, and it made number one for three weeks in a row. Thankfully, it died a natural death soon after.

The guys tried to get me to sing it at the pub, and I told them I would if they could get Frank Sinatra to join me. I never did have to sing there.

May Day or May 1st was a hoot at Oxford. The campuses and a good part of the city turned into a huge street fair. People came from all over the country. There were the maypoles with traditional dances. There were Morris dancers everywhere.

The choir sang "Hymnus Eucharisticus" atop Magdalen Tower at sunrise. The tower was so tall you couldn't hear the choir up top, so they held up a sign to say when the choir was done so we could applaud. This was followed by twenty minutes of bell ringing, not from the tower but from a group with handbells.

When that was finished, Morris dancers collected the crowd and led a procession across the Magdalen Bridge and down High Street to Radcliffe Park where they commenced dancing.

That was at sunrise. We had been at it all night. We had breakfast at 4 a.m. at Taylor's on High Street. The pubs were open all this time, so the crowd was feeling no pain. I stuck with coffee as I was losing a night's sleep.

We had dressed for the occasion. My face was green, and my hair looked like the branches of a tree. My robe looked like the bark of a tree. I looked like I was the Green Man stepping out of Beltane into the world.

What a makeup artist hired from Warner Brothers at Leavesden can do is a wonder. It cost a mint but was well worth it. With my height, I stood out. I spent a good amount of my time posing with people for their pictures. It was good fun.

For my efforts, I was given a lot of kisses. For the record it was all women, but of all ages, sizes, and shapes. I recognized them later by the green smudges on their cheeks. I had a small jar of green cream to refresh my look.

The guys took the easy way out and wore robes to make them look like Druids accompanying me. Their faces were painted blue, and they wore circlets of flowers. We were a hit.

I burned out right after lunch and retreated to my garage. There, I took a nap and then drove home. I took a shower with green running everywhere. After that was finished, I dressed casually for dinner. Grandmum was not the stickler that Mum had become.

Grandmum worried that the viscountess business might go to her head. I disagreed. Mum would never forget who she was or where she came from. She was an actress and was performing as expected. I know the beast.

After dinner, I put on my RAF mess dress with medals and escorted Iris Butler to a ball at her school. Her boyfriend was out of town on business and sent his regrets. He was the one who suggested I escort her. We had a good time and I got to dance with a lot of different girls. My gongs and how I had earned them were a topic of conversation. It kept the subject away from me, the actor and rich guy.

I slept in the next day. It was a Monday, but I didn't care about classes. When I asked later, I found out that neither did any of my dons, as none of them showed up.

Mum and Denny's birthdays were both on May 19. For Mum, I had shipped to her a complete Scottish outfit I had seen in Edinburgh. It was in the Jackson tartan and included the kilt, blouse, sash, tam, sporran, long socks, shoes, and what I knew she would like best, a sgian dubh.

I bought Denny a more prosaic German Hasselblad camera. While I considered it prosaic, it was arguably the best camera in the world.

Mary's birthday was on May 28, a week later. What do you get a young lady who is turning six, has already been in movies and on TV, and has her own clothing line? It was easy. With Mum and Dad's permission, I had the State Coach refurbished and then pictures taken.

The pictures were staged with it being pulled with six white horses and our staff in livery alongside. She was promised a ride when she came to England. Of course, that wouldn't be until the summer school break. In the meantime, Grandmum was getting out and about to the local bingo hall, so we all dressed up one mild evening in May and took her to bingo in style.

They would be talking in the bingo hall about that for years. While we were parading, people came out of the stores to see what was happening. She leaned out the window and gave the Queen's wave. That little side-by-side motion they make. It was a hoot.

Of course, pictures were taken and sent to the papers. The scandal sheets said it was a disgraceful sendup of the Queen. The staider *Times* reported it as good, clean fun. Someone got a quote from Elizabeth. "If my coach breaks down, maybe they will lend me theirs."

When I wasn't flying for the Messenger Service, I flew my plane every weekend. A weekend trip to one of the guys' houses was a flying trip, with a ride arranged from the local airport. I also was doing the tourist thing as much as possible.

I would fly to Dublin, rent a car, and end up kissing the Blarney Stone. Next weekend it would be to Cologne to see the cathedral. Man, it was big; I felt like an ant. Then it was down to Aachen to see Charlemagne's iron crown and drink from the public water fountain which had been flowing for over two thousand years.

Then I went back to the Louvre to spend some real time there and at Notre Dame. Sometimes I had company, but many times I did not. The touring explains how I ended up in Cannes one week in May. I was invited as an actor with films in release and one about to be released. I had called Mr. Monroe and asked him about the festival.

He told me to go and enjoy myself but not expect much. None of my films were entered as they were crass commercial products. They were deemed as having no artistic value and those who worked on them as common tradesmen.

I couldn't wait. What a chance to see world-class arrogance up close!

What I found was a bunch of overinflated egos who attended boring parties to talk about themselves. I guess that is what made them boring. I wasn't invited to that many events or even those considered upscale. My title did get me into enough of them to know that this would be my first and only festival.

I stayed in Nice as that was as close as I could find a room for the weekend. It was only seventeen miles. I stayed at the Hotel Negro. Even there, it took a phone call from my concierge at the Plaza in London to the hotel to secure a room. Who knows what sort of horse trade was done for that?

It was across the street from the Mediterranean Sea. I was going to lie out on the beach as my California tan was now a distant memory. When I saw the black rocks that they called a beach, I decided that was not the best idea. I did sit and look at the scenery for quite a while. Did you know they go topless in France?

I had arrived Friday morning, and by Sunday afternoon, I had had enough of the in-crowd. I had thought about staying over until Monday, even skipping class to do so. It shows how bad it was that I skipped the festival events to attend a calculus lecture. Getting drunk and throwing up in the street wasn't my idea of a good time.

There was another downside to the festival. Producers were there looking for money for their next picture. The word was out that I had some money, thank goodness not how much, and I was approached on three different projects.

As politely as I could, I told them all my funds went into a trust as I was still a minor. So, I lied. Much later, I recognized one of the projects that had actually made it to the screen. It was a total bomb.

Then there were the so-called actresses. I don't talk about it much, but I do get propositioned on occasion by women who are washed up or want to get into the industry. They are easy to recognize and scare the heck out of me. Run, Rick, run.

I think my perfect girl would have the elegance of Anna Romanov, the beauty of Sharon Bronson, and the personality of a small-town Ohio girl. What were my chances of finding that?

When I got home from school that Friday, there was a note to call Mr. Norman no matter the time. I called him immediately. The RAF had ordered me as a seconded flight officer to appear at Barkston Heath tomorrow morning at ten hundred hours in the Queen's Messenger plane. There would be an Air Marshal Steed waiting at flight operations. No other information was available.

With a bit of trepidation, I flew to Barkston Heath on time for my meeting with Air Marshal Steed. He was waiting for me as told.

A big bluff-hardy sort of guy, he would have looked good in a Walrus mustache. Well, as good as any guy could look.

I reported in as per the RAF procedure.

"Well, at least you know how to report. Now, do you know how to fly?"

I must have looked puzzled because he added, "I have heard many things about you as a boy wonder, except what sort of pilot you are. I want to check you out today."

My thought was that someone had too much time on their hands, but of course, my response was, "Yes, sir."

We went out to the Greyhound, and I performed a walk around as though I had never seen the aircraft before. Luckily, the wings hadn't fallen off or the tires gone flat in the last fifteen minutes.

Since my fuel state was good, we entered the aircraft, and again, I pretended this was a true check ride. It might have been for all I knew.

Receiving permission, I taxied to the runway and went through all the radio chatter that was appropriate for taking off.

After we were in the air, the air marshal gave me instructions on where and how to fly. It was virtually the same as all my previous check rides in this aircraft type. We flew around for forty-five minutes, and the air marshal told me to get us on the ground as quickly as possible.

I asked if it were an emergency, and he said no; he was satisfied that I could fly and get him back down quickly as he had things to do.

I radioed the control tower and asked for permission to land immediately at the air marshal's request. I was given clearance to land on runway 06 at once.

Now, I was a little resentful for having to go through this exercise, so I took the Air Marshal at his word and got him down quickly. I landed on runway 06 the same way I had in the California brush fire. Dive bombed down, flared out as fast as I could and set it down hot, and then jammed the brakes and airfoils to a complete stop.

It felt like we had dived into the earth but somehow ended up sitting on the runway.

"Was that fast enough, sir?" I asked as though butter wouldn't melt in my mouth.

The air marshal was working his jaw as though to speak, but nothing came out.

Finally, "That will be all."

I dropped him off at flight operations. I had to go in and file a flight plan for my return to Oxford. I wondered what that had been all about.

A squadron leader approached me. "I saw that landing you gave old Steed. He is probably in the loo about now. Well done."

"I hope he won't get too upset."

"Did you notice Air Marshal Steed does not have his pilot wings? He is purely administrative and hates anyone who can fly. I think he was trying to find something to use as a complaint about you."

"I just followed his order to get him down as quickly as I could."

"The tower has noted that he gave that order, so you won't have any problems there."

After that, we introduced ourselves.

"Oh, by the way, Rick, never try a stunt like that under my command. You could have torn the wings off."

"No disrespect, sir, but the plane is built for it, and I have done precisely that once before."

"Do you have time for lunch?"

"Yes, sir."

"Fine, I will buy, and you can tell me about the last time you did that landing. It must be quite a story to tell."

At lunch, we were joined by three other officers, and I told them about the brush fire in California and how the FAA was upset until they realized I knew the aircraft's capabilities.

They wanted to know how I had that much knowledge as that wouldn't have been covered in flight school. That brought up my training with Mr. McGarry. One of the officers, Flight Lieutenant Hale, had read about Mr. McGarry's history as a Flying Tiger.

After lunch, I headed home. I think that the luncheon conversation did a lot for my reputation within the RAF. At least I would be known as the pilot who sent Steed to the loo.

Dad's birthday was on June 5. He had recently taken up sporting clays. I called his club in Los Angeles, and they gave me the measurements that had been taken for him to order a custom-made shotgun. It hadn't been ordered yet in March, so I had time to order a bespoke gun from Purdy for him. I had to pay a premium to have it made so quickly.

The premium was more than a new T-bird, but it was for Dad. I had to let Dad know that I was buying him the gun so he wouldn't go ahead with his order. When I mentioned Purdy, he was pleased as punch.

There was a significant disparity in the cost of the gifts I had bought everyone, but at this money level, it was the thought that counted.

Chapter 36

June was going to be a busy month. I was to be Mark Downing's best man at his wedding to Sharon Bronson. The wedding would be in California. I would be getting off the plane and going to his bachelor party.

The wedding was on Saturday, June 11th, so, I had to leave London early Friday morning. Then, I had an interview early Monday the 13th with a possible new agent Mr. Baxter recommended. I didn't see why I needed an agent, considering I wasn't planning any movies shortly.

Mr. Baxter was very insistent that I have one. I yielded to his knowledge and experience in the industry. Plus, I felt like I owed him for what he had done for my family. If nothing else, keeping Mary gainfully employed and out of trouble earned him a lot.

As soon as I could, I had to get to Denver on Monday after the interview to start the practice rounds for the US Open. Dad arranged a charter flight for me that would set down at a private airfield near Cherry Hills so I wouldn't have to fight the Stapleton traffic.

Then there was school and the fact that I would miss a full two weeks. The only saving grace was that I was leaving at the beginning of the revision period. With my notes, I felt like I could do this on my own. After the Open, I had to hightail it back to London for my Knights of the Garter investiture. That was on Monday, June 20th.

In preparation for the KG ceremony, the Palace had ordered my complete outfit, and that would be waiting for me at my suite at the Plaza. I had questioned the wisdom of buying that suite, but it had been useful several times now.

I explained my June schedule to the guys at the Dog and Crown on our first June Thursday night get-together. I went wild that night and drank half a pint. It took that to describe the month. They agreed it was a crazy schedule and better me than them, though they saw the possibilities of a lot of birds at the US Open.

Then I would only be able to look and not touch as I wouldn't have time, pity. I thought they had one-track minds. I hardly ever thought about girls.

The days went by, and all of a sudden, I had a flight to the US the next morning. The trip would be a transpolar flight on TWA, directly from London to Los Angeles. That cut down on the flying time from when I first started flying from the US to England.

Packing for the trip was easy. I pointed out what I wanted to take on Saturday and Mr. Hamilton had it folded and put in my suitcase. I was amazed at how nice everything looked when he was done. It would have looked like the clothes hamper on wash day if I had attempted it.

As they say in the RAF, I flew my Cessna to London at o'dark hundred on Friday. I parked the plane in a rented hangar space on the private side of the field. They would wash and fuel it while I was gone.

My luggage and I were taken to the main terminal, where I checked in at the curb. Since I had tickets in hand from an earlier purchase, there was no waiting in line. I went directly to the TWA Ambassador Club, where I picked up my boarding pass and had my first coffee of the day. Well-earned, I might add.

I had just barely finished my first cup, and it was time to board the airplane. I and two other people were led through a back hallway and allowed to board immediately. I had no idea who the other people were and didn't care.

As the boarding process started for the rest of the passengers, I ordered more coffee and started through my revision notes. I had to be serious about this on the trip if I were going to pass my exams.

It was my bad luck that a chatty guy sat next to me. I was in the window seat, and he seemed determined to talk across the top of the world. He interrupted my study so often that I finally told him that I had to study for upcoming exams and would he please leave me alone.

Not only couldn't he take a hint, but he couldn't take a direct request. I finally pushed the call button and explained my problem to the stewardess. There was an open seat across the aisle, so she moved him over there. Now he could pester someone else.

You could tell the jerk was complaining about me being anti-social. The man in the seat beside him rang his call button and ended up sitting beside me in blessed silence for the rest of the trip. I am so glad that you only run into people like that on rare occasions. I shudder to think what a flight would be like if there were more like him on board. I hope Mum and Dad let me use their jet when they get it for trips like this.

I took a three-hour nap over the North Pole. I had to sail the Arctic someday so I could get the Order of the Blue Nose.

We landed on time in LA. I felt so tired and grungy. A limo had been put on, and I was taken directly to Jackson House, where I showered and changed clothes. I gave Mary and Mum a quick hug and shook hands with Dad and my brothers, then got back in the limo to go to Sharon's small town. I arrived there at eight o'clock in the evening.

I had started my journey twenty-five hours ago and even though I had a nap, I was tired. Mark, his two brothers, and several of his friends were waiting for me, so we went to a local bar where the back room had been reserved for his party.

I was glad that none of those present were crazy drunks. My contribution to the party was traditional. They wheeled in a large cake that had a stripper inside. She did her act, kissed us all on the cheek, and left. All in all, it was a staid party.

The next day saw the ceremony go off without a hitch. I was glad to see that Sharon had finally reconciled with her parents. During the reception, Mark and Sharon thanked me for my impact on their lives. Sharon had decided to drop out of the acting business and become a housewife.

In private, I was told that I would be invited to a christening in about seven months. Good for them.

The paparazzi had not found out about the wedding, so it was a pleasant affair. At the reception, I danced with the maids of honor, but they were all older than me and most of them married. You can't win them all, but dang!

When the bride and groom left for their honeymoon to parts unknown, I made my departure back to LA. I was so glad to get to bed, I was asleep by nine o'clock. Of course, I was wide awake at five o'clock, which wasn't too bad. I was able to get a good run in after doing my exercises.

The agent candidate had agreed to meet me at the Calabasas Country Club for brunch and an interview. This was a typical Hollywood meeting. I liked that it was more informal, and you could better understand how people were.

My sense of Clark Miller was that he was a solid person who took his work seriously. I was upfront with him about my movie plans or lack thereof. He had a question for me.

"Are you aware that *Over the Ohio* is being talked about as an Oscar contender even though it hasn't been released and that you will be nominated as Best Actor?"

"Oh, come on, it's a B movie."

"It may have started life like that, but the reviewers who have watched the in-house release take it as a serious movie with a powerful message. Your role is the key to the whole movie as it highlights the dichotomy of the day."

"I think the nation as a whole is awakening to the fact that the settlement of America was more than Pilgrims and Cowboys and Indians. This movie reveals the good and bad of both sides and how the conflicts were unavoidable."

"You either have to go in hiding from all the offers you receive or hire an agent. I would like the job if at all possible. Even if you never do another movie, as your agent, doors will open for me."

I liked that attitude, so I asked him what money he was looking for as an agent. I told him since he would benefit from being associated with me, he certainly would take less. After we stopped laughing, we came to terms with a standard agent's agreement. It was not as good as I had with Mr. Baxter, but that was a special arrangement.

I tried to get him to accept points instead of five percent, but he pointed out that I told him I might never make another movie. I countered that you won't get a commission anyway if that is so. He thought about it and decided that the points were an excellent incentive, but it would be predicated on me getting points in the movie.

I countered that it was his job as my agent to negotiate points for us. We went back and forth for over an hour. We finally ended up saying he would take points if he could get them and if not, his regular fee. It was fun going back and forth sitting outside on the veranda in the California sun; it sure beat the English rain and a smoky pub.

The girls wore short dresses and tennis shorts, much better than a girl in an anorak.

We finished up, and Clark told me he would have a contract written up and provide copies to me and my lawyer. He knew my law firm through Mr. Baxter. I wasn't sure about the whole thing, but it wouldn't cost me anything to have an agent on my behalf, so why not?

I felt good about getting him to accept points in a picture. It would be a real incentive to negotiate hard.

After lunch, I drove home and over to the Forestry Service airfield. My chartered flight arrived right on time, and I was off to Denver.

The flight was uneventful. The plane, a converted DC 3, had a pilot and copilot, so there was no room for me in the cockpit, but they let me watch over their shoulder after we took off. There wasn't a flight attendant, but they had a cooler with soft drinks and snacks. I ended up serving the crew. Did that make me a stewardess?

Going over the Rockies was a little rough, but these old birds were tough as nails and could handle it. I bet some would still be flying fifty years from now.

After bouncing around a little, we landed at the small airfield near the Cherry Hills golf course. I grabbed my overnight bag and walked to the little shack they called a terminal. My real luggage was being shipped separately. I hoped it made it.

John Jacobs was waiting for me. We gave each other a guy hug and went to my hotel. It was a small operation, not part of any chain, but very well kept with all the modern conveniences. It even had color televisions in each room.

It was too late in the day to play, so John and I went over to the club, where he showed me where my locker with my clubs and gear was. The place was a beehive of golfers. You could tell the difference between the pros and the amateurs; the pros were calm and appeared at home. The amateurs were like cats on a hot tin roof, nervously moving everywhere and looking lost.

I tried to act calm and pretend I was at my home course. Having John there helped a lot because he was now familiar with the entire club and guided me around.

I went to the driving range and, starting with my low irons, worked my way up to the driver. My time in England had been well spent as I wasn't tightened up from lack of practice. After that, it was an hour on the putting greens. It was a traffic jam out there. The result was that most people were putting too fast, trying to keep out of each other's way. This wasn't learning; this was developing bad habits.

Once John pointed out that I was starting to do the same thing, I called it a day. After cleaning up and changing clothes in the clubhouse, I took John and his wife Linda out to dinner. It was a fun relaxed meal at a Mexican restaurant. It was more TexMex than Mexican, which was fine with me.

It had colorful furniture and posters on the wall. The floor was tile, and the lobby had an adobe water fountain. Despite the kitsch look, it was a classy place, and the food really good.

John tried to get me to eat a raw jalapeno pepper, but I wasn't going to fall for that again.

His wife Linda told me they were having a great time, and she could handle this life easily. They had plans for a family, but nothing was happening yet, not from a lack of trying. This was too much information.

We did talk about what would happen if I won the Open. It meant that I would try for the grand slam as an amateur next year. I had no desire to turn professional. As John put it, I probably couldn't afford the cut in pay if I went pro.

I let that line go. I wouldn't take a cut in pay as I owned the company, but it would take up too much time.

We called it an evening after dinner, and after taking a walk around the hotel area, I went to bed for a good night's sleep. I still had some jet lag to sleep off.

Chapter 37

Monday morning, I got ready for my first practice round. The goal of this round was for John to familiarize me with the course.

The first hole is a 346-yard par 4 with a slight dogleg left. It is possible to drive the green. I think they set it up this way to lull the players into a false sense of security.

Number two is a 410-yard par 4. Trees line the entire right side of the fairway, while bunkers guard the left side. A lake protects a reasonably flat green on the left side of the green. It would be quite easy to go from the beach to the water.

Hole number three is 348 yards, a short par 4. Most of the Open players are capable of driving the green. The tabletop green falls off in all directions with closely mown grass, so it is difficult to get a wedge to hold, let alone a driver. If you go long, Little Dry Creek comes into play.

The fourth hole is a 426-yard par 4. A dogleg-left requires a well-placed tee shot to the right side of the fairway, as overhanging trees on the left half of the fairway can send a ball awry. A short-iron second shot will allow some birdies, but a two-tiered green complicates it.

Hole five is 538 yards and a par 5. Being a short par five, it is deceptive as it requires an accurate tee shot if one tries for the green in two. The tee shot has a creek to the right, deep bunkers to the left, and a narrow fairway of only 26 yards between the two hazards. The green has the most slope of any on the course and is unforgiving. Shots left and short will end up in a deep bunker, and long shots will leave a virtually impossible chip or pitch because of the slope.

Number six is 174 yards and a par 3. Being a short par 3 gives a chance at making a birdie. Because of bunkers surrounding the green and a small creek to the left, it requires an accurate short iron. A severe slope from front to back requires one to keep the ball below the hole. Again, a shot over the green will leave a near-impossible second shot, placing one in bogey territory.

Hole seven is 411 yards and a par 4. Most players will hit a fairway wood off the tee to avoid going through the fairway on this dogleg left. Cutting the dogleg will reduce yards, but then you have to get past the large bunker complex that guards the left side of the hole. The green has a soft slope from back to front once you clear the bunker. On the left, there is a severe fall off to the right. So, shortcutting is very high risk and only to be done if I need to make up some strokes.

The eighth hole, 233 yards par 3, is where the course starts to show its teeth. The hole requires an accurate fairway wood to avoid large bunkers both left and right of the green. Poor shots to the right bring Little Dry Creek into play. It is easy to turn this possible birdie into a bogey.

On nine is a 430-yard uphill par 4, which is one of the most difficult holes at Cherry Hills. A long and accurate tee shot is required. A crowned fairway brings the deep rough on the left into play or a large bunker on the right. You can only see the top of the flag on the second shot and there is a severely sloped green guarded by a large bunker in the front.

The first nine holes are 3315 yards with a par of 35.

Number 10 is a 444-yard par 4. An accurate tee shot is needed to the fairway, which is severely sloped from right to left and guarded by a large bunker and trees on the right side. The second shot is to a right-to-left-sloping green which has bunkers on both sides. If the pin is on the right side, it will be a difficult, high-risk shot.

The 11th is 563 yards and a par 5. It takes a long hit to reach this par five in two strokes. I hope to use this to my advantage. The tee shot is uphill on the fairway, guarded by a bunker on the left and out of bounds just off the right side of the fairway. A large cross bunker 110 yards short of the green prevents most players from going for the green in two. The large green is severely sloped from back to front. Putts above the hole should be avoided as you can roll right off the green.

Number 12 at 212 yards is a par 3. Shots that land just short of the green will roll back into a pond guarding the front. Anything long leaves a virtually impossible pitch. The green is divided in the middle with a severe mound, so being in the right quadrant is a must.

Thirteen is a 385-yard par 4. It is a straight-away, which requires an accurate tee shot to avoid the deep grass mounds on the left and the large fairway bunker to the right. A successful drive leaves a short iron to a small and tricky green—anything over the green guarantees a bogey.

The 14th hole is a 470-yard par 4 and the most challenging hole on the course. The hole has a slight dogleg left and along the widest fairway on the course. One would think this is an easy hole. The second shot is downhill, with the green guarded by Little Dry Creek to the left and a large bunker to the right, all manageable. It is a severe green, and putting is a real challenge.

Number 15 is a 196-yard par 3. It plays slightly downhill to a small green guarded by bunkers on both sides. Shots moving too far left could end up in Little Dry Creek, which is closer than it looks from the tee. The green has a subtle movement from back to front.

Hole 16 is 402 yards and a par 4. A fairway wood off the tee is needed to stay out of Little Dry Creek, which works its way through the right side of the fairway and then cuts across the middle of the fairway. The second shot is played with the ball below the player's feet to a green that slopes the opposite way. A severe green is guarded with bunkers on the front left and the right half.

The 17th is a 548-yard par 5 with water short of the green. There are also two sets of cross bunkers protecting the green. An accurate tee shot is needed to allow a chance to go for the island green in two.

This is a moderate risk for me. The green looks easy but has mild ridges.

On 18, a 468-yard par 4, water runs down the left side of the fairway, and high rough guards the right side. The second shot plays uphill with the clubhouse in the background. Large bunkers on both sides protect the challenging green.

The back nine is 3688 yards and a par 36. The course is a par 71.

John had been around this course many times and knew it well. I was in a threesome, just like the tournament would be. We didn't talk to each other as we all were intensely quizzing our caddies about the course.

Everyone was polite, but not much on the chit-chat. The tension was already building.

The players had a dinner that evening with required attendance. It was a chance for the organizers to be recognized for their hard work. I arrived late enough to avoid the cocktail hour. It was your typical rubber chicken meal. I sat next to another amateur and a club pro. The amateur, Robert somebody, and the pro, Bill someone, came from the East Coast and exchanged mutual acquaintances throughout the meal. I was pretty much left out of it. I was asked where I was from, and I was torn between Hollywood and Oxford. Using my British accent, I went with Oxford.

They wanted to know if I played for the university, and when I told them no, it ended my role for the meal. After the speeches and awards, I skipped the after-dinner cocktails and cut out to my hotel. I wonder how many golfers would fail because of the cocktail hours and the many parties being held.

I had received several written invitations from people I didn't even know for parties at their houses. I supposed they had looked me up, associated me with my movies, and wanted a Hollywood star at their party. I declined all of them. I was here for one reason.

On Tuesday, my tee time was scheduled at 11 a.m., so I had time for my entire exercise routine, the driving range, and the practice putting green.

John and I agreed that today I should be working on all the risky shots to see how I would do.

On the first hole, a 346-yard par 4 with its slight dogleg left, I was able to drive the green, setting up a possible eagle. I birdied, which was a good start.

I stayed in the middle of the second fairway with a 340-yard drive on this 410-yard par 4, leaving an easy wedge to the fairly flat green, making another birdie. This isn't a tough course at all! I made that comment to John, and he set me straight really quickly.

I drove the green on number three and had it promptly roll back off the green. Fortunately, it didn't go long, so I ended up with a par. Maybe John was right about the course.

On the fourth hole, a 426-yard par 4, I had a well-placed tee shot to the right side of the fairway and avoided the overhanging trees on the left half of the fairway. My short-iron second shot ended up on the wrong tier of the two-tiered green, so I had a bogey.

The fifth fairway is 538 yards and a par 5. My tee shot ended up dead center of the 26-yard-wide fairway, so it was accurate enough to go for the green in two. Getting on the green in two was my last good thing on the hole. I four-putted as I landed upslope from the hole. My first putt went way past. My second came up short, and then I left it on the lip. Not what I needed to win.

On the next fairway, which is a 174-yard par 3, I nailed the green and made the bird.

Hole seven is a 411-yard par 4. I cut the dogleg, which went okay. I even hit the green but hit the slope wrong and fell off to the right, leaving me with a bogey. John and I agreed that we would play the hole without shortcutting the dogleg unless I was in trouble.

I came back on the eighth hole, landing on the green of the 233-yard par 3, and ending up with another bird.

On the 430-yard ninth hole, my tee shot was good, staying in the middle of the crowned fairway. Even at 345 yards after its roll, I could only see the top of the flag. This is where John's knowledge came into play as he could tell me where to aim to land correctly on the severely sloped green. Today, I had to aim it at 10:30 as pilots would describe the direction. My aim and distance were good, but I ended up two-putting for par.

I ended up even for the front nine. We grabbed a sandwich and a Coke from the table set up for the players. I bet half the field ended up with indigestion from the way we had to scarf our food.

On number 10 is a 444-yard par 4. I almost fell apart when my tee shot drifted and ended up in a bunker. I came out okay but well short of the green. My third shot got me on where I two-putted for a bogey. This was with the pin in the center of the green. If it had been on the right side, I would have been in real trouble.

The 11th hole, a 563-yard par 5, allowed me to redeem myself as I made the green in two. I was below the hole, and I put it for an eagle.

On 12, after landing on the green, I needed three putts for a bogey.

Thirteen was a no-brainer for me, up the middle, shot iron to the green, and two-putted in for par. This is a good candidate for a bird if I could get my putting under control.

The 14th hole, a 470-yard par 4, the toughest hole on the course, gave me no problems at all. I was on in two and just missed a bird.

Number 15 is a 196-yard par 3. It went well with a bird.

I used a fairway wood on the 16th to stay short of Little Dry Creek. The hole is 402 yards and a par 4. I didn't have a problem with having the ball below my feet. That may have something to do with my height—I'm just guessing. My shot clung to the green, and I two-putted for a par.

I birdied 17, a 548-yard par 5, making the island green in two, leaving a five-foot putt, which I drained, my best putt of the day.

Eighteen was a par, getting on in two and two-putting. This left me two-under for the day. John told me that probably would not win the tournament. He thought it would have to be at least four-under to win.

I wasn't discouraged because I had taken some risky shots. If avoided, it would have left me four-under.

I watched TV that night, and to this day, I can't tell you what was on. I had no trouble falling asleep and waking up early. After my morning routine, I went to the course where John had me on the practice green using the same techniques as he did at Calabasas. It helped.

We went out later in the afternoon for my Wednesday practice round. I had just thought the other players weren't talkative. They all appeared to be wound tight as a drum. Of course, I was relaxed and at ease. Yeah, of course I was.

Wednesday's round was a repeat of Tuesday's, except I played with reduced risk to see what score I would get. I turned 5 and 10 from bogeys to pars. This gave me four-under for the day. I was ready to play.

Chapter 38

On Thursday morning, the 65th playing of the US Open started with a field of one hundred and fifty players. I had been assigned to the morning wave. That meant I would tee off this morning and tomorrow in the afternoon wave. I don't know if this was good or bad. I wouldn't have time to get a case of the nerves this morning, but I would have plenty of time tomorrow, especially if I performed poorly today.

We teed off every eleven minutes. I was in line for the tee half an hour in advance after leaving the official's tent, where we had to obtain our cards and find out who was in our threesome.

The way they assigned threesomes was strange. John, who had time to find these things out, explained it was entirely at the whim of the tournament organizers. Usually, it was a small committee, but it could be just a single person. There was nothing prim and proper about it. They would put three highly rated pros in a group because people wanted to see them head-to-head, and TV people liked it.

They were just as likely to put the three shortest players in one group and the three tallest in another or mix and match. Koreans might go together to satisfy their home audience. Then there was the group that wasn't acknowledged; they would place the three most obnoxious golfers together. They were known as the three Ps. It was a game to guess which group they were in.

My group included two other amateur college kids who probably had no business being on the course. Shortly after I was in place, one of my group members showed up. He was a good-looking guy and could prove it as he had a model-type woman hanging all over him. They weren't in line for five minutes, and an official gave him a warning about unbecoming conduct.

At the very last minute, our third player showed up. He came in walking like he owned the place. The officials had been getting nervous about him appearing. The TV cameras were turned onto us, waiting to see what happened.

Showboat told us that he was working to plan to get as much publicity as possible, so when he won the tournament and turned pro on the spot to collect his first winnings, he would be in line for sponsors.

His plan only had one flaw, and it was a big one. By the draw, he was first up, and he promptly shanked his shot so far out that he had a lost ball penalty. That was the end of Showboat. He finished up ten over.

Loverboy was next and had a solid drive that almost made the green. It should be an easy up-and-out for him. My drive made the green and stuck to leave me a three-foot putt.

Loverboy made the green but ended up two-putting for par. I made my birdie putt.

I had to hand it to Showboat; he never gave up or showed a temper. If he settled down, I bet he could play golf, or how would he have gotten here in the first place?

The fifth was the only hole on the front nine that gave me a scare. On my drive, I missed the fairway and ended up in a bunker to the right. That left me getting on in three, where I promptly three-putted. This gave me my first and only bogey for the day.

From there, my day was a repeat of my last practice round. I ended up one-under for the day, which left me in a good position for tomorrow's round. If I could hold it together, I would cut. John helped keep me centered all day.

Friday was nerve-racking all morning. I didn't tee off until 1:22. I tried to sleep in but woke up at daybreak. I had my exercise, a five-mile run, cleaned up, and breakfasted by nine o'clock. All I had to do was worry until John caught up with me.

He took me to the driving range, where I worked through my clubs, and then to the practice green. I saw Mr. Palmer there and got up the nerve to say "Hello." He looked blankly at me for a moment and then said, "I don't remember your name, but we have met before. I think it was in Ohio at a high school tournament."

I was amazed that he remembered that much.

"Yes, you told me how the grass will change direction due to the sunlight."

He laughed and told me, "I hope I don't live to regret that."

We then went our ways. I saw Ben Hogan but wasn't brave enough to introduce myself. Jack Nicklaus was there, but he had so many people following him you couldn't get nearby. He was the favorite of all the amateurs who entered.

After that, John drove me to a quiet restaurant away from the course. We ate a leisurely lunch while I answered his questions about Oxford. By the time we got back to the course, I was relaxed. Whatever I paid John wasn't enough. That thought reminded me that we needed a plan going forward if I did well.

We had talked about it with his wife, but no firm decisions had been made. I guess it could wait until after tomorrow or even longer, as I would be high on adrenaline. I certainly had enough adrenaline highs to know it was not a good time to make long-term plans. High like that, you could take on the world.

When it was time to tee off, Loverboy was there sans girl, and Showboat was fifteen minutes early. Today would be serious if we were to cut. Showboat was in trouble at ten over, and he had his work cut out for him. We talked a little before our turn, and he seemed like a nice guy who had thought too much.

Today, we all had decent drives, with mine being the only one sticking on the green.

For me, the round was a replay of yesterday without the bogey on five. I made a clean and easy par there. That left me two-under for the day and three-under for the tournament.

The cut ended at five over, so sixty of us would advance to the final rounds. Showboat wasn't one of them. He made a valiant effort, recovering four strokes, but at six over, he missed it.

Loverboy would be there at a plus-four. His girl was waiting at the 18, and they took off. I hoped for his sake that their night wasn't too good. Showboat, whose name was Bob Means, and I shook hands, and he wished me luck. I told him there would always be next year.

He replied he had a plan already. It involved tan shoes with pink shoelaces, a polka dot vest, and a Panama with a purple hatband. My look must have been priceless as he laughed and walked away. At least the guy had a sense of humor.

The press finally figured out that I was the actor Sir Richard Jackson. At the tournament organizer's request, I gave a brief interview. Yes, I was proud to be part of this fine event. I had hopes, but this was truly a world-class field, and I would make no rash projections when people like Arnold Palmer and Ben Hogan were in the hunt. I appreciated the effort put in by the fine people who organized this tournament. I also believed in God, the American Way, and apple pie.

I didn't say any of the last, but it would have fit in.

At the end of the two rounds, Mike Souchak led at seven-under. This was going to be hard to beat if he could maintain his lead.

I was paired with Ben Hogan and Jack Nicklaus, and that was frightening. All of a sudden, this was very real. We teed off later in the day.

Jack remembered me from the Ohio Junior Championship. That seemed like forever ago, but it was only two full years. Mr. Hogan was polite but a little reserved. I think playing with two young golfers was strange to him. Maybe it made him feel old. Yeah, and I have a bridge in Brooklyn.

We teed off at 10:38. There were only two groups after us. I would like to say I tore up the course but was able to go from three-under to four-under, which was very much in the hunt. Mike Souchak had a bad round, giving back two of the seven strokes. He was still in the lead.

At the 18th, I recognized first Mum and then Dad in the crowd. Mum stood out as she chose to wear her complete kilt ensemble. If you looked closely, she even had the dagger in her right sock.

Dad was with her in a more conservative golf shirt. They greeted me with hugs as I came off the green. Mum looked around, saying, "Now, where did she get to?"

Mary had accompanied them but had wandered off. It isn't good when you can't find your six-year-old daughter. It didn't take long to find her. All I had to do was look where the press was. As the center of attention, my sister was all smiles being interviewed on TV.

We pushed up front to hear her answer a question.

"I'm rooting for my brother Ricky, but you know he is playing against some of the best golfers in the world. Jack Nicklaus is great, and Mr. Hogan and Mr. Palmer are plain scary as golfers. To help Ricky, I wore a new frock from my latest collection. Don't you like it?"

As she said that, she gave a little model spin to show it off.

The lady TV person asked Mary, "Who told you to say that?"

"Miss Wallace, my publicity agent."

"What would you say if you used your own words?"

"Go, Ricky! Beat their butts!"

And that ended that interview. Mum took charge of her wayward daughter. The press started to approach her with questions, but her glare told them otherwise.

I ducked back, grabbed a sandwich and Coke, and went back to golf. It is much safer.

As I approached the final round, I realized I knew where I wanted every shot to land on this course. Now, it was the execution. If I missed a shot, I couldn't let it get to me and had to move on. At least I didn't have the pressure of a paycheck weighing on me. If I won, the person in second place, if a pro, would get the money, so I wasn't depriving anyone.

To start the last round, I ran a string of four birdies, a par on five, then birds on six and seven. I then took a par on eight and nine. I was now eight- under and leading the tournament.

I hit into the rough on 10 and ended up with a bogey. I followed that with a birdie on 11. I got conservative from there and parred up through 16. At 17, I thought my world was coming to an end. I was on in two as per plan. I then three-putted for a bogey. The green that was considered easy almost did me in as I misread a slight ridge in the green. What should have been my par putt missed by an inch! It ended up as a tap-in, but still, it was a bogey.

I was now six-under. John and I had estimated that winning the tournament would take a five-under or better.

It was with great trepidation that I approached 18.

As I was walking up to the tee block, John said, "Hey, Rick, if you screw it up, they can't take away your birthday."

I gave a short laugh at that, and I felt a weight come off. It wouldn't be the end of the world, so just do it.

And that is what I did, a textbook par to end up at six-under.

Mr. Arnold Palmer, who had started the day tied for fifteenth, made an incredible charge and ended up five-under. Mike Souchak faded at the end.

Mr. Palmer was nice when he congratulated me. He said there is always next year. He was wrong. It took him two more years before he won the US Open, his first of three times in his career. Jack

Nicklaus had shaken my hand and told me he hoped I wasn't turning pro. I told him that wasn't the plan.

That question came up in the news conference afterward. The reporters had expected me to declare myself a pro immediately to collect the $14,400.

My reply was simple: I don't have time to play golf professionally as I'm attending Oxford University, and with my acting career, I don't need the money. I didn't want to get into the real money that was Jackson Enterprises.

I just smiled when asked if I intended to enter the major tournaments next year to try for the grand slam as an amateur. It hadn't been done since the legendary Bobby Jones.

"We will see."

After all the presentations and the biggest trophy I had ever received, I joined my family with John and his wife for a steak dinner at the Brown Palace in Denver. The food was great. The décor was a little dark for me, but I was used to smoke-darkened rooms from the Middle Ages.

We did have a serious talk about next year. John and his wife were up for almost anything to get ready. He was going to start his homework on getting qualified on the following courses: Augusta, Georgia, for The Masters on April 6-10, 1961; the US Open at Oakland Hills Country Club, Birmingham, Michigan, on June 15-17; then the British Open at the Royal Birkdale course in Southport, England, July 12-15; and last was the PGA Championship, July 27-31 at the Olympia Fields Country Club, Olympia, Illinois.

He told me he knew what he had to do to caddie at all the courses but the Royal Birkdale. I told him I may have an in there and would get back to him.

We did a very rough tabletop budget, and we let John and Linda know I didn't expect them to skimp. John laughed and told me the way this was going, he would make a million before he was thirty. I was glad for him. He earned it all when he reminded me they couldn't take away my birthday.

As we were leaving the restaurant, there were many requests for autographs. This didn't surprise me, and I gave them out easily. What did surprise me was the line of little girls getting Mary to sign. She took it very seriously, asking who they wanted it made out to. She did have to ask most of them how to spell their names. I don't mean last names; I mean, Linda, Ellen, and others. Her seriousness was so cute.

Chapter 39

From the restaurant, I was driven back to the Cherry Hill airport, where I took a small charter to Stapleton to catch a direct flight to London.

TWA was ready for me at check-in. The Airline of the Stars had photographers waiting at the Ambassador Club and again at the gate. I went through all the correct motions but just wanted to get on the plane and digest the events of the day.

A gentleman sat next to me and minded his own business. I got down to studying, but my thoughts wandered.

The US Open is like many other major events, such as the circus coming to town. It is here, and the biggest thing around, and then it is gone. All that would be left by now would be a few hospitality tents.

The golfers would be moving on to the next tournament, the caterers to the next event. Even the birds that had hovered over the trash cans would have moved on to the next free meal.

There would be no threesomes waiting at the tee box. The driving range and practice green would also be empty. There would be no customers in the pro shop. The course would have the quiet of a slow summer day.

It reminded me of a day in 1955. I think it was then that Dad and Uncle Wally took me to Lima, Ohio to see the Barnum Bailey Ringling Brothers Circus. It was the last time they toured with the Big Top, a true three-ring circus. After that they only appeared in colosseums.

The next day, when the circus left town, only three circles of sawdust were left from the three rings. We had stayed overnight, so I saw it on the way home. It left me with a memory of how great-appearing things can disappear overnight.

Uncle Wally tried to convince me that there had been a murder the night before and that the body was buried under one of the rings. They had the elephants trample the ground so you wouldn't know it had been dug up.

If it had been anyone but Wally, I might have believed them.

After that bit of introspection, I went back to my studies. This lasted until the pilot announced they were pleased to have onboard today the winner of this year's US Open, Sir Richard Jackson. That set off the parade of people asking for autographs. I even had to change to the aisle seat with the other guy so he could have some peace.

It finally died down, and I spent the rest of the flight reviewing my coursework notes. Exams were like golf tournaments. They came and were a big deal, then left with the wreckage of student's hopes and dreams in their wake. After that, nothing was left but the smooth flow of centuries in Oxford's academic life.

It must be the letdown after a major life event; I was positively melancholy today.

When we landed early Sunday morning, I felt dirty, grungy, and plain out of sorts with a headache, so I was glad to get to my hotel suite. It was proving to be one of my better investments, unlike the Beach House, which my family said was fantastic, while I hadn't seen it since it was finished. They had spent several days at the beach and assured me it was great fun. Did I mention I'm tired and grumpy?

I took a shower and napped until noon. At the front desk, a stack of phone messages had somehow found me, many of them congratulatory, many wanting interviews, and even sponsorship offers if I changed my mind and went pro.

President Eisenhower and the Queen both sent messages.

I took a long walk through the City of London. I wasn't up to going to a park and running. I let the city's sights and sounds pass by, and I calmed down from the last week. Wow, I had won the US Open. I think it was just starting to sink in.

I may not run fast enough for football, but I can hit a golf ball. I had read somewhere about compensating. I must be overcompensating.

I called Mr. Norman's private number after lunch. He told me a car would pick me up at seven in the morning. My regalia were in place at Windsor Castle. All I had to do was show up in a suit and tie.

After waking at five, getting a light workout in, and then cleaning up and eating breakfast, I was dressed and waiting for the limo, which pulled up promptly at seven.

Traffic wasn't terrible like Los Angeles, so we made the drive quickly. Mr. Norman was waiting for me and escorted me to a dressing room where I donned the outfit of a member of the Order of the Garter. First was the actual garter, which is worn on the left calf. It is a dark blue velvet strap-on.

Then, the velvet mantle, a dark blue long cape lined with white taffeta.

Then there was the hat. Not something you would see every day. Not that the mantle wasn't unusual, but the hat was something else. It was what Henry VIII wore in most of his portraits, except it also had a plume of white ostrich and black heron feathers.

During the investiture ceremony, I would receive the collar, a pure gold 30-troy-ounce chain with the Great George medallion suspended, showing St. George slaying the Dragon.

When I was shown into the room where the current Knights were waiting, I realized two things: I was the only new knight, and all of them were more than fifty years older than me!

Prince Philip was kind enough to take me in hand and introduce me around. The other knights were all lord lieutenants, field marshals, the head of the Bank of England, and heads of large businesses.

I was in august company. I felt overwhelmed as if I had snuck under the circus tent rather than paid at the door. My looks must have told the prince that, as he told me, "You are the only Knight here for bravery. An argument could be made you are the only true Knight present."

Maybe not the former field marshal who ran the entire British forces during World War II, but most of them.

That put a different slant on it, but I was still in over my head. That was until the businessmen started asking about Jackson Enterprises and the container business. While I didn't run the business, it was mine, and I had the final say. Maybe I was equal to some of them. One even asked me to attend a golf outing. I told him I would get back to him.

We all entered the throne room at Windsor and knelt to our Queen. I was called forth, and she tapped my shoulder with a real sword this time. When she did, she winked at me! Then, the Collar and Medallion of the Order were placed around my neck. I was handed a box with the Lesser George and sash, which I would wear on my uniforms at official functions and a ribbon for my daily wear.

We had what they called a luncheon and what I would call a banquet with the Queen presiding. I wasn't near her, so I didn't have a chance to make my manners to her.

After eating, we marched down the hill to the George Chapel. Along with us were the Military Knights. The path was lined with soldiers in antique uniforms and many an invited onlooker.

In the chapel, I had my stall with a plate on the end bearing my coat of arms. I had just joined one of the most powerful private clubs in the world. Our current twenty-two members made the US Senate look like a boys' club. Well, except for me. I hoped to grow into the role.

When it was all done, I returned my regalia for safekeeping except for the Lesser George star and sash on which I would wear it, plus the ribbons for my uniform.

It was a shame my parents couldn't be there, but they had prior commitments and were tired of living on airplanes like me. My grandmum was there and had a great time. The Queen Mum accompanied her, and they chatted a dozen a minute. I suspect they just couldn't understand what this younger generation was coming to.

Later, Grandmum told me they talked about the latest soaps on the telly. Go figure.

The royals and most of the other players in today's pageant were off to the races, the Royal Ascot races. I went back to school. Another circus parade was finished. I had to wonder, is that all there is?

At school, it took the rest of the week to settle back in and get into the revision routine. The guys wanted to know all about the golf tournament, and were many girls there? And the investiture, and were many girls there? The answer was I had no idea about golf as I had been focused on my play.

Yes, I noticed many girls, granddaughters probably, but never had the opportunity to speak to any as my peers the old fogies took my attention either about business or golf.

When asked about the business, I told them I thought I had bought another steamship line sight unseen. That took them aback until they realized I was giving them the piss for being pests.

I studied like my academic career depended on it, which it did for the next two weeks. Like all study times, there is never enough. Too quickly, the days of the exams were upon me. The entire last week of June, I was either taking an exam or swotting for the next one.

When the last one was finished, I hurried home to The Meadows and had dinner with Grandmum, who assured me I had passed all my exams. I was returning to the US on the morrow. There was no packing required as I now had my kit on both sides of the ocean. I suppose someday I will have complete wardrobes around the world.

I went to say good night to Grandmum, but she was talking about the soaps on the phone with her new best friend.

The next morning, I drove to Oxford Airport and then flew my plane to Heathrow. Mr. Norman knew I was out of the Messenger business for the summer break. He had arranged for an RAF pilot to fly the Greyhound if needed.

Boarding good old Try Walking Again, I settled in for the long flight, wondering what the summer would bring.

Finished for now.

Back Matter

To be continued in Book 9: The Cold War The Richard Jackson Series[1]

https://www.enelsonauthor.com/

For information on hiring Janet E. Rupert to edit your fiction project, email:

janeteditorrupert@gmail.com

---

1. https://d.docs.live.net/f59a06b92f374959/Desktop/Jackson%20Stories/eBooks/

9.%09https:/www.amazon.com/gp/product/B08BJLD3Z5

Other books by Ed Nelson
The Richard Jackson Saga
Book 1 The Beginning
Book 2 Schooldays
Book 3 Hollywood
Book 4 In the Movies
Book 5 Star to Deckhand
Book 6 Surfing Dude
Book 7 Third Time is a Charm
Book 8 Oxford University
Book 9 Cold War
Book 10 Taking Care of Business
Book 11 Interesting Times
Book 12 Escape from Siberia
Book 13 Regicide
Book 14 What's Under, Down Under?
Book 15 The Lunar Kingdom
Book 16 First Steps
In the Richard Jackson World
Mary, Mary
Stand-Alone Story
Ever and Always
Cast in Time Series
Book 1: Baron
Book 2: Baron of the Middle Counties
Book 3: Count
Book 4: Earl
Book 5: Earl of the Marches

Did you love *Oxford University*? Then you should read *Cold War* by Ed Nelson!

In the early 1960s the Cold War intensifies as does Rick's involvement. The KGB and the East Germany Stasi start it, but Rick finishes it. Trying to capture him is one thing, kidnapping Mary is another. As his life at Oxford becomes routine, his duties as a Queen's Messenger prove challenging to the extreme. This tongue in cheek saga is all true, give or take a lie or two.